The
Postcard
Killers

A complete list of books by James Patterson is on pages 426–27. For previews of upcoming books by James Patterson and more information about the author, visit www.JamesPatterson.com.

The Postcard Killers

A NOVEL BY

James Patterson

AND

Liza Marklund

LITTLE, BROWN AND COMPANY

NEW YORK   BOSTON   LONDON

Little, Brown and Company
Hachette Book Group
237 Park Avenue, New York, NY 10017
www.hachettebookgroup.com

First Edition: August 2010

Little, Brown and Company is a division of Hachette Book Group, Inc. The Little, Brown name and logo are trademarks of Hachette Book Group, Inc.

The characters and events in this book are fictitious. Any similarity to real persons, living or dead, is coincidental and not intended by the author.

Library of Congress Cataloging-in-Publication Data
Patterson, James.
    The postcard killers / James Patterson and Liza Marklund. — 1st ed.
        p. cm.
    ISBN 978-0-316-08951-7
    1. Police — Fiction.   2. Americans — Sweden — Fiction.   3. Women
journalists — Fiction.   4. Couples — Crimes against — Fiction.
5. Stockholm (Sweden) — Fiction.   6. Serial murderers — Fiction.
I. Marklund, Liza. II. Title.
    PS3566.A822P67 2010
    813'.54 — dc22   2009051755

10 9 8 7 6 5 4 3 2 1

RRD-VA

Printed in the United States of America

Prologue

One

Paris, France

"IT'S *VERY* SMALL," THE ENGLISHWOMAN said, sounding disappointed.

Mac Rudolph laughed, put his arm around the woman's slender neck, and allowed his hand to fall onto her breast. She wasn't wearing a bra.

"Oil on a wooden panel," he said. "Thirty inches by twenty-one, or seventy-seven centimeters by fifty-three. It was meant to hang in the dining room in the home of the Florentine merchant Francesco del Giocondo. But da Vinci never got it finished."

He felt her nipple stiffen under the fabric of the blouse. She didn't move his hand away.

Sylvia Rudolph slid up on the other side of her, her hand easing its way under the woman's arm.

"Mona Lisa wasn't her name," Sylvia said. "Just Lisa.

3

Mona is an Italian diminutive that can be taken to mean 'lady' or 'her grace.'"

The woman's husband was standing behind Sylvia, his body pushed up against hers in the crowd. Very cozy.

"Anyone thirsty?" he asked.

Sylvia and Mac exchanged a quick glance and a grin.

They were on the first floor of the Denon wing of the Louvre, in the Salle des États. Hanging on the wall in front of them, behind nonreflective glass, was the most famous portrait in the world, and the guy was thinking about beer?

"You're right," Mac said, his hand gently gliding down the Englishwoman's back. "It is small. Francesco del Giocondo's dining room table can't have been very large."

He smiled over at the woman's husband.

"And you're right, too. It's time to drink some wine!"

They found their way out of the museum, down the modern staircase toward the Porte des Lions, and stepped out into the middle of a Parisian spring evening.

Sylvia inhaled deeply, breathing in the intoxicating mix of exhaust fumes, river water, and freshly opened leaves, and laughed out loud.

"Oh," she said, hugging the Englishwoman, "I'm so glad we met you. Honeymoons are all very well and good, but you have to see a bit of the world, too, don't you? Have you had time to see Notre-Dame yet?"

"We only got here this morning," her husband said. "We've hardly had time to eat."

"Well, we must do something about that at once," Mac

said. "We know a little place down by the Seine. It's wonderful, you'll love it."

"Notre-Dame is fantastic," Sylvia said. "One of the first Gothic cathedrals in the world, strongly influenced by naturalism. You're going to *love* the South Rose Window."

She kissed the woman on the cheek, lingering for a second.

They crossed the river on the Pont d'Arcole, passed the cathedral, and arrived at the Quai de Montebello just as someone started playing a melancholy tune on an accordion.

"Order whatever you like," Mac said, holding the door of the bistro open. "It's on us. We're celebrating your honeymoon."

Two

THEY GOT A COZY TABLE for four overlooking the river. The sunset was painting the buildings around them blood-red. A *bateau-mouche* glided past, and the accordionist switched to a more cheerful tune.

The tetchy Brit thawed out after a couple of bottles of wine. Sylvia felt his eyes on her and undid another button of her thin blouse.

She noted that the Englishwoman was stealing glances at Mac, at his fair hair, honey-colored skin, girlish eyelashes, and well-built biceps.

"What a magical day this has been," Sylvia said when Mac had paid the bill and she was pulling on her backpack. "I *have* to have a *souvenir* of this evening."

Mac sighed theatrically and put a hand to his forehead. She sidled up to him and cooed, "I think Dior on Montaigne is still open."

"This is going to be *expensive*," Mac groaned.

The British pair laughed out loud.

They took a taxi to Avenue Montaigne. Mac and Sylvia didn't buy anything, but the Brit pulled out his credit card and bought a hideous silk shawl for his new wife. Mac settled for a couple of bottles of Moët & Chandon from a nearby wineshop.

Out in the street again he took out a joint, lit it, and passed it to the Englishwoman.

Sylvia put her arms around the Englishman's waist and looked him deep in the eyes.

"I want," she said, "to drink these bottles together with you. In your room."

The Brit gulped audibly and looked at his wife.

"She can play with Mac at the same time," Sylvia whispered, and kissed him on the lips. "It's perfectly all right with me."

They hailed another taxi.

Three

THE CENTRAL HOTEL PARIS WAS a clean, simple spot in Montparnasse. They took the lift to the third floor and tumbled, giggling and slightly stoned, into the room, which looked out on the Rue du Maine.

The walls were sunshine yellow. In the middle of the thick sky blue carpet was an enormous double bed.

"I'll get this bubbly stuff opened at once," Mac said, taking one of the bottles of champagne into the bathroom. "No one go anywhere."

Sylvia kissed the Englishman again, more seriously this time, using her tongue. She noticed his breathing get quicker. He probably had a full erection already.

"I expect you're a big boy, aren't you?" she said in a seductive voice, her hand moving along his leg, up toward his crotch.

She could see the Englishwoman was blushing, but she said nothing to stop this from proceeding.

"Bottoms up!" Mac said, coming back into the room with

four improvised champagne glasses on the tray that had held the toothbrush glasses.

"Here we go!" Sylvia cried, swiftly taking one of the glasses and knocking it back.

The British pair were quick to follow her example. Mac laughed and went around refilling the glasses.

Then he lit another joint, which was perfectly rolled.

"How long have you been married?" Sylvia asked, inhaling and passing the marijuana cigarette.

"Four weeks," the woman said.

"Just imagine," Sylvia said, "all those lovely nights ahead of you. I'm jealous."

Mac pulled the Englishwoman to him and whispered something in her ear. She let out a laugh.

Sylvia smiled. "Mac can keep going for ages. Shall we try to beat them? I think we can."

She leaned over and nibbled at the man's earlobe. She noticed his eyelids were already drooping. The Englishwoman giggled, a low, confused sound.

"Only a minute or so now," Mac said. "We're close now."

Four

SYLVIA SMILED AND SLOWLY UNDID the man's shirt. She managed to get his shoes and trousers off before he collapsed on the bedspread.

"Clive," the woman slurred. "Clive, I love you forever, you know that..."

Then she, too, fell asleep.

Mac had managed to take all her clothes off—apart from her underwear. He removed the underpants now, carried her to the bed, and laid her down next to her husband. Her hair, a little shorter than Sylvia's but more or less the same color, spread out like a fan.

Sylvia picked up her purse. She riffled quickly through the credit cards, then looked more closely at the passport.

"Emily Spencer," she read, checking the photo. "This is good, we look similar enough. That makes it easier."

"Do you think she's related to Lady Di?" Mac said, as he pulled off her wedding ring.

Sylvia gathered together Emily Spencer's clothes, valuables, and other important belongings and stuffed them in her backpack.

Then she opened the bag's outer pocket and pulled out latex gloves, chlorhexidine, and a stiletto knife.

"Mona Lisa?" she asked.

Mac smiled. "What else? Perfect choice. Help me with the cleaning first, though."

They pulled on the gloves, got some paper towels from the bathroom, and set about methodically wiping down everything they had touched in the room, including the two unconscious figures on the bed.

Sylvia stared at the man's genitals.

"He wasn't that big after all," she said, and Mac laughed.

"Ready?" she asked, pulling her hair up into a ponytail.

They took off their own clothes and folded them and put them as far away from the bed as possible.

Sylvia started with the man, not for any sexist reasons, just because he was the heavier of the two. She sat behind him and hauled him into her lap, his slack arms flopping by his sides. He grunted as though he were snoring.

Mac straightened the man's legs, crossed his arms over his stomach, and handed Sylvia the stiletto, which she took in her right hand.

She held the man's forehead in the crook of her left arm to keep his head up.

She felt with her fingertips for the man's pulse on his neck and estimated the force of the flow.

Then she thrust the stiletto into the man's left jugular vein. She cut quickly through muscle and ligaments until she heard a soft hiss that told her that his windpipe had been cut.

Five

UNCONSCIOUSNESS HAD LOWERED THE BRIT'S pulse
and blood pressure, but the pressure in his jugular still made
the blood gush out in a fountain almost three feet from his
body.

Sylvia checked that she hadn't been hit by the cascade.

"Bingo," Mac said. "You hit a geyser."

The force of the flow soon diminished to a rhythmic pulsing. The bubbling sound as the air and blood mixture seeped
from the severed throat gradually faded away until finally it
stopped altogether.

"Nice work," Mac said. "Maybe you should have been a
doctor."

"Too boring. Too many rules. You know me and rules."

Sylvia carefully moved away from Clive, propping him
against the cheap headboard. She got blood on her arms
when she arranged the man's hands on his stomach, right on
top of left, but didn't bother to wash it off yet.

"Now it's your turn, darling," she said to the doped-up Englishwoman.

Emily Spencer was thin and light. Her breathing had almost stopped already. Her blood scarcely spurted at all.

"How much champagne did she actually drink?" Sylvia asked as she arranged the woman's small hands on her stomach.

She looked down at her bloody arms and went into the shower. Mac followed her.

They pulled off the latex gloves. Carefully they soaped each other and the stiletto, rinsed themselves off, and left the shower running. They dried themselves with the hotel's towels, which they then stuffed into the top of Sylvia's backpack.

Then they got dressed and took out the Polaroid camera.

Sylvia looked at the bodies on the bed, hesitating, deciding if the look was right.

"What do you think about this?" she asked. "Does it work?"

Mac raised the camera. The brightness of the flash blinded them momentarily.

"Works pretty damn well," he said. "Maybe the best one yet. Even better than Rome."

Sylvia opened the room's door with her elbow and they stepped out into the corridor. No security cameras, they'd made sure of that on the way up.

Mac pulled his sleeve down over his fingers and hung the DO NOT DISTURB sign outside the door. The door closed with an almost inaudible click.

The sounds of the night faded into silence. The gentle patter of the shower inside the room could just be heard above the hum of the ventilation system.

"Stairs or elevator?" Mac asked.

"Elevator," Sylvia said. "I'm tired. Murder is hard work, darling."

They waited until the doors had closed and the elevator was descending before they kissed.

"I love being on honeymoon with you," Sylvia said, and Mac smiled brilliantly.

Part One

Chapter 1

Thursday, June 10
Berlin, Germany

THE VIEW FROM THE HOTEL room consisted of a scarred brick wall and three rubbish bins. It was probably still daylight somewhere up above the alley, because Jacob Kanon could make out a fat German rat having itself a good time in the bin farthest to the left.

He took a large sip from the mug of Riesling wine.

It was debatable whether the situation inside or outside the room's thin pane of glass was more depressing.

He turned his back on the window and looked down at the postcards spread out across the hotel bed.

There was a pattern here, wasn't there, a twisted logic that he couldn't see.

The killers were trying to tell him something. The bastards who were cutting the throats of young couples all over Europe were screaming right in his face.

They were shouting their message, but Jacob couldn't hear what they were saying, couldn't make out their words, couldn't understand what they meant, and until he could work out their language, he wouldn't be able to stop them.

He drank the rest of the wine in his mug and poured some more. Then he sat down on the bed, messing up the order he had just arranged for the postcards.

"Let's look at it this way, then. Let me see who you are!"

Jacob Kanon, a homicide detective from the NYPD's 32nd Precinct, was a long way from home. He was in Berlin because the killers had brought him here. He had been following their progress for six months, always two steps behind, maybe even three or four.

Only now had the magnitude of their depravity started to sink in with the police authorities around Europe. Because the killers carried out only one or two murders in each country, it had taken time for the pattern to emerge, for everyone except him to see it plainly.

Some of the stupid bastards still didn't see it, and wouldn't take help from an American, even a fucking smart one who had everything riding on this case.

He picked up the copies of the postcard from Florence.

The first one.

Chapter 2

THE POSTCARD SHOWED THE BASILICA di San Miniato al Monte, and on the back was the now familiar quote. He read the lines and drank more wine, then let the card fall and picked up the next one, and the next, and the next.

Athens: a picture of the Olympic Stadium from 2004.

Salzburg: an anonymous street scene.

Madrid: Las Ventas.

And then *Rome, Rome, Rome...*

Jacob put his hands over his face for a few seconds before getting up and going over to the rickety desk by the wall.

He sat down on the Windsor chair and rested his arms on his notes, the notes he had made about the various victims, his interpretations, the tentative connections he had made.

He knew very little about the Berlin couple yet, just their names and ages: Karen and Billy Cowley, both twenty-three, from Canberra in Australia. Drugged and murdered in their rented apartment close to Charité University Hospital, for which they had paid two weeks in advance but which they hadn't had the chance to fully enjoy. Instead, they had their throats cut and were mutilated on their second or possibly third day in the apartment.

It was four days, maybe five or six, before they were even found. *Stupid, arrogant German police! Acting like they knew everything, when they knew so little.*

Jacob got up, went over to the bed again, and picked up the Polaroid picture of the couple that had been posted to the journalist at the *Berliner Zeitung.* This was the point where his brain had reached the limit for what it could absorb.

Why did the killers send first postcards and then grisly photographs of the slaughter to the media in the cities where they carried out their murders?

To shock?

To get fame and acclaim?

Or did they have some other intention? Were the pictures and postcards a smoke screen to conceal their real motive? And if so, what the hell might that be?

What the hell, what the hell, what the hell?

He examined the photograph, its macabre composition. There had to be a meaning, but he couldn't see what it was.

Instead, he picked up the picture of the couple from Paris.

Emily and Clive Spencer, just married, propped up next to each other against a pale-colored headboard in a Montparnasse hotel room. They were both naked. The streams of blood that covered their torsos had gathered in congealed little pools around their genitals.

Why?

Chapter 3

JACOB REACHED FOR THE WEDDING photograph he had asked Emily's mother to send him.

Emily was only twenty-one years old. Clive had just turned twenty-six. They were a stunningly beautiful couple, and the wedding photo radiated so much happiness and romance. Clive was dressed in tails, tall and handsome. Maybe a touch overweight, but that suited his status as a stockbroker in the London markets.

Emily looked like a fairy-tale princess, her hair in big ringlets framing her head. Slim and fragile, she looked quite enchanting in her ivory dress. Her eyes shone at the camera.

They had met at a mutual friend's New Year's party in Notting Hill, in one of those narrow trendy houses where the film with Hugh Grant and Julia Roberts had been shot.

Emily's mother hadn't been able to stop crying when Jacob talked to her on the phone.

He could neither comfort nor help her. He wasn't even formally involved in the case, after all. As an American police officer, he had to be careful not to get involved in the work done by the authorities in other countries.

That could have diplomatic consequences and, even worse, could lead to his expulsion from the country.

A wave of despondency washed over Jacob with a force that took his breath away and made the mug of wine in his hand shake.

He quickly emptied it of its contents and went and poured some more. *Pathetic*, he knew.

He sat down at the desk once again, his back to all the photographs and postcards so that he didn't have to look at them.

Maybe he should go and shower. Head down to the communal bathroom at the end of the corridor in the hope that there was some hot water left. *Did he even have any soap? Christ, had he even used soap since he arrived in Berlin?*

He drank some more wine.

When the bottle was empty, he picked up the pictures of the dead couple from Rome. He placed them in front of him on the desk and put his 9-millimeter Glock 26 beside them, just as he always did.

The killers had sent two pictures of the murder in Rome: one image of the two naked victims and a close-up of two of their hands.

The woman's left and the man's right.

He picked up the picture of the hands and traced the shape of the woman's graceful hand with his finger, smiling as it reached the birthmark at the base of her thumb.

She played the piano, was an expert on Franz Liszt.

He breathed out deeply, let go of the picture, and picked up his gun.

He ran the palm of his hand over the dull plastic of the grip and put the muzzle in his mouth. It tasted of powder and metal.

He closed his eyes and the room slid gently to the left, the result of far too much Riesling.

No, Jacob thought. *Not yet. I'm not done here yet.*

Chapter 4

Friday, June 11
Stockholm, Sweden

THE POSTCARD LAY NEXT TO a harmless invitation to a *boules* tournament—the newsroom against a rival newsroom—and another invitation to a wine-tasting evening with the culture crowd.

Dessie Larsson groaned out loud and tossed the cards for the pointless social events into the recycling bin. If people paid more attention to their work instead of playing with balls and scratching one another's back, maybe this newspaper would have a future.

She was about to get rid of the postcard the same way but stopped and picked it up.

Who sent postcards these days, anyway?

She looked at the card.

The picture on the front was of Stortorget, the main

square in Stockholm's Old Town. The sun was shining and the sky was blue. People were eating ice cream on the benches, and the fountain in the middle was purling with water. Two cars, a Saab and a Volvo, stood parked in front of the entrance to the Stock Exchange Building.

Dessie turned the card over.

TO BE OR NOT TO BE
IN STOCKHOLM
THAT IS THE QUESTION

WE'LL BE IN TOUCH

What sort of insane crap was this?

She turned the card over and looked at the picture once more, as if it might give her a clue to the cryptic words on the back.

Ice cream was licked, water purled. Neither the Volvo nor the Saab had moved.

People need to get a life, she thought as she tossed the card into the recycling bin.

Then she went over to her desk in the crime section.

"Has *anything* happened in Stockholm today? Anything at all?" she asked Forsberg, her dumpy, disheveled news editor, as she put her backpack on the desk and set her bicycle helmet down next to it.

Forsberg looked up over his glasses for a fraction of a second, then went back to the newspaper in front of him.

"Hugo Bergman has written a big piece. The People's Party want a European FBI. And they've found another pair of young lovers murdered. In Berlin this time."

What sort of nonsense has Hugo Bergman come up with now? Dessie thought, sitting down at her desk. She took her laptop out of her backpack and logged into the paper's network.

"Anything you want me to do more work on, boss man?" she wondered out loud, clicking on the news about the double murder in Berlin.

"Talk about sick bastards, these killers," the news editor said. "What the hell's wrong with people like that?"

"Don't ask me. I specialize in petty criminals," Dessie said. "Not serial killers. Nothing big and important like that."

Forsberg stood up to get a cup of coffee from the machine.

The victims in Berlin were Australians, Dessie read. Karen and William Cowley, both twenty-three and married for a couple of years. They'd come to Europe to get over the death of their infant son. Instead, they had run into the notorious murderers who were killing couples all over Europe.

The postcard had been sent to a journalist at a local paper. The picture was of the site of Hitler's bunker, and there had been a Shakespeare quote on the back.

Dessie suddenly gasped. She felt almost like she was having a heart attack, or how she imagined that might feel.

To be or not to be...

Her eyes were pinned to the recycling bin in front of her.

"Forsberg," she said, sounding considerably calmer than she felt. "I think they've arrived in Stockholm."

Chapter 5

"SO, DESSIE, YOU'VE NO IDEA why the postcard was sent to you in particular?"

The police had taken over the conference room behind the sports desk.

Police superintendent Mats Duvall sat on the other side of the table, looking at her through a pair of designer glasses.

An old-fashioned tape recorder, the sort that actually used a cassette, was slowly winding on the table in front of her.

"Not the faintest idea," Dessie said. "I don't get it at all. No."

The newsroom was cordoned off. A team of forensics officers had taken the postcard, photographed it, and sent it off for analysis. After that, they had laid siege to the mail room.

Dessie didn't understand what they were expecting to find there, but they had a whole arsenal of equipment with them.

"Have you written any articles about this? Have you reported on any of the other murders around Europe?"

She shook her head.

The superintendent looked at her coolly.

"Can I ask you to reply verbally so that your response gets picked up on the tape?"

Dessie sat up in her chair and cleared her throat.

"No," she said, a little too loudly. "No, I've never written about these murders."

"Is there anything else you might have done to provoke them into contacting you specifically?"

"My obvious charm and flexibility?" she suggested.

Duvall tapped away at a small gadget that Dessie assumed was some sort of electronic notepad. His fingers were long and thin, the nails well manicured. He was dressed in a suit, a pink shirt, and a gray-on-blue striped tie.

"Let's move on to you: how long have you been working here at *Aftonposten*?"

Dessie clasped her hands in her lap.

"Almost three years," she said. "Part-time. I do research when I'm not here."

"Research? Can I ask what in?"

"I'm a trained criminologist, specializing in property crime. And I've done the extension course in journalism at Stockholm University, so I'm a trained journalist as well. And right now I'm writing my doctoral thesis.... Glad you asked?"

She had let the sentence about her thesis trail off. Focusing on the social consequences of small-scale property break-ins, it had been placed on the back burner—to put it mildly. She hadn't written a word of it in over two years.

"Would you describe yourself as a high-profile or famous reporter?" the superintendent asked.

Dessie let out a rather inappropriate laugh, partly through her mouth, partly her nose.

"Hardly." She recovered slightly. "I never write about the news. I come up with my own stories. For instance, I had an interview with Burglar Bengt in yesterday's paper. He's Sweden's 'most notorious' burglar. Found guilty of breaking into three hundred eighteen properties, and that doesn't include—"

Superintendent Duvall interrupted her, leaning in closer across the table.

"The usual scenario is that the people who sent the postcard carry on a correspondence with the journalist. You may get more mail from the killers."

"If you don't catch them first," she said.

She met the policeman's gaze. His eyes were calm, inscrutable behind his shiny glasses. She couldn't tell if she liked or disliked him. Not that it mattered.

"We don't know the killers' motives," he said. "I've spoken to the security division, but we don't think you need personal protection for the time being. Do you think you need it?"

A shiver ran up Dessie's spine.

"No," she said. "No personal protection."

Chapter 6

SYLVIA AND MAC WERE STROLLING happily, arm in arm, through the medieval heart of Stockholm.

The narrow cobblestoned streets wound between irregular buildings that appeared to lean toward one another. The sun was blazing in a cloud-free sky, prompting Mac to take off his shirt. Sylvia stroked his flat stomach and kissed him passionately on the mouth and elsewhere.

The streets opened out and they emerged onto a little triangular square with an ancient tree at its center. Some pretty, blond girls were jumping rope on the cobbles. Two old men were playing chess on a park bench.

The huge canopy of the tree cast shadows over the whole square, filtering the sunlight onto the cobbles and facades of the houses. They each bought an ice cream and sat down on an ornate park bench that could have been there beneath the tree for hundreds of years.

"What an amazing trip this is. What an adventure we're having," Sylvia said. "No one has ever lived life like this."

The air was clear, crystal clear, and birds were singing in the branches above them. There was no urban noise, just the girls' laughter and the rhythmic sound of the jump rope hitting the cobbles.

The square was an oasis surrounded by five-hundred-year-old buildings in muted colors, their hand-blown windows shimmering.

"Shall we do the National Museum or the Museum of Modern Art first?" Sylvia asked, stretching out along the length of the bench, her head in Mac's lap, as she leafed through her guidebook.

"Modern," he said between bites of his ice cream. "I've always wanted to see Rauschenberg's goat."

They took the street north out of the square and passed a huge statue of St. George and the Dragon. A minute later they were down on the quayside again, opposite the sailing yacht *af Chapman,* which was lying at anchor off the island of Skeppsholmen.

"There's water everywhere in this city," Mac said, amazed.

Sylvia pointed to the island directly behind the Grand Hôtel.

"Are we walking, or shall we take a steamer?"

Mac pulled her close and kissed her.

"I'll go anywhere, anyhow, any way, as long as I can be with you."

She pushed her hands down under his belt and stroked his bare buttocks.

"You look like a Greek god," she whispered, "with a very nice tan."

In the Museum of Modern Art the first thing they looked at was Rauschenberg's world-famous piece *Monogram,* a stuffed angora goat with a white-painted car tire around its middle.

Mac was ecstatic to see it in person.

"I think this is a self-portrait," he said, lying down flat on the floor alongside the goat's glass case. "Rauschenberg saw himself as a rudely treated animal in the big city. Look at what it's standing on, a mass of found objects, newspaper clippings about astronauts, tightrope walkers, and the stock fucking exchange."

Sylvia smiled at his enthusiasm.

"I think all of his 'combines' are a kind of narrative about the big city," she said. "Maybe he wants to say something about how human beings are always trying to master new environments."

When Mac was done with his veneration, they went on to look at the Swedish art.

At the back of the Modern, through one long corridor and a couple of shorter ones, they found the motif for the next murders.

"Perfect," Mac said.

"Now all we have to do is find two people in love," Sylvia said. "Just like us."

Chapter 7

DESSIE LARSSON DRAGGED HER RACING bike through the lobby of her ancient apartment building and chained it to the drainpipe in the courtyard.

The bike ride through Stockholm City Centre had not managed to blow away her sense of unease. The intense questioning had taken up most of the day. The police had gone through every article she had written since the first murder took place in Florence eight months ago.

Whatever it was that had made the killers choose her as the recipient of the postcard, there was no obvious explanation in any of the articles.

Superintendent Duvall had looked completely frustrated when he let her leave.

She wandered back into the lobby, ignored the elevator, and took the stairs up to the third floor. The leaded windows facing onto the courtyard made the staircase gloomy in the half-light. Her steps echoed between the stone walls.

She had just reached her apartment and pulled her keys out of her backpack when she froze.

There was a man standing in the shadows by her neighbor's door. She opened her mouth to scream, but no sound came out.

"Dessie Larsson?"

She dropped her keys and they landed on the marble floor with a clatter. Her mouth was dry, her legs ready to run.

He had a beard and long hair, and he smelled. He put his hand inside his jacket and Dessie felt her knees about to buckle.

I'm going to die.

He's going to pull out a big butcher's knife and cut my throat.

And I never did find out who my father was.

The man held a small disk toward her, a blue-and-yellow badge with the letters NYPD on it.

"My name's Jacob Kanon," he said in English. "I'm sorry I scared you. I'm on the homicide unit in the Thirty-second Precinct of Manhattan, in New York City."

She looked at the disk. *Was that supposed to be an American police badge?* She had seen them on television only. This one looked like it could easily have been bought in a toyshop.

"Do you speak English? Do you understand anything I'm saying?"

She nodded and looked up at the man. He was hardly any taller than she was, with broad shoulders and strong biceps, and he was blocking her escape route down the stairs.

He had a powerful presence but appeared to have lost weight recently. His jeans had slid down and were hanging on his narrow hips. His suede jacket was good quality but badly creased, as though he'd been sleeping in it.

"It's really important that you listen to what I've got to say," he said.

She looked carefully at his eyes, which were bright blue and sparkling. Quite the opposite of everything else about him.

"They're here, and they're going to kill again," he said.

Chapter 8

JACOB FELT THE ADRENALINE PULLING like barbed wire through his veins.

He had never been so quick out of the gate before, only a day or so behind them: before the murders took place, before the pictures of the bodies, before their flight to yet another city.

"I have to find a way into the investigation," he said. "At once, right fucking now."

The reporter stumbled a little and steadied herself against the wall behind her. Her eyes were wide and watchful. He'd frightened her badly. He hadn't meant to.

"If I'm the killers' contact," she said, "who's yours?"

Her voice was dark, a little hoarse. Her English was perfect but spoken with a strange accent. He looked at her in silence for a few moments.

"Who interviewed you?" Jacob asked. "What's his name, what unit's he on? Is there a prosecutor involved yet? What safety measures have been taken? *Someone's going to die here in Stockholm.*"

The woman backed away another few steps.

"How did you know I received the card?" she asked. "How did you know where I live?"

He looked at her carefully. There was no reason to lie.

"Berlin," he said. "The German police. It was the *deutsche Polizei* who told me another postcard had turned up, sent to a Dessie Larsson at *Aftonposten* in Stockholm, Sweden. I came at once. I've just gotten in from the airport."

"So, what are we doing here? What do you want with me? I can't help you. I'm nobody."

He took a step closer to her, she took a step to one side. He checked himself.

"They have to be stopped," he said. "This is the best chance yet.... They picked you. So now you're *somebody*."

Chapter 9

"I'VE BEEN FOLLOWING THESE BUTCHERS since the murders in Rome last Christmas," he said.

Suddenly he turned away and looked out through the leaded glass farther down the stairs. The fading sunlight was making red, green, and dark blue spots dance on the marble steps.

He closed his eyes and put his hand over them, the colors burning into his brain.

"Sometimes I think I'm right behind them. Sometimes they slip past me, close to me, so close I can almost feel their breath."

"How did you find me? I asked you a question."

He looked at the reporter again. She wasn't like the others. She was younger, about thirty, less high-strung. Plus, all the others had been men—apart from the female reporter in Salzburg whom he hadn't managed to make contact with yet.

"I got your address from directory inquiries. The taxi

driver dropped me off at the door. Like I said, I'm a detective."

He knotted his hands in frustration.

"You have to understand how important this is. How far have the police gotten? Have they made contact with the Germans? Tell them *they have to talk to Berlin,* the best inspector there is called Günther Bublitz. He's a decent man. He cares."

The woman lowered her head, peering at him from beneath her hair. Her fear seemed to have subsided, and her gaze was steady and calm now. She was impressive in her way.

"This is my home," she said. "If you want to discuss anything about the postcard or the killers or the police operation, you'll have to come to my workplace tomorrow."

She nodded toward the stairs.

"I'm sure you'll find your way, Detective. You can get the address from directory inquiries."

He took a step closer to her and she held her breath.

"I've been chasing these bastards for six months," he said, almost inaudibly. "No one knows more about them than I do."

The woman braced herself against the wall, then forced her way past him. She picked up her keys from the floor and clutched them hard in her hand.

"You look and smell like a garbage dump," she said. "You've no authority with the Swedish police. You're just chasing these killers....Sorry, but that seems a bit... obsessive."

He brushed his hair back hard and closed his eyes.

Obsessive? Was he obsessed? Of course he was.

He saw the Polaroid picture in front of his eyes, the man's and woman's hands, the beautiful fingers that were almost touching. The blood that had run down their arms and gathered around the fingernails. *"Love you, Dad! See you at New Year's!"*

He opened his eyes and met her gaze.

"They killed my daughter in Rome," he said. "They cut Kimmy's and Steven's throats in a hotel room in Trastevere, and I'm going to chase them until Hell freezes over."

Chapter 10

DESSIE HEARD THE MAN'S HEAVY footsteps disappear down the stairs as she double-locked her door. She blew out a deep breath.

It was Friday evening, and she was alone again. Worse, she'd just been scared shitless by an American detective who tragically had lost his daughter.

She took off her sneakers, hung up her jacket, and put her bike helmet on the hat rack. She pulled off the rest of her clothes as she walked to the bathroom and got into the shower.

Jacob Kanon, she thought. He hadn't meant her any harm, that much was obvious. What would have happened if she had asked him in? What would she have lost as a result? Would she have gotten a news story?

She shook off the idle thoughts and turned the tap to run the water ice cold. She stood under the jet until her toes started to go numb and her skin stung.

Wrapped in a big dressing gown, she walked across the

tiled floor into the living room. She sank onto the sofa and reached for the television remote control but held it idly in her hand.

Why had the killers picked her? What the hell had she done? She wasn't a star reporter by any means.

Were they actually in the city right now?

Were they looking for their next victims, or had they already set to work? Had the letter containing the photographs of the dead bodies already been sent?

She got up off the couch and went into the kitchen. She opened the fridge door and found a few withered carrots and a moldy tomato. Jeez. She really must do some shopping.

Coming home usually made her thoroughly calm and relaxed. Not this night.

Her apartment lay on Urvädersgränd, an old street on the island of Södermalm, in the heart of the onetime working-class district that had recently been transformed into over-priced homes for the hip middle class to buy. Sweden's national poet, Carl Michael Bellman, had lived in the building next door for four years in the 1770s. She tried to feel the winds of history.

It didn't work too well tonight. Another Friday at home. Why was that?

She went over to the stereo and put on a CD of German hard rock. *Du, du hast, du hast mich* . . .

Then she sat down and stared at the telephone. She had a pretty good reason for making the call.

She was neither lonely nor abandoned. She had just

turned down the chance to invite a man into her apartment—a dirty, unshaven man, admittedly—so she wasn't the slightest bit desperate. Right?

She picked up the receiver and dialed the number of Gabriella's cell phone.

Chapter 11

GABRIELLA ANSWERED WITH HER USUAL unfriendly grunt.

"Hi," Dessie said. "It's me."

She could hear Gabriella breathing.

"It's not what you think," Dessie said. "I don't want to be a nuisance, and I haven't changed my mind..."

"I've been expecting you to call," Gabriella said, sounding strictly professional. "Mats Duvall pulled me onto the investigating team this afternoon. I think you and I can deal with this like grown-ups.... Right, Dessie?"

Dessie breathed out. She had lived with police inspector Gabriella Oscarsson for almost a year. Maybe they had been in love, maybe not. Three months ago Dessie had ended the relationship and Gabriella had moved out of the apartment. It hadn't been an amicable split. Was it ever?

"Have you heard anything?" Dessie asked, which meant in plain language, Have you found any bodies with their throats cut?

"Nothing. Not yet."

Not yet. So they were expecting something. They believed the postcard was real.

"I was contacted by an American cop here this evening," Dessie said. "A Jacob Kanon. Do you know anything about him?"

"He's been working with the Germans," Gabriella said. "We've had confirmation that he's with the New York force, and that his daughter was one of the first victims. In Rome. Where did you say you met him?"

Dessie sighed with relief. At least he was who he said he was, even if he smelled.

"He looked me up," she said.

"*Why?* Why did he look you up? What did he want with you? He came to the apartment?"

All the old irritations came crashing back on Dessie like a fist in the stomach. All these questions, the insinuations, the same accusing tone that had finally driven her to finish it with Gabriella.

"I really don't know," Dessie said, trying to sound calm and in control of the situation.

"We're thinking of talking to him to see what he knows," Gabriella said, "so you're free to interview him if you like."

"Okay," Dessie said, feeling that it was time to hang up.

"But we're looking after this case, not some freelancing Yank," Gabriella said. "And be careful, Dessie. These are murderers, not your usual pickpockets and burglars."

Chapter 12

Saturday, June 12

SYLVIA RUDOLPH TILTED HER HEAD to one side and smiled beautifully. Her eyes lit up.

"You have to let us show you our very favorite place in Stockholm. They've got the most wonderful cakes, and their hot chocolate cups are as big as bathtubs."

The German couple laughed, their mood lightened by the thick joint the four of them had just shared.

"It's on Stortorget, the square in the Old Town that's got a ridiculously dramatic history," Mac said, putting his arm around the German woman. "The Danish king, one Christian the Tyrant, had the whole of the Swedish nobility executed there in November fifteen twenty."

"More than a hundred people lost their heads," Sylvia said. "The mass murder is still called 'the Stockholm Bloodbath.'"

The German girl shuddered.

"Ugh, how horrid."

Mac and Sylvia exchanged a quick glance and smiled at each other. "Horrid?" This from someone whose forefathers started two world wars?

The Rudolphs held each other's hand and walked quickly up toward Börshuset, the old Stock Exchange Building, and the Nobel Museum located in it. The Germans followed them, giggling and stumbling.

In the café, actually called *Chokladkoppen*, "The Chocolate Cup," they ate cinnamon buns and drank homemade raspberry juice.

Sylvia couldn't take her eyes off the German woman. She really was incredibly beautiful. Unfortunately she was light blond, almost platinum, but that could be sorted out somehow.

"Oh, I'm so glad we met you two," Sylvia said, hugging the German man. "I have to have a souvenir of today! Mac, do you think the jeweler in that department store is still open?"

Mac sighed, raising his eyebrows as he always did at this point in their script.

"Oh, dear," he said. "This is going to be expensive."

The German took out his wallet to pay for the pastries, but Mac stopped him.

"This is on us!"

Chapter 13

THEY WALKED DOWN TO THE quayside together, following the water until they came to the greenery of Kungsträdgården. The German woman seemed to have gotten the munchies badly after the marijuana, because she stopped to buy an ice cream at one of the kiosks along the way.

Sylvia took the opportunity to sidle closer to the man while his girlfriend was busy licking her ice cream.

"She's amazing," Sylvia said, gesturing toward the woman, who was dripping melted ice cream on her clothes. "If I were you, I'd really want to give her a token of my appreciation..."

The German smiled, a little uncertain. He was not exactly a bad specimen either. He looked like a handsome villain from some film, maybe a member of the old Baader-Meinhof Gang, something like that.

"'Appreciation'? How do you mean?"

Sylvia kissed him on the cheek and touched his left wrist.

"She hasn't got a nice watch..."

Sylvia suggested they get a little cash, so they stopped at the bank. She hung on to the man, memorizing his PIN as he keyed it in at the ATM.

NK, the department store, was crowded, and they had to take a number at the jeweler. Sylvia pulled the German woman over to the perfume department while the men picked out the right watch. They each bought a bottle of Dior's J'adore.

The woman let out a series of very cute squeals of joy when she opened her present.

Sylvia took the opportunity to pop into a branch of Systembolaget, the state-owned chain that had a monopoly on selling alcohol throughout Sweden, and bought two bottles of Moët & Chandon.

"This deserves a celebration," Sylvia cooed, twining her arm around the German man's waist. "I want to drink these with you, somewhere where we can be alone."

The German looked slightly confused but definitely interested.

Sylvia laughed softly.

"I mean all four of us," she said. "Do you know anywhere we could go?"

He looked at her full breasts and gulped audibly, then nodded.

"We're renting a house in the archipelago. Our rental car's actually in a garage not far from here."

Sylvia kissed him on the lips then, letting her tongue play over his front teeth.

"So what are we waiting for?" she whispered. "Let's go to your house."

Chapter 14

THE NEWSROOM WAS NEARLY ABANDONED for lunch.

Forsberg, the news editor, was sitting chewing the end off a ballpoint pen and reading telegrams. Out in the mail room, two twitchy forensic investigators had settled in to intercept any letters the killers might send.

Dessie was sitting with a mass of printouts about the double murders throughout Europe over the past eight months spread out on her desk. She had been there since seven o'clock that morning and had been told to stay until the last postal delivery arrived, sometime in the late afternoon. She had agreed to put together a summary of the murders that another reporter could build a story on.

The case in Berlin, the latest one, was deeply tragic to her.

The killers had not been content merely to murder the Australians. They had also mutilated their bodies. It was not clear from the articles Dessie had found precisely what they had done to the couple.

She picked up another printout and started making her way through the Spanish newspaper article.

The killings in Berlin seemed to be a replica of those in Madrid, except for the bit about mutilation. An American couple, Sally and Charlie Martinez, had been found with their throats cut in their room in the Hotel Lope de Vega. They had been in Spain on their honeymoon.

The postcard had been sent to the newspaper *El País,* and it was of the bullfighting arena Las Ventas.

She leaned closer to the grainy printout.

It looked like a round building with two towers with flags on top. Some cars and some pedestrians were in the picture. There was no information about what had been written on the back of the card.

"How's it going, Dessie? Have you caught them yet?"

She put the printout down.

"Jealous?" she asked, looking up at Alexander Andersson, the paper's high-profile, sensationalist reporter.

Andersson sat down on her desk and made himself comfortable. Dessie could hear her printouts getting crumpled beneath his backside.

"I've been wondering about something," he said smoothly. "Why did the killers send the card specifically to you?"

Dessie opened her eyes wide in surprise, mocking Andersson.

"God," she said. "You really are quick. Did you come up with that question all on your own?"

Andersson's smile stiffened somewhat.

"People don't usually read anything you write," he said. "It's a bit of a surprise..."

Dessie sighed and made up her mind not to get angry. She reached for a copy of that day's paper. There was nothing about the postcard in it. Andersson walked away without saying anything else.

The paper's management, after serious pressure from the police, had decided not to publish the details. But Andersson had written a sloppy article about the murders around Europe. It contained a large number of loaded words like *terrible* and *unpleasant* and *massacre* but not many facts.

Dessie lowered the paper.

I've been chasing these bastards for six months. No one knows more about them than I do.

Why hadn't she heard from Jacob Kanon today? He had been so keen to talk yesterday evening.

She stretched her back and looked out across the newsroom.

Presumably his not getting in touch again had something to do with her behavior—the fact that she was always so brusque and never let anyone get close to her.

She shook off her feelings as ridiculous, then leafed through the printouts again.

She ran her fingers over the pictures of the victims.

The victims in Rome.

This was her, this was what she looked like before she was murdered. Smiling, shy, fair curly hair.

Kimberly Kanon.

Jacob Kanon's daughter.

She had her father's bright blue eyes, didn't she?

Chapter 15

THE WIND HAD DROPPED BY the time they stepped into the bright sunshine outside the house the Germans had rented in the archipelago. Yachts with slack, chalk white sails glided slowly past in the sound below as Sylvia waved to an older man piloting a large yacht.

Mac filled his lungs with air and stretched his arms out toward the islands, trees, water, and glittering sunlight.

"This is wonderful," he exclaimed. "I love Sweden! This could be my favorite country so far."

Sylvia smiled and threw him the car keys.

"Can you find the way back out of here?"

Mac laughed loudly. He shoved the backpack onto the backseat of the rental car, pulled on a new pair of latex gloves, got in behind the wheel, and put the car in gear.

As they turned left onto the gravel track, Sylvia opened the window to let the fresh air into the coupe.

The landscape was sparse, yet simultaneously beautiful and tastefully minimalist. The green of the deciduous trees was still tender, almost transparent, the sky clear blue as glass. Shy flowers that had only just emerged from the frozen soil swayed in the turbulence caused by the car as it flashed by.

They passed two cars just before they crossed the bridge leading back onto the mainland. Neither of the drivers seemed to take any particular notice of them.

"Party time tonight," Sylvia said, stroking Mac's neck. "Are you up for it?"

"I want you here, right now," he whispered sexily.

She ran her hand slowly across his crotch, feeling how hard he was.

When they were on the motorway heading north toward Stockholm, Sylvia put on a new pair of gloves. She reached into the backseat for the backpack and started to go through the dead Germans' valuables.

"Look at this," she said, taking out an ultramodern digital camera. "A Nikon D3X. That's pretty neat."

She rummaged through the woman's jewelry.

"A lot of it's rubbish, sentimental, but this emerald ring is okay. I guess."

She held it up to the sunlight and examined the gemstone's sparkle.

"He had a platinum Amex," Mac said, glancing at the things spread out on the floor of the car and in Sylvia's lap.

"So did she," Sylvia said, waving the metallic card.

Mac grinned.

"And we've got the Omega watch itself, of course," Sylvia

said, triumphantly holding up the German woman's recently purchased gift. "And it's even in the original packaging!"

"The cheap Kraut bastard was thinking of buying her a Swatch," Mac said.

They burst out laughing, heads thrown back, as they passed through the commercial center of Stockholm.

"We're *back*," Sylvia said in an eerie voice.

Chapter 16

THIRTY-FIVE MINUTES LATER MAC MADE a turn into the long-term parking lot at Arlanda Airport. Just to be safe, Sylvia wiped down the surfaces she might have touched with her fingers: the buttons that controlled the side windows, the instrument panel, Mac's seat.

Then they left the car among a couple of thousand others, a dark gray Ford Focus that even they lost sight of after walking just a few meters. It would probably be there for weeks before anyone noticed it.

The free bus to the airport's terminal buildings was almost empty. Sylvia sat on one of the seats, Mac standing beside her, wearing the backpack. No one paid any attention to them. Why should they?

They got off at International Terminal 5 and went straight to the departure hall.

Sylvia had managed to get a fair ways ahead before she noticed that Mac wasn't right behind her. Now where was he?

She turned all the way around and saw him standing and looking up at one of the large screens where departures were listed.

She hurried back quickly.

"Darling," she whispered, sidling up to him. "What are you doing?"

Mac's light gray eyes were staring fixedly at the flashing destinations.

"We could take a plane," he said.

Sylvia put her tongue in his ear.

"Come on, baby," she said in a low voice. "We've got lots left to do. Today is party time!"

"We could go home," Mac said. "We could stop this game of ours now. Quit while we're ahead. Retire as legends."

She wound her arm around his waist and blew softly on his neck.

"The train leaves in four minutes," she said. "You. Me. We're on it."

He let her lead him off to the escalators, down into the underground, and out onto the platform. Only when the doors had closed and the express train had set off for the center of Stockholm did Sylvia let go of him.

"Legends," she said, "always die young. But not us."

Chapter 17

Sunday, June 13

A UNIFORMED SECURITY GUARD STOOD up in a glass cubicle over to Jacob's left. He pressed a button and said something incomprehensible in a metallic loudspeaker voice.

"I don't speak Swedish," Jacob said. "Can you tell Dessie Larsson that I'm here?"

"What about?"

"The postcard killings," he said, holding up his New York police badge. "I'm homicide."

The man pulled his stomach in and yanked up his baggy trousers.

"Take a seat for a moment."

He gestured toward the row of wooden benches over by the door.

The stone floor of the *Aftonposten* lobby was slippery from the rain outside.

Jacob slid a couple of steps before getting his balance back, along with his dignity. He straightened his shoulders, wondering if perhaps he was not entirely sober yet.

With a groan, he sank onto the nearest bench. It was hard and cold.

He had to pull himself together. Never before, never during all those years raising Kimmy, had he let himself sink this low. The previous day had vanished in a haze of vodka and aquavit. The Swedes also had something they called *brännvin,* a spirit made from potatoes that was pure dynamite.

Hoping he wasn't about to be sick, he rested his head in his hands.

The killers weren't far away. Even though he felt hazy about many things, he could sense their proximity.

They were still walking the city's streets, hiding in the rain, and had probably already found their next victims — if they hadn't already dealt with them . . .

Jacob shivered slightly and realized how cold and wet he was. His hands were filthy. There was no shower in his room in the youth hostel where he was staying, and he hadn't bothered trying to find the shared bathroom. The building depressed him. It was an old prison, and his room was a cell from the 1840s, which he was sharing with a Finnish poet. He and the poet had squeezed onto the lower bunk of the bed and drunk their way through the vodka, aquavit, and *brännvin,* and afterward the poet had gone into the city to dance the tango somewhere.

Jacob had spent the night throwing up into the wastepaper basket and feeling miserable. There wasn't enough alcohol in the whole of the country to drown his thoughts about Kimmy and her murder.

He beat on his forehead with his fists.

Now that he was so close to the bastards, his own failings were overtaking him.

He got gingerly to his feet and set off toward the glass cubicle again. The soles of his shoes had dried and had a better grip on the floorboards.

The glass box was empty now. The guard had gone off somewhere. *Shit.*

Shielding his eyes from the glare of the glass with his hands, he tried to see into the newsroom. As far as he could tell, there was no one about.

What sort of fucked-up place was this? Wasn't this supposed to be a newspaper?

He walked back to the security post and buzzed the alarm. No response, no one anywhere.

He put his finger on the buzzer and held it there. The guard finally approached, holding a mug of coffee in one hand and a pastry in the other.

"Hello!" Jacob called. *"Can you please call Dessie Larsson and tell her I'm here?"*

The guard glanced at him, then turned his back and started talking to someone out of sight.

Jacob banged the glass wall with the palm of his hand.

"Hello!" he yelled. "Come on! It's a matter of life and death!"

"You're too late," said a voice behind him.

He spun around to see the journalist standing in the

stairwell behind him. Her face was white, her green eyes tired. There were dark rings around them.

"The picture arrived this morning," she said. "The forensics team already took it away."

He stepped toward her and opened his mouth, but he couldn't get a single question out.

"A man and a woman," Dessie Larsson said. "Their throats were cut."

Chapter 18

DESSIE OPENED THE DOOR TO the newsroom with her card and code.

"I'm not going to offer you anything to drink," she said over her shoulder. "If you'd turned up yesterday, you might have gotten a cup of coffee, but you lost your chance. This way..."

She headed off to the right through the office, aiming for the crime desk.

"I'm not here for coffee," Jacob Kanon said behind her. "Have the bodies been found?"

He was in a bad mood and stank like hell. Nice guy.

"Not yet," said Dessie. "Give us a little time, will you. Murder is a bit less common here than in New York. Suicide is our specialty."

She sat down behind her desk and pointed to the wobbly metal chair in front.

"When was the letter posted?" he asked.

"Yesterday afternoon, at the central Stockholm post office. We don't usually get mail on a Sunday, but the police ordered an extra delivery."

He sat down on the chair and leaned forward, his elbows on his knees.

"Did you see the picture?" he asked. "What did it show? Were there any particular characteristics? Anything that could identify the crime scene?"

Dessie looked carefully at the man in front of her. He looked even worse in daylight than he had in the gloom of the stairwell. His hair was a mess and his clothes were dirty. But his blue eyes were burning with an intensity that brought his whole face alive. She liked something about him— maybe the intensity. Probably that.

"Just a Polaroid picture, nothing else."

She looked away as she passed him a copy of the picture. Jacob Kanon took it with both hands and stared at the bodies.

Dessie was trying to look calm and unaffected. Violence didn't usually bother her, but this was different.

The victims were so young, their deaths so cold and calculated, so inhuman.

"Scandinavian setting," the policeman stated. "Pale furniture, pale background, blond people. Did they take the envelope away?"

Dessie swallowed.

"Forensics? Of course they did."

"Have you got a copy?"

Dessie handed him a photocopy of the ordinary oblong envelope. The address was written in neat capital letters across the front.

DESSIE LARSSON
AFTONPOSTEN
115 10 STOCKHOLM

She looked uncomfortably at her own name.

"They won't find anything on it," Jacob Kanon said. "These killers leave no fingerprints, and they don't lick the stamps. Was there anything on the back?"

She shook her head.

He held up the picture of the bodies.

"Can I have a copy of this?"

"I'll print a new one for you," Dessie said, clicking the command through her computer and pointing at a printer some distance away. "I'm going to get a coffee," she said, getting up. "Do you want one?"

"I thought I'd lost my chance," Jacob Kanon replied, heading off toward the printer to get the picture.

Dessie went over to the coffee machine with a gathering feeling of unreality. She pressed for coffee with milk for herself, and black, extra strong for the American. He looked like he needed it.

"They have to make a mistake sometime," Jacob said as he took the coffee. "Sooner or later they'll get lazy, or overconfident, or just unlucky. That moment can't be far off now. That's what I'm thinking."

Dessie pushed the terrible coffee away from her and fixed her gaze on the American.

"I've got a lot of questions," she said, "but this one will do for a start: Why me? Why did they pick me? You seem to have a lot of answers. Do you know why?"

At that moment her cell phone began to vibrate. She looked at the display.

Gabriella calling.

"It's one of the police team," she said.

"One of the team on this case? Answer it, then!"

She took the call and turned her chair so she had her back to Jacob Kanon.

"We think we've found the victims," Gabriella said. "A German couple out on Dalarö. It's a real mess."

Chapter 19

DESSIE TOOK A DEEP BREATH.

"Who found them?" she asked in Swedish.

Jacob Kanon walked around her desk so that he was in front of her again.

"The cleaner," Gabriella said through the phone. "We've got a local patrol out there now."

"Have they found the victims?" Jacob asked.

Dessie turned away from him again, twisting her body.

"Are you sure it's the couple in the picture?" she asked.

"They've found them, haven't they?" the American persisted, annoying her.

"Who's that talking in the background?" Gabriella asked.

"The coroner will find traces of several different substances in the victims' blood," Jacob Kanon said loudly, right next to the phone. "Partly THC and alcohol, but also a drug that will be identified as—"

"When did the murders take place?" Dessie asked, putting her finger in her ear to shut out the noisy American.

"I'm worried about you," Gabriella said. "These killers mean business. I want you to take special care."

Jacob Kanon grabbed Dessie's office chair and swung it around so that her knees ended up between his.

"Get the address!" he said, looking her right in the eyes. "Get the address of the crime scene right now."

"What's the address of the crime scene?" Dessie asked, flustered, feeling the warmth from his legs through the thin fabric of her trousers.

"Are you at the paper? Is that the crazy Yank?"

Gabriella's voice turned shrill and accusing again.

"What's he doing there? You let him come into the news-room? Why?"

Dessie avoided the man's bright blue eyes, feeling her irritation at Gabriella bubbling over. She was very close to shouting at her.

"The address, Gaby. This is a newspaper, and these murders are news. We'll have to send someone out there."

"What? Since when are *you* a newshound?"

A stubborn streak that should have vanished when she was three years old welled up inside her and made her cheeks burn.

"Would you rather we sent Alexander Andersson? I can arrange for that."

Gabriella Oscarsson gave her an address out on Dalarö.

"But whatever you do," she said abruptly, "don't bring the Yank with you."

Then she hung up.

Dessie put her cell down. Jacob Kanon let go of her chair and took a step back.

"Where is it? Where's the crime scene?"

"Forty-five minutes away," Dessie said, looking at her watch. "South of here, on an island."

She walked around the desk, hoisted her knapsack onto her back, picked up a pen and notepad, and stopped in front of Jacob Kanon.

"Shall we go?"

Chapter 20

IT HAD STOPPED RAINING, BUT the pavement was still wet. The tires hissed as Dessie steered the Volvo from the newspaper's auto pool through the puddles outside the paper's garage. She braked at the main entrance and opened the passenger door for Jacob Kanon.

The stench of him once he shut the door was quite dreadful. This was a big mistake.

"God," she said, opening the window. "Haven't you learned to use soap and water in America?"

He fastened his seat belt.

"We're in good time," he said. "Almost as quick as the police. That's a good source you've got."

Dessie switched gears and drove off. She paused for a moment before replying.

"She's my ex."

The American sat in silence for a moment.

"Your ex, as in..."

"Girlfriend, yes," Dessie said, concentrating on the thin traffic.

Why was it so hard to talk about it? It was 2010.

She put her foot down to avoid having to stop at a red light. She peered up at the sky to see if the clouds were showing any sign of breaking up, which they weren't. She turned on the car radio and found *Gentle Favorites*. She tried to sing along but didn't know half the words.

"What about you?" she asked, to put an end to the silence. "Have you got a girl?"

"Not anymore," he said, looking out through the windshield.

"If you tried showering occasionally, maybe she would have stayed."

"She was murdered. In Rome."

Shit, shit, shit, what an idiot she was.

"Sorry," she said, staring straight ahead now.

"Don't worry about it," he said, looking at her. "Kimmy was my family. It was just her and me."

So, what happened to the mother? Dessie thought, but she decided to keep her mouth shut this time.

They headed south along Route 73 in silence, passing the Tyresö road and the vast suburb of Brandbergen. The American leaned forward to study the huge, ugly concrete buildings.

She peered intently at the road signs and found the exit for Jordbro. The motorway vanished, replaced by a minor road, the 227.

Not far now.

She felt her pulse rise. She had been to a lot of crime scenes. She was used to broken patio doors and overturned drawers, but she had never been to the site of any murder, let alone a really bad one.

"When we get there," Dessie said, "what can we expect to find?"

Jacob Kanon looked at her, his eyes sparkling.

"Blood," he said. "Even small amounts of blood look huge when they're spread across furniture and floors. You know the stain on the wall when you squash a mosquito? We're talking about large amounts here."

Dessie clutched the wheel harder and took the hard right toward Björnö.

Chapter 21

THE MURDER HOUSE WAS ON the shore by the sound, facing the island of Edesö. Dessie didn't want to be here.

It was small, ordinary, yellow, with carved detailing on the veranda and a little hexagonal tower topped by a pennant. A white picket fence with a gate lined the road. Freshly green birches framed the house, marsh marigolds edging the gravel drive up to the door.

A policeman was busy cordoning off the site with blue-and-white tape down by the shore.

A second officer was talking into his cell phone by the corner of the house.

Dessie stopped by the fence. She held up her compact digital camera and took a few pictures of the house.

Jacob Kanon pushed past her, opened the gate, and snuck under the plastic cordon.

"Hang on," Dessie said, stuffing the camera in her pocket. "You can't just—"

"You there!" called the policeman who was tying the

cordon around a rowan tree down by the shore. "You can't come in here, it's closed to the public."

Jacob Kanon held up his police badge as he sped up, heading straight for the house.

Dessie was half running behind him on trembling legs. "Jacob—stop!" she called.

"New York Police Department," Jacob called back. "They want to talk to me about the investigation. It's all set."

The policeman with the cell stared at them but kept hold of his phone.

"Jacob," Dessie said, "I don't know if—"

The American kept going and climbed up onto the veranda. He took a quick look around and kicked off his shoes.

The outer door was wide open. Jacob stopped at the threshold. Dessie caught up with him and instinctively put her free hand up to cover her nose and mouth.

"Bloody hell," she said. "What's that smell?"

Chapter 22

TO THEIR RIGHT WAS A half-open door that seemed to lead to a small kitchen. Ahead and to the left they could see people moving, the floor tiles creaking as they walked about.

"*Hello*," Jacob called out. "My name's Jacob Kanon and I'm an American homicide officer with information about this case. I only speak English. I'm now entering the crime scene."

Dessie fumbled her way out of her shoes, still covering her nose and mouth, desperately trying not to retch. She saw Jacob pull on a pair of thin gloves that he took out of his jacket pocket and then open the door in front of them.

From her position behind his back she saw Mats Duvall, the superintendent who had questioned her on Friday, turn around and stare at them. He was wearing a light gray suit with a mauve shirt and bright red tie, and he had blue coverings on his shoes. He was holding his electronic notepad in his hand.

Gabriella was standing by the window, writing something on her own pad. Outside in the sound a yacht glided by.

"What the hell?" Gabriella said, taking a couple of quick steps toward them.

Jacob held up his badge.

"I'm not here to sabotage things," he said quickly. "I've got important information that will help your investigation. I know more about these killers than anyone else does."

He stepped to one side to let Dessie into the living room. She stopped beside him and caught sight of the sofa. *My god, dear god.*

The bloody bodies were still sitting and looked frozen in their peculiar pose.

The blood covering their bodies was dark, almost black. It had run onto the floor, down into the cracks in the wood, to be sucked up by a colorful rug. The woman's light blond hair hanging down across her breasts was stiff with blood.

The man was lying in her lap, half on the floor, just like in the photograph. The opening in his throat was like a gaping gill, Dessie thought. The wound to his windpipe had been so violent that his head had almost come away from his body.

Dessie felt her blood pressure sink into her toes and grabbed at Jacob to stop herself from falling.

"So you're Jacob Kanon," Mats Duvall said, looking the American up and down. "I've heard about you."

He didn't sound aggressive, just curious.

"You'll find at least one empty champagne bottle

somewhere in here," Jacob said, "probably Moët and Chandon. Four glasses, and in two of them you'll find traces of the drug cyclopentolate. It a muscle relaxant used in eye examinations to dilate the pupil."

Gabriella took a couple of long strides across the room and stopped right next to Jacob Kanon.

"You're trespassing on a crime scene," she said and pointed back at the door. "Get out of here!"

"Eyedrops?" Mats Duvall asked.

Jacob looked at the Swedish detectives, ready to fight his side of the ring.

"In the States it's sold under several different names," he said. "Ak-Pentolate, Cyclogyl, Cylate, and a couple more. In Canada it's also known as Minims Cyclopentolate. You can get it here in Europe, too."

Dessie could feel the room starting to spin. There was a very good chance that she'd throw up. That was pretty much all she was thinking about now.

"So the killers drug their victims?" Mats Duvall said, stepping over and putting his hand on Gabriella's shoulder. "With eyedrops in the champagne?"

Gabriella cast a furious glance at Dessie and moved even closer to Jacob Kanon.

"And cut their throats once they're unconscious," he said. "The killer is right-handed and uses a small, sharp implement. He does it from behind, sticking the knife right into the left jugular vein, then cutting deeply through the sinews and windpipe."

He mimed the act with his arms as he spoke. He'd obviously done it before.

Dessie realized that all the colors and sounds were starting to fade away.

"Pulse and breathing probably stop after a minute or so," Jacob said.

"Sorry," Dessie said, "but I have to get out."

She went out onto the gravel drive, raised her face to the sky, and took several long, deep breaths. Her first big case, she thought, and probably her last.

Chapter 23

"THEY'RE CHARMING, PLEASANT PEOPLE, THESE killers," Jacob said to Dessie, stretching his back in the thin sunlight. "They find it easy to make new friends. Are you sure you don't want a cinnamon bun?"

Dessie shook her head, letting the American eat the last one.

They were sitting on the terrace of the Hotel Bellevue on Dalarö, with a coffeepot, cups, and an empty plate in front of them. There was a sharp wind from the sea.

It was really too cold to be sitting outside, but Dessie couldn't bear Jacob Kanon's body odor after feeling sick at the murder scene.

"So, you think there's two of them? A couple—a man and a woman? Why?"

Jacob nodded, chewing hungrily on the bun. He seemed completely unaffected by the grisly scene they had just witnessed.

"A couple is less of a threat. They're probably young,

attractive, a pair of carefree travelers meeting others doing the same thing. People who drink champagne, smoke dope, live it up a bit..."

He drank some coffee.

"And they probably speak English," he said.

Dessie raised her eyebrows quizzically.

"The postcards. They're written with perfect grammar, and most of the victims have been native English speakers. I'm guessing the rest have been fluent."

Dessie pulled her long hair up into a bun on her neck and pushed her pen through it to keep it up. Her notepad was already full of information about the victims, the murders, and the killers.

"These postcards," she said. "Why do they send them?"

Jacob Kanon looked out over the water. The wind pulled at his messed-up hair.

"It's not unusual for pattern killers to communicate with the world around them to get attention," he said. "There are lots of examples of that."

"They kill to get in the paper?"

Jacob Kanon poured himself some more coffee.

"We had our first Postcard Killer in the U.S. over a hundred years ago, a man named John Frank Hickey. He spent more than thirty years killing young boys along the East Coast before he was caught. He sent postcards to his victims' families, and that was what gave him away in the end."

He drained his cup again and seemed strangely content.

Dessie was freezing her ass off in the bitter wind.

"But why me?" she asked.

Chapter 24

JACOB KANON DID UP HIS suede jacket, the first sign that he felt *anything*.

"You're talented, ambitious, and your career comes first above almost everything else in your life. You're well educated—really too well for the type of journalism you're involved in, but that doesn't seem to bother you."

Dessie made an effort to look cool and neutral as she sipped her coffee.

"Why do you think that?"

"Am I right?"

She cleared her throat quietly.

"Well," she said. "Maybe a bit. Some of that is true. Continue, please."

He gave her an indulgent look.

"It's not rocket science," he said. "I think I've worked out what they do when they pick their contacts."

Dessie wrapped her arms tightly around herself. Everything about this was so creepy and unreal.

"What?"

"They buy the local papers the day they decide to set to work. The paper, and the reporter, with the biggest crime news that day is the one they pick as their contact."

Dessie blinked several times.

"Burglar Bengt," she said. "My interview with Burglar Bengt was on the front page of *Aftonposten* on Thursday."

Jacob Kanon looked out at the sea.

"But how could you know?" she said. "That bit about ambition and education?"

"You're a woman and you write about typically male subjects. That requires talent, and also stubbornness. Where I come from, crime reporting isn't very highly regarded, even if it sells papers. That's why the journalists involved in it tend to be competent but not too hung up on prestige."

"That's not always the case," Dessie said, thinking of Alexander Andersson.

Jacob Kanon leaned toward her.

"I need to work with you," he said. "I need a way into the investigation and the media. I think I can get them this time. I do."

Dessie got up, holding down the payment with the coffeepot so it wouldn't blow away.

"Have a bath and burn your clothes," she said. "Then we'll see."

Chapter 25

THE STORY HAD QUICKLY GROWN into something unusual—a top international news story playing out right there in Stockholm.

All the top boys and girls at the paper were keen to have a headline that might get quoted on CNN or in the *New York Times*. Photographers swarmed around the picture desk, waiting for a crumb to fall their way. Poor Forsberg sat there tearing at his remaining strands of hair, talking into two cordless phones at the same time.

Alexander Andersson held court in the newsroom, reading out loud from his own articles.

For the first time in history the editor in chief, Stenwall, had come into the paper on a Sunday. Dessie saw him sipping a cup of coffee in his glass box.

She went over to her desk, got out her laptop and camera, and downloaded the pictures she had taken of the yellow house in the archipelago, then sent them to the picture desk.

She wrote down all the facts about the case and the killers that could be used as a basis by some other reporter.

"How was it out there?" Forsberg asked, suddenly materializing beside her desk.

"Terrible," Dessie said, typing on her laptop. "Worse than I could ever have imagined."

"Is it the same killers?"

"Looks like it," she said, turning the computer so the news editor could read her background material.

He started skimming her copy. "Eyedrops?" Forsberg said.

"There were several previous cases in Sweden where women were drugged with eyedrops in their drinks. In Mexico City the drops are used by prostitutes to knock out their clients. At least five men have died there, probably more."

"From eyedrops in their drinks?" Forsberg said doubtfully. "Sounds like the stuff of mystery novels."

Dessie let go of the keyboard and looked up at him.

"Some girls put the drops directly on their nipples."

Forsberg shuffled his feet and dropped the subject. She always won with him—if she needed to.

"How much of this can we publish?"

"Hardly anything," Dessie said, going back to her computer. "The police want to suppress the information about the drugs, champagne, and other stuff they found at the crime scene. We can give the cause of death, though, and information about the victims. Their families were told at lunchtime."

Forsberg sat down on the edge of her desk. He liked Dessie but was thoroughly confused because of her fling with Gabriella. Everyone was.

"The victims?"

Dessie stared at her screen, at the bare facts she had put together about the dead couple.

"Claudia Schmidt, twenty years old. Engaged to Rolf Hetger, twenty-three, both from Hamburg. Arrived in Stockholm on Tuesday, renting the house on Dalarö through an agency on the Internet. Rented a car at the airport, a Ford Focus. Car missing.

"They probably met their killers somewhere in town and invited them home," Dessie said. "We're getting photographs from *Die Zeit*. You'll have everything in two to three minutes."

"What are your sources? I need those as well, Dessie."

She looked at him coolly.

"Confidential," she said. "What are we going to do with the information about the postcard and the picture of the bodies?"

Forsberg stood up.

"The police have us on a short leash, so we still can't use it. Did you take pictures of the house?"

"Of course. Just as backup. They're with the picture desk. So sick."

She held up the copy of the postcard of the Stock Exchange.

"Do you know what the American cop calls them? 'Postcard Killers.'"

"Cool headline," Forsberg said. "Almost even lines."

Dessie looked at her watch.

"The last mail has just arrived. If there's nothing there, I'm going to go."

"A date?" Forsberg teased.

"Actually, yes," Dessie said, "and I'm already late."

Chapter 26

SHE REALLY HAD BEEN ASKED out, something that wasn't exactly commonplace. In a way she had been looking forward to this evening: someone actually wanting to take her out to dinner at a fancy restaurant with candles and white napkins.

Right now, though, she would have given anything to get out of going.

Several weeks ago she had been contacted by Hugo Bergman, a successful crime writer and columnist, who needed help with the credibility of one of his characters: an incorrigible petty thief who had ended up the victim of a global conspiracy. As partial thanks for her work, he had offered to take her out to dinner.

Flattered, she had said yes. Hugo Bergman was famous, rich, and fairly good-looking. Also, he'd invited her to the Opera Cellar, one of the fanciest eateries in town.

She parked her bike outside the entrance, the smell of the

corpses from Dalarö still in her nostrils. She took off her helmet, let her long hair down, and went in.

In her shapeless trousers and sweaty top, she was as wrongly dressed as she could have been, but there had been no time to go home and change for dinner.

The maître d' showed her to the table. The magnificent dining room with its cut-glass chandeliers, painted ceiling, and tall candles made her feel messy and clumsy, like the country bumpkin she often felt that she was since coming to Stockholm.

Chapter 27

"DESSIE," HUGO BERGMAN SAID, HIS face lighting up. He stood and kissed her on both cheeks in the continental fashion.

Dessie gave a forced smile.

"Sorry I'm late, and a mess," she said, "but I've been out at a double murder all day."

"Ah," Hugo Bergman said. "These stupid editors. Blood and death, their daily bread. But who am I to moralize?"

Bergman laughed at his own joke.

"It was really rough," Dessie said, sitting down. "The victims, a young couple from Hamburg."

"Let's not talk about that anymore," the author said as he poured red wine into the glass in front of her. She noticed that the bottle was half empty.

"I've already ordered," he said, putting his glass down. "I hope you eat meat."

Dessie smiled again.

"I'm afraid I don't," she said. "I'm against the commercial exploitation of animals."

Hugo Bergman inspected the wine list.

"Well," he said. "You can eat the mashed potatoes. They haven't been exploited. What about this one, the Château Pichon-Longueville-Baron from nineteen ninety-five?"

This last sentence was directed at the waiter who had silently glided up to their table.

Bergman turned back to her. "Did you read my article about the workload of public prosecutors, by the way? Goodness, I've had a really positive response to it."

Dessie continued to smile until her mouth was starting to ache. She really was trying. Tossing her hair and fluttering her eyelashes, she listened attentively and laughed politely at the writer's attempts to be witty and sophisticated.

The food was good, or at least the mashed potatoes were.

Bergman got more and more drunk from the ridiculously expensive wines he went through. He actually had some difficulty locating the dotted line when it came to signing the credit-card bill.

"You're a very beautiful woman, Dessie Larsson," he slurred when they came out into Kungsträdgården in front of the restaurant.

His heavy breath struck her in the face.

"Thank you," she said, unlocking her bicycle, "for everything."

"I'd love to see you again," he said, and tried to kiss her.

Quickly Dessie put on her bike helmet, thinking, That

ought to work as a passion killer. But Bergman didn't give up so easily.

"I've got a writer's pad in the Old Town," he slurred at her. "A penthouse..."

Dessie took a quick step to the side and got on her bike.

"Thanks for a fantastic evening," she said, turning her back on him and pedaling off.

It was so bloody typical. Anyone who was interested in her was a control freak, a self-obsessed idiot, or a single-minded sex maniac.

She glanced back over her shoulder when she reached the next intersection. Hugo Bergman was standing there swaying where she had left him, fumbling with his mobile phone. He had probably forgotten about her already.

"Asshole," she whispered into the wind. "It's your loss."

It was a cool, still evening. The clouds had drifted away and the sky was light even though it was after eleven.

People were walking along the quayside, talking and laughing. The sidewalk bars were open, offering blankets and halogen heaters to anyone feeling cold.

She breathed the white summer night into her lungs and cycled slowly past the Royal Palace, crossed the intersection at Slussen, and then stood up on the pedals to climb up Götgatsbacken.

She carried the bike up the steps to Urvädersgränd, unlocked the door, and parked it in the courtyard.

She had time to unlock and open the door to her apartment before she noticed the man standing watching her from the shadows.

Chapter 28

SHE HEARD HERSELF GASP. THAT was starting to become a habit, a very bad one.

"I've done what you said," Jacob Kanon said, stepping toward her with his arms outstretched.

She looked at him. He had shaved and washed his hair.

"H and M," he explained.

He was wearing the same jeans, the same jacket, but possibly a new T-shirt. It was hard to tell: it was black, just like the previous one.

"Fantastic," Dessie said. "What a transformation."

"They sell soap as well," he went on.

"I hope you didn't wear yourself out shopping," Dessie said. "What do you want?"

He looked at her with his sparkling eyes.

"The Swedish police will be making a huge mistake if they don't listen to me," he said. "They won't catch these killers, even if they trip over them. The Germans did nearly everything right and still didn't catch them."

Dessie closed the door to her apartment. She stayed out in the hallway with him. She wasn't afraid of him anymore, just a bit leery.

"This type of murder investigation is the worst to try to clear up," the American went on. "The victims are picked at random, there are no connections between them and the killers, no obvious motives, no shared history going back more than a few hours. And the killers are traveling like ordinary tourists, which means that no one notices their absence, no one cares when they come and go, no one notices if they act strangely . . ."

He appeared sad, restrained, and not quite sober, but something in him seemed entirely genuine. He wasn't putting it on, he wasn't exaggerating.

Maybe it was the contrast to Hugo Bergman's supercilious sense of self-congratulation that made Dessie notice it. And now that she could see what he looked like behind all the grime, he was actually pretty good-looking. And those eyes of his were something.

Watch yourself, she thought and crossed her arms.

"What's this got to do with me?" she asked.

Jacob held up a small sports bag that she hadn't seen before.

"All we've got is a pattern," he said. "I've got copies of the pictures of most of the bodies in here, and postcards from almost all of the murders. The killers are communicating through these pictures, but I can't work out what they're saying. Can you help me?"

"I don't know anything about murder," she said.

He laughed, a sad, hollow laugh.

"Who else can I turn to?"

Of course. He was here, outside her door, because he had nowhere else to go.

"Look," she said, "I'm tired and I have to be up in a couple of hours."

The timed lights in the stairwell went out. Dessie didn't bother to switch them on again.

"You've been working late," Jacob Kanon said in the darkness. "Has something happened? They didn't kill again, did they?"

She realized to her surprise that her mouth was dry.

"I've been on a date," she said.

She could see only his silhouette against the lead-framed window in the stairwell.

"With Hugo Bergman," she went on. "A famous crime writer. Maybe you've heard of him?"

Jacob pressed the light switch again and the lights came on.

"Time's passing," he said. "The killers usually stay only a few days in a place once they've already done their killing. They're probably still here, but they'll soon be moving on."

He took a step closer to her.

"Kimmy dies," he said. "Kimmy dies over and over again, and we have to stop them."

Dessie backed away.

"Tomorrow," she said. "Come to the paper tomorrow. If you're lucky I'll get you a cup of coffee from the machine."

He rubbed his eyes with his free hand and looked like he was about to say something but changed his mind.

Instead he disappeared down the marble staircase.

Chapter 29

DESSIE WENT IN AND CLOSED the door behind her, put the safety lock on, and clenched her fists.

She pulled off her clothes and thought about taking a shower but dropped the idea.

She crept under the covers in her double bed without turning the lights on.

The room was gloomy but not dark. The sun had gone down but would be up again in a few hours. She lay there quietly, looking around her bedroom.

Restless, she threw off the covers, pulled on a dressing gown, and went out to the kitchen.

She drank a glass of water and then went into what was once the maid's room, a little cubbyhole behind the kitchen where she had set up her office. She switched the computer on, hesitating a few moments before opening her half-finished doctoral thesis.

Who knew if it would ever get finished?

She sighed. She was actually extremely interested in her

research subject, so she didn't know why she never got it done. She had already spent several years of academic life on it, studying minor criminals and their thought processes, patterns of behavior, and motives.

She had grown up among petty thieves on a farm out in the forests of Norrland in the north of Sweden.

The great majority of her family hadn't done an honest day's work in the whole of their miserable lives.

She scrolled up and down the text, reading sentences and whole paragraphs at random.

Maybe she could get going on it again, finish it, and finally get her degree.

Why on earth did she find it so difficult?

Everything she did ended up half done, no matter whether it was work or relationships.

She switched off the computer and went back into the kitchen.

The perfect partner didn't exist, she knew that much, and, god knows, her knowledge was based on extensive research. The idea of finding your other half was a myth and a lie. You had to compromise, make allowances, be tolerant.

Gabriella was a great girl, beautiful and sexy and seriously in love with her.

There had been nothing wrong with Christer either. If he hadn't asked for a divorce, she'd probably still be married to him.

She drank another glass of water and looked at the clock on the wall. 1:43.

Why had she told the American she'd been on a date?

Why had she mentioned Bergman's name? Was it that she wanted Jacob Kanon to know that she dated men as well? Why would she want him to know that?

She put the glass down on the draining board and realized that she was quite hungry. All she had eaten were those damn mashed potatoes!

Chapter 30

THE POET HAD GONE BACK to Finland, leaving Jacob alone in his cell.

There was no space for a chair or table in the narrow room, so he had settled down on the Finn's abandoned lower bunk. He had put his pistol and the framed photograph of Kimmy on the deeply recessed windowsill. He'd bought the gun in Rome with the help of an old cop friend who had retired to Italy.

He leaned forward and ran his finger along his daughter's smiling cheek.

This was the picture he had given the press after she died, taken the day she'd been accepted at Juilliard.

Jacob got up, went over to his duffel bag, and opened a bottle of wine. He stood with the bottle in his hand, staring out at the light summer night.

There was a small beach under his window. A few alcohol-fueled youngsters wearing mortarboards were noisily soaking one another without taking their clothes off.

He let his eyes roam over the dark water.

Kimmy didn't like swimming.

All the other kids on the block loved going down to Brighton Beach, but Kimmy never learned to swim well. Instead she preferred the big forest parks on Staten Island, or up in Westchester or Putnam County, with their teeming wildlife, especially deer.

There was only one thing she loved more than her graceful deer, and that was his aunt Isabelle's piano. Kimmy would go and play on it after school every afternoon, and every day in the summer. She was gifted, so Jacob paid for lessons with the best teacher available in Brooklyn.

But that afternoon a couple of years ago when she told him she'd applied to Juilliard, the most famous college in the world for music, drama, and dance, he'd felt almost terrified. He'd never heard of anyone from Brooklyn's Bay Ridge area even getting close to being accepted there. He'd checked: only five percent of all applicants got in.

But Kimmy was special. She specialized in Franz Liszt, one of the most technically demanding composers in the world, and she had chosen his suggestive piano concerto Totentanz no.1 as her audition piece.

He had been so proud that he'd burst into tears when the acceptance letter came—and back in those days, he hardly ever cried. Not like the present.

Kimmy had met Steven on her very first day at Juilliard, a budding classical composer. They got engaged and decided to get married as soon as they graduated.

Steven was a great guy, but Jacob thought they should see something of the world before they settled down.

So he had given them a trip to Rome as a Christmas present.

They were murdered the day before they were due to return to New York.

Jacob took a deep breath and found himself back in the narrow cell at the hostel.

The shrieking kids on the beach had vanished.

He sank onto the lower bunk with Kimmy's picture in his lap.

He had identified her dead body in the cold room of a mortuary on the outskirts of Rome on New Year's Day, the first day of what had been the very worst year of his life.

This year.

He picked up his pistol and put the muzzle in his mouth, just as he had done so many nights before, tasting the powder and metal, taking comfort from the idea that there could be an end to this. One slight movement of his finger and his desperate loss and longing would be over.

But not yet. Not until he found her murderers.

Chapter 31

Monday, June 14

THE PAPER *AFTONPOSTEN* WAS STUCK in a downward sales and readership spiral that was probably hopeless. In an attempt to break it, the management was making increasing use of unusual and risky innovations. Usually they failed.

On other occasions everyone busted their butt to get things moving.

This was one of those days.

Dessie had parked herself at her desk with the first edition that day.

Aftonposten had filled practically the whole paper with the Dalarö murders.

The front-page headline was "Butchered by the Postcard Killers." The photo that dominated the paper was a beautiful picture of the two young Germans. Claudia Schmidt and Rolf Hetger were in each other's arms, laughing happily toward the camera.

Dessie leafed through to the paper's heavyweight news spread, pages 6 and 7. "Death in the Archipelago" was the dramatic headline.

And the picture editors had chosen one of her shots of the yellow wooden house.

It came out quite well, actually, with the contradiction between the idyllic veranda and the heavily clouded sky.

She ran her eyes over the text. It was written by Susanna Gröning, one of the paper's star female reporters.

Page 8 had an updated run-through of the killings around Europe, with maps and graphics.

Page 9 was written by Alexander Andersson under the heading "Postcard Killers — Vicious Murderers Killing for Kicks."

Andersson referred to "anonymous sources close to the investigation" who claimed to have "a clear picture of the killers."

The Postcard Killers were at least two men, seriously deranged, probably with PTSD, according to the sources. They killed purely for pleasure, and they enjoyed seeing people suffer. The extent of the violence indicated that at least one of the men was very well built and extremely strong. Seeing as the victims were usually well-off tourists, the motive was similar to that of terrorism: the killings were an attack on Western lifestyles.

Dessie read the text twice with growing astonishment, and finally, anger and disgust.

Then she got up and went over to the news desk. The group around Forsberg were laughing loudly at something as she approached.

"Alexander," she said, holding up page 9. "Where did you get this from?"

The reporter raised an eyebrow and smiled her way.

"Are you after my sources?"

"No need," Dessie said. "They're completely *worthless*."

Alexander Andersson's smile died and he stood up. Dessie felt all the men looking at her. They expected her to get her ass kicked now, didn't they?

"This doesn't make any sense," she said. "There's nothing in the investigation to suggest terrorism or killing for kicks. Quite the opposite."

"And you know that, do you, just because they sent you a postcard?"

Several of the men laughed and waited for more from Andersson. Dessie felt the blood rush to her face.

"This article is completely wrong, I know that much. If you really have got a source, they must be several miles from the center of the investigation."

Forsberg stood up and took hold of Dessie's arm. "Come."

Chapter 32

"COME ON," FORSBERG SAID. "LET'S go through what you're doing today. In the other room."

Alexander Andersson took a step toward her.

"If you know so bloody much, why aren't you writing anything?"

She pulled loose from Forsberg and stared daggers at the reporter.

"I know you might have trouble understanding this," she said, "but my goal in life really isn't to get a big-picture byline. I could care less."

She went back to her desk then, followed by Forsberg.

"You've got to be careful with Alexander," she said to the editor. "He's faking it."

"Dessie," Forsberg said, "listen to me. I've got a job for you. Have you read Hugo Bergman's article on public prosecutor workloads?"

Dessie looked at the news editor and blinked.

"The one we published on Friday?"

"It's caused a real stink," Forsberg said, handing her a bundle of printouts. "Call Bergman and get an interview, and check with the different regional prosecutors to see how many cases they've actually got at the moment. Can you do that?"

Dessie made no move to take the printouts. She could see Hugo Bergman in her mind's eye, swaying like a tree outside the Opera Cellar, where she'd left him the night before.

"You're trying to get me off the murders," she said. "That's what this is, right?"

The news chief sat on her desk and lowered his voice.

"Dessie," he said, "there are people asking why you were sent that postcard. They're wondering what sort of contacts you've got with the underworld."

She swallowed, couldn't believe her ears.

"I'm here today only because the police told me to be here," she said. "I'm supposed to be off Monday and Tuesday. I'm not claiming any kind of copyright on these murders, but if—"

She was interrupted by a shout and then a loud commotion in the lobby. It sounded like something breaking, something large and solid.

Forsberg stood up.

"What the hell is that?"

A furious male voice could be heard through the office walls. The words weren't clear, but they didn't need to be.

"Wait here," Dessie said and ran toward the door as fast as she could.

Chapter 33

JACOB KANON WAS STANDING AND yelling inarticulately at the enclosed glass cubicle where Albert, the security guard, had taken cover. Dessie fumbled with the door and rushed out into the lobby.

"You're calling her right now!" the American detective was screaming. *"You're going to pick up the phone now and tell her I'm here, you fucking—"*

"What are you doing?" she asked breathlessly, grabbing him by the shoulder.

Jacob Kanon spun around and stared at her. He fell silent in the middle of a word that sounded suspiciously like *motherfucker,* then breathed out.

"Have you heard from the police today?" he asked "What are they saying? *Tell me.*"

Dessie looked over her shoulder into the newsroom, then took a firm grip of the man's arm and pulled him toward the outside door.

"Your credibility is already pretty low," she said, pushing

him into the revolving door. "You won't make it any better by standing here shouting at poor Albert. And whatever did you *break*?"

They emerged into the sunshine.

"A wooden bench," the American said sullenly. "It hit one of the radiators."

She gave him a skeptical look, then burst out laughing.

"You're crazy," she said.

Chapter 34

SHE FELT HIM LOOKING STRANGELY at her as they walked off in the direction of Fridhemsplan.

They went into an empty taxi drivers' café a few hundred meters from the newspaper office.

"I'm serious," the policeman said as they sat down in a corner with their coffee. "The Swedish police are way too rigid in their thinking. They'll never catch the killers if they carry on like this. They're acting like amateurs. Trust me on this."

Dessie stirred her coffee, the spoon clinking noisily against the china.

If anyone was being rigid, it was she. Her behavior in the newsroom just now wasn't exactly smart. She had to stop being so blunt, and finally, dumb.

"I can't help you," she said. "I'm not even working on the killings for the paper. There are other people assigned to the story."

Jacob Kanon leaned across the table, his eyes sparkling brilliantly again.

"Can't you try to get back on the story?"

Dessie looked at the American. His interest in the case was beyond dispute. Unlike her he was dedicated, he had a burning passion, he had a purpose to what he was doing.

What did she have to lose by writing a few commonplace articles about murder? Doing some normal interviews like any good reporter.

"Maybe I could interview you about Kimmy," she said thoughtfully.

That wasn't actually a bad idea. A father in mourning speaking out, his grief for a much-loved daughter...

She reached for her pen and notepad.

"Tell me what Kimmy was like as a girl. How you reacted when you found out she was —"

Jacob Kanon smashed his fist on the table so hard the cups jumped. Dessie dropped her pen with a start.

The waitress behind the counter glanced quickly in their direction, then looked away again. Whatever this was, she didn't need any of it.

"I'm not giving any interviews about Kimmy," Jacob said.

Dessie sat in silence for several moments before she spoke.

"I just meant as a way of—"

"I'm a homicide detective," he interrupted. "I talk to people, I attempt to solve crimes, but I don't do interviews. Not about anything."

"I don't want to ask you in your capacity as a policeman, but as a father."

He looked at her with his strange, piercing eyes. Then he grabbed his sports bag. He pulled out a bundle of papers and slapped a photocopy on the table between them.

"This is Kimmy," he said.

Dessie heard herself gasp.

Chapter 35

TWO YOUNG PEOPLE LAY DEAD as if broken on the floor of a hotel room.

Their throats had been cut with the same brutality as in the murders on Dalarö. The wounds gaped dark red, the floor was drowning in blood.

Dessie's mouth went dry again and her pulse was racing in a terrifying way.

"The blood's still bright, fresh," Dessie said. "They were alive just a few minutes before."

"Yes, that's correct," said Jacob, "they'd just died."

She forced her breathing to stay calm, regular. It wasn't really helping.

Jacob put another picture in front of her.

"Karen and Billy Cowley," he said. "Look at them, Dessie. What do you see?"

The young Australian couple who had come to Europe to get over the death of their young son hadn't just had their throats cut. They were sitting upright, side by side, their heads leaning back against what must have been the head of a bed. Their left eyeballs had been stabbed, blood and fluid running like red mascara from the sockets.

"The couple in Amsterdam had their right ears cut off," Jacob said, putting a third picture in front of her. "Their names were Lindsay and Jeffrey Holborn."

She looked at the pictures, forcing herself to see beyond the blood and violence.

"They're telling us something," Jacob said angrily. "The killers are talking through these pictures. I'm sure of it. Look at this one, from Florence."

A double bed: a young woman on the left, a young man on the right. The picture was taken from above, which meant the photographer must have been standing on the bed, right between the dead bodies.

"What do you see?" Jacob asked.

The man and woman were lying in the same position, their bent legs parallel a little to the left, their right hands on their ribcages and their left ones over their genitals.

"They couldn't have been lying like this when they died," she said.

Jacob nodded.

"I know," he said, "but why?"

Dessie picked up the picture from Paris. The two victims were sitting with their hands on their stomachs.

"They look like they've just eaten too much," Dessie said.

They were posing. *The corpses were posing.* They were saying something, or at least representing something. What

114

was it? If the cops figured that out, they just might catch them.

She looked at Jacob.

"Let me see the one I was sent," she said.

He gave her the picture from Dalarö. She took it and could still feel the smell of the hot living room.

The woman, Claudia, was sitting upright against the back of the sofa. In her lap was a cushion that had probably been white to start with. She was leaning over the man, Rolf, who was lying on the cushion in her lap.

The man was lying in a strange position. One knee was drawn up, and his fingers were spread out above his heart. In his right hand he was holding something that looked like a sign—or a spatula.

"It's definitely been arranged," she said.

"Does it mean anything to you?"

Dessie looked at the picture for a long time.

"I recognize something," she said. "I just don't know where from. I can't put my finger on it."

"Concentrate," Jacob said.

She stared at the picture until the focus started to blur.

"Sorry," she said. "It's not coming."

He looked at her with his very blue eyes for several long seconds.

Then he gathered the pictures together and without another word left her sitting at the café table.

Chapter 36

JACOB GOT OFF THE BUS outside the central police headquarters on Kungsholmen in the middle of Stockholm.

On his first night in Stockholm he had walked around the huge complex that housed the central Swedish police authority ten times or more, feeling like a nut, not caring in the least.

Various different sections had been added over the course of the past century, giving the building an extremely schizophrenic appearance. The eastern section looked like some Disney castle, the southern bit was functional concrete, the northern section was a concrete monstrosity, and the western piece was inherited from the same Soviet era as the suburb he and Dessie had passed on the way to the crime scene on Dalarö.

The unconventional-looking building hadn't made the people inside particularly flexible—he knew that much already. The investigating team refused to take his calls. The receptionist kept putting him through to an automated message box that acted as the telephone tip-off line.

Enough was enough, though.

Now he was going to get inside, no matter what the cost to his reputation.

He clenched his fists and steeled himself for the upcoming confrontation.

The entrance was in the old, communist part of the complex. He walked into the lobby and got a sense of déjà vu. Like the *Aftonposten* lobby, it had a stone floor, pale wood, and a glass cubicle.

He hoped the similarities would end there and cleared his throat as he laid his police badge on the desk.

"Jacob Kanon, NYPD," he said as calmly as he could manage. "I'm here to see Superintendent Mats Duvall. It's about the murders on Dalarö."

The overweight woman on the other side of the desk looked impressed at the sight of his police badge.

"Is he expecting you?"

"He should be," Jacob replied, entirely truthfully.

"I'll just call him," the plump woman said, picking up the phone.

"No need," Jacob said. "I'll find him myself. He's on the fifth floor, isn't he?"

He had studied the building from outside and counted seven floors in the office section.

"Fourth floor," the woman said, putting the receiver down as she clicked open the inner door.

He took the elevator up to the fourth floor and exited into a narrow corridor with a low ceiling and humming strip lighting. He took several steps before knocking on a random door. He stuck his head into a small office and said, "Hello, excuse me, but Duvall, can you tell me where he is?"

A woman with a ponytail and glasses looked up in surprise.

"He's in a meeting about Dalarö at the moment," she said. "Conference Room C, I think."

"Thanks," Jacob said and turned back. He had already passed Conference Room C.

He retraced his steps, slipped into the room, and closed the door behind him.

There were ten people inside, the core of the investigating team: Mats Duvall, Gabriella Oscarsson, a woman in her fifties in a suit, two fairly young women, and five men of varying ages. There were thermoses of coffee and refreshments on the table.

Coffee cups stopped in midair, hands stiffened, and ten pairs of eyes stared at him.

"Your investigation is about to go seriously wrong," he said, pulling up a chair and sitting right down at the table with them.

Chapter 37

THERE WAS A DEATHLY SILENCE in the room.

He had managed to get their attention, though. Now he had about ten seconds before he would be thrown out.

"You've probably worked out that the victims' passports and wallets are missing," he said. "Jewelry, cameras, and other valuables are gone. Their bank accounts have been emptied, their credit cards taken right to the limit with cash withdrawals. When you go through their credit-card transactions, you'll discover at least one large purchase before the cash withdrawals take over."

He paused. No one moved.

"What you're looking for is a very attractive couple around twenty-five years old," he went on. "Maybe even younger. A man and a woman, English speaking. They're well off, probably white, posing as normal tourists."

Mats Duvall cleared his throat. Then he spoke in nearly perfect English.

"I should explain to my colleagues that this man is a

homicide detective from the New York police. His name is Jacob Kanon, and he has been tracking all the investigations since New Year's. He has personal reasons—"

"My daughter, Kimberly, was one of the victims in Rome," Jacob said.

He looked around the group. Their shock at his appearance had started to turn to anger in a few of the faces. One of the older men, a bald man in a suit and vest, seemed particularly irritated.

"This is Sweden," the bald man said now. "The Swedish police are responsible for official business here. We don't need any lessons in investigative technique, not from the FBI, nor from any other New York cowboys."

"Cross-border cooperation is absolutely vital if these killers are going to be stopped," Jacob said. "All we've got to go on is their pattern, and we need coordination for that to become clear."

"That isn't necessarily true," the bald man said. "What we need is a decent, honest investigation, and we're very good at that here in Sweden."

Jacob stood up so abruptly that his chair toppled over behind him.

"I'm not here to take part in some pissing contest," he said in a gruff voice. "And New York doesn't have cowboys, by the way!"

The bald man in the vest also stood up. His forehead was sweating and his eyes were narrow and small.

"Evert, let him speak."

The woman in the suit had said this. Her voice was low and calm. She stood up and walked over to Jacob.

"Sara Höglund," she said, holding out her hand to him. "Head of the National Crime Investigation Department. You'll have to excuse Prosecutor Ridderwall, he's an extremely dedicated judicial investigator."

The prosecutor sat down and ran his hand angrily over his scalp.

The woman in the suit looked Jacob carefully up and down.

"Detective Kanon from New York City," she said. "What district?"

"Thirty-second," Jacob replied.

Her eyes lit up in recognition.

"Harlem," she said.

He nodded. The police chief knew her NYPD.

She turned to Mats Duvall.

"We need all the help we can get on this case," she said. "Formalize Mr. Kanon's status with Interpol. These bastards have to be stopped."

Jacob clenched his fists in triumph.

He was on board, and his intuition had been correct—something was going to break here in Stockholm. He hoped it wasn't him.

Chapter 38

WASHINGTON CONFIRMED JACOB'S STATUS AND Berlin verified that he had been linked to them in their investigation into the German case, and a couple of phone calls later, he was formally accepted as part of the group, albeit on strictly limited terms.

"You've got no mandate to make your own decisions on police business," Mats Duvall clarified. "You can't be armed, so I must ask you to hand over your sidearm. And you have to be accompanied at all times by a Swedish colleague."

Jacob looked at him steadily.

"I haven't got my sidearm with me. You'll get it, though," he said. "Who am I going to be working with?"

Mats Duvall looked at everyone.

"Gabriella, you've been on the case from the start?"

Gabriella Oscarsson tightened her lips until they formed a harsh line.

"Good," the superintendent said, distributing sheaves of photocopies around the table.

The atmosphere in the room was tense and uncomfortable. Serious run-throughs of an entire case like this almost always contained elements of hierarchical squabbling, and Jacob realized that his actions hadn't made things easier.

Mats Duvall cleared his throat and continued going through the victims' credit-card transactions. He spoke in English for Jacob's benefit. None of the others objected, but they couldn't have liked it.

The last purchase had been made in the NK department store around lunchtime on Saturday. Claudia Schmidt had been shopping at the perfume counter, and Rolf Hetger in the jewelry department.

After that, there was a gap of a few hours before the cash withdrawals began.

Jacob studied the printout. It was in Swedish, but the times and amounts were clear enough. And it was the same damn pattern as in the other cities.

In fewer than six hours, the killers had managed to trick their victims out of their bank cards, drug them, kill them, steal their possessions and rental car, drive off in the vehicle, and start emptying their bank accounts.

"The Germans died between the perfume counter and the cash withdrawals," he clarified.

Prosecutor Ridderwall leaned forward across the table.

"The preliminary autopsy results haven't been able to pinpoint the exact time of death," he said. "Are we really going to sit here and *guess?*"

Jacob put the papers down and looked at the fat little man, at his aggrieved expression and small, hostile eyes. He needed to set some firm boundaries with these people from the beginning.

"Are we going to run through the investigation," he said, "or are the two of us going to go outside and fight in the yard? I like to fight, by the way. Golden Gloves in Brooklyn."

Gabriella gave an audible sigh and muttered something that sounded like "Good god."

The prosecutor didn't reply and remained seated. So Jacob picked up the papers again.

Rolf Hetger had spent 22,590 kronor in the jewelry department—almost $3,000.

"What did he buy?" Sara Höglund asked.

"We've got people at NK right now," the superintendent said. "We'll know soon."

They moved on to the next sheet and went through the cash withdrawals. The addresses meant nothing to Jacob.

"Where are these cash machines?"

"In the city center."

Jacob nodded. Thus far the killers were following the pattern *exactly*. That was good news, he believed.

"Some of the machines have camera surveillance," Gabriella Oscarsson said. "We've requested the recordings for the times in question."

"What did the cameras in the other cities show?" Mats Duvall asked.

Jacob fished out a notebook from his sports bag. He replied without opening the book; he knew the answer by heart.

"A tall man with brown hair, a cap, and sunglasses. He's wearing a dark, medium-length coat, and light shoes."

"Every time?" the superintendent asked.

"Every time," Jacob said.

They went through the valuables that, according to the victims' families, had probably been stolen from Dalarö.

"The make of camera? What karat ring?" Jacob asked.

"The parents are going to go through old receipts," Gabriella said, irritated. "They've just lost their kids. Surely some level of sympathy..."

Jacob looked at her and felt his jaw clench.

Silence fell on the room. Finally Sara Höglund took over.

"How do we proceed from here? Suggestions?"

Jacob swiveled in his chair for a few seconds before replying.

"We have to break their pattern somehow," he said. "We have to provoke them to start making mistakes."

Sara Höglund raised her eyebrows. "*How* do we do that?"

"By using the communication channel they've already opened," Jacob said.

Ten pairs of eyes looked skeptically at him.

"The postcard to the paper *Aftonposten*," he said. "The killers obviously want to communicate—and now we're going to give them a reply."

Gabriella Oscarsson lifted her eyes to the ceiling. Mats Duvall nodded in encouragement.

"Go on."

Jacob looked at each and every one of the people at the table before answering.

"I've been thinking about this for a while. Get Dessie Lars-son to write an open letter to the killers and have it pub-lished in tomorrow's paper. Have her offer to interview them."

Evert Ridderwall snorted indignantly. "Why on earth would the killers respond to something like that?"

Jacob looked steadily at him.

"Because we're going to offer them a hell of a lot of money," he said.

Chapter 39

SYLVIA SIGNALED THE WAITER OVER with a well-manicured hand and a small, delicate wave. She was playing rich girl again today.

"We'd like to look at the wine list again," she said, then giggled and leaned against the shoulder of the beautiful Dutch woman sitting next to her. "It feels so naughty, doesn't it, drinking wine at lunchtime?"

The Dutch woman cackled and nodded. "Very good wine, too."

They were sitting in Bistro Berns, a high-class French restaurant with a rather vaudevillian atmosphere, situated by the Berzelii Park in the middle of town.

Sylvia and the Dutch woman had eaten *chèvre chaud* with a beetroot and walnut salad, and the men had each had *boeuf bourguignon,* and now they were ready for another bottle of red, the good stuff.

"I think the financial crisis will lead to the sort of clear-out that the capital markets really need today," the Dutchman said, looking important.

He was terribly keen to impress Mac, and Mac was playing along and pretending to be interested in his every pronouncement. Mac kept getting better with each new couple they met.

"That's the positive scenario," Mac said. "On the other hand, maybe we ought to learn from history. Financial worries at the turn of the last century didn't break until after the First World War."

"God, you're both soooooooo boring," Sylvia groaned, waving the waiter over again. "Well, I'm going to have a sinfully rich dessert. Anyone joining me?"

The Dutch woman ordered a crème brûlée, and the men asked for coffee.

"Have you heard what happened here?" Sylvia asked, pouring more wine into their glasses. "Two tourists were murdered on some island."

The Dutch woman's brown eyes opened wide. She was absolutely gorgeous, this one.

"Is that true?" she said in horror. "Was it in the papers?"

Sylvia shrugged.

"I can't understand what the papers say. It was a girl in the hotel who told us. Isn't that right, Mac, that two tourists were murdered on an island near here?"

Mac nodded. "Yes, that's right. Two Germans. An awful business, apparently. Their throats had been cut."

Now Mr. Dutch Boyfriend's eyes opened wide as well.

"Their throats were cut?" he said. "We had a case like that in Holland actually. In Amsterdam, not all that long ago. That's right, isn't it, Nienke?"

"Is it?" the Dutch woman said, licking dessert off her spoon. "When was that, then?"

"They're being called the Postcard Killers," Mac said. "They've sent a postcard to some newspaper here."

"That's sick," the Dutch woman said, scraping her bowl for the last remnants of the brûlée. "Where did you get that blouse?"

This directed at Sylvia. The murdered Germans were already gone from the Dutch woman's pretty little blond head.

"Emporio Armani," Sylvia said. "There's a great boutique, fabulous. It's just around the corner from here, on Biblioteks-gatan."

She stood up, walked around the table, and settled down on Mac's lap.

"Darling," she cooed, "it's such a lovely day. I'd really love a souvenir, something to remember it by..."

"No," Mac said, standing up quickly.

Sylvia almost fell on the floor.

"What?" she said, laughing, as Mr. Dutch Boyfriend stood up and helped steady her. "Do you think it would be too expensive?"

"No, Sylvia," he said. "Not now. Not today." His lips curled in irritation.

Sylvia laughed and wound her arm around the Dutch-man's shoulder.

"Ooh," she said, "what a killjoy he is. I think you're much more fun."

She stretched up on tiptoe and kissed him full on the lips.

"We've got to go now, Sylvia," Mac said, taking hold of her other arm.

Chapter 40

"HANG ON," THE DUTCHMAN SAID, handing Mac his card. "Get in touch if you fancy going out for a meal one evening. We'd enjoy it."

"Sure, we'll do that!" Sylvia called as Mac pulled her out of the restaurant.

When they were out of sight, Sylvia pulled herself free of his grip.

"I presume you have a good explanation," she said, stroking his arm.

Mac didn't answer at first. Then he said, "Why did you bring up the murders? We don't make mistakes like that."

"It wasn't a mistake. The city is too hot now. We couldn't kill them. Though, Christ, I wanted to. I wanted to cut them both."

The Berzelii Park was crawling with people with ice creams and bicycles and buggies.

Sylvia sidled closer to Mac and kissed his neck. "Are you

angry with me?" she whispered. "How can I make it up to you?"

"We've got some work to do," he said tersely. "We still have to get out of Stockholm."

She sighed theatrically but took hold of his hand, sucking his finger and then kissing him on the lips.

"I'm your slave," she whispered. "I just don't want to end up in prison. I couldn't bear to be without you, Mac."

They walked across the bridge over Strömmen back to the Old Town. Sylvia had both her arms around Mac's waist, which made it hard to walk as she stumbled along the edge of the quay.

Finally Mac cheered up and put his arm around her shoulders. "You're forgiven."

They walked to the 7-Eleven on Västerlånggatan, tucked in among all the medieval buildings, and Sylvia bought the day's papers while Mac got half an hour on the Internet.

"Is there anything about Oslo?" Sylvia asked.

Mac tapped quickly on the keyboard.

"Nope," he said.

Sylvia turned to pages 6 and 7 of *Aftonposten,* recognizing the house in the picture.

"You know something?" she said. "We left the Dutch couple with the bill."

Mac laughed. Then he logged in and set to work.

Chapter 41

THE SHOP ASSISTANT AT NK was a forty-year-old woman from Riga named Olga. She had bleached-blond hair and big earrings, held a goldsmith's diploma, and was fluent in five languages. Swedish wasn't one of them. She had gotten the job in the jewelry section of the department store during the tourist season to take care of foreign customers.

Two days before, she had sold an Omega watch, a Double Eagle Chronometer in steel and gold with a mother-of-pearl case, to the murdered German tourist Rolf Hetger.

Now she was sitting in the interrogation room on the fourth floor of Stockholm's police headquarters, clearly ill at ease.

Jacob studied the woman from his position by the wall.

She looked considerably older than her forty years. The question was, Why was she so nervous?

"Can you tell us about your encounter with Rolf Hetger?" Mats Duvall asked.

The Latvian licked her lips.

"He wanted to look at a watch. That's pretty much it," she said. "There was another man with him. They spoke English to each other. They were both very stylish."

She blushed.

"Can you describe the other man's appearance for me? Please."

"The American? He was blond and really fair. He looked like a film star. He was very charming. Humorous, attentive."

She looked down at the table.

Jacob felt his muscles tense: the killer was a flirtatious American? Of course he was.

"What made you think the fair-haired man was American?" the superintendent asked.

Olga fingered one of her earrings.

"He spoke American," she said.

"Are you sure of that?"

She blushed deeper.

"He sounded...he looked...like that nice actor with long hair...from *Legends of the Fall*."

Mats Duvall looked confused.

"Brad Pitt," Jacob said.

The superintendent cast a surprised glance in Jacob's direction.

"What happened at the store? Tell us everything. Please."

"They looked at watches. The German was thinking of buying a Swatch at first, but the American persuaded him to buy a different one. So that's what he did."

Over 22,000 kronor for an impulse buy, Jacob thought. The killer was very persuasive.

"Did Rolf Hetger sign for it or use his PIN?"

Olga breathed deeply for a few seconds.

"He used his code."

"And where was the American while this was going on? The purchase transaction."

"He was standing right next to him."

"Do you think you'd recognize the American if you saw him again?"

She hesitated, then nodded.

"Why's that?" Mats Duvall asked.

Olga looked at him, confused. "What do you mean?"

"You must have hundreds of customers every day. How come you remember these two in particular?"

"Not hundreds," she said and seemed slightly annoyed, "and not many of them buy expensive Omegas."

She looked down and Jacob could tell that she was lying.

Olga remembered the men because they were young, wealthy, handsome, and had flirted with her.

He knotted his hands. This was what he'd been waiting for: a mistake. They'd been sloppy and had made themselves visible. They had finally left a trail. Now could he follow it?

"Have you got the equipment to do electronic composite pictures?" he asked.

"Two floors down," Mats Duvall replied. "We can do anything you can do in America."

They ended the session.

Chapter 42

A POLICE INSPECTOR TOOK THE woman to the expert whose computer was full of noses, eyes, and hairlines.

"That went pretty well," Mats Duvall said as they walked back toward his office. "A breakthrough, really. A victory for street-level policing."

"Partly," Jacob said. "Olga wasn't being completely honest with us."

Mats Duvall raised his eyebrows. "What do you mean?"

"She isn't Latvian. I know Latvians from my old neighborhood," Jacob said. "I think she's from farther east, Russia or Ukraine, which means she's here on a false passport. And she isn't forty. She's more like fifty. I'd find a way to hold her, question her more. She knows something she isn't telling us."

The superintendent sat down behind his desk and switched on his computer.

"We don't just hold people as we like in this country, and

certainly not on the basis of vague suppositions about false passports."

"It's not because of the passport," Jacob said, making an effort not to shout. "We've scared the hell out of her. Didn't you see that? She'll disappear as soon as she gets the chance."

Mats Duvall typed something on his computer and didn't reply.

Jacob took a couple of long strides toward the superintendent's desk and leaned over the screen.

"This is the first time anyone's seen the killer and remembered him so clearly," he said. "If she disappears, then so do our chances of identifying him."

Mats Duvall looked at his watch.

"Time to head off to *Aftonposten* again," he said.

Chapter 43

DESSIE COULDN'T BELIEVE HER EARS.

"You can't be serious," she said. "I can't do that. The paper can't do it."

She was sitting at the table in the conference room behind the sports desk. She was there with the editor in chief, Stenwall, Forsberg, the news editor, Jacob Kanon, Gabriella, and Mats Duvall.

"This doesn't have to be a unanimous decision," Robert Stenwall said. "The editorial team is agreed, so the matter's set. We're publishing a letter to the killers tomorrow. We all feel the letter should come from you. You're the one they chose to contact, after all."

Dessie stood up at the table. She was beside herself.

"Offer money to those *bastards?* Can't you see how unethical that is?"

"We believe this is a good way of getting them to communicate," Mats Duvall said. "The murderers want mass-media coverage. Otherwise, they wouldn't send those letters and postcards."

Dessie looked at their faces. They were closed, their eyes turned away. They had already made their decision, she realized, without even consulting her.

"It isn't the media's job to do the work of the police like this," she said. "We're supposed to report murders, not solve them."

"We see this as a chance to do both at the same time," the editor in chief said in a rather strained voice. "People are dying, Dessie."

She crossed her arms over her chest.

"Then I think you should sign the letter," she said. "Why should I have to put my name to it?"

Forsberg twisted uncomfortably in his chair. He didn't like disagreements.

"*They chose you*," Mats Duvall said. "It won't have anything like the same impact if someone else does it."

She stared at the floor.

"This is wrong," she said. "It's wrong to pay them for their crimes."

"Dessie," Gabriella said, "come on. They won't get any money. It's just to lure them in."

"And if I refuse?"

Suddenly Jacob stood up, took her arm, opened the door, and pulled her into a corner of the sports section.

Dessie looked back over her shoulder and had time to register the editor in chief's surprised expression and Gabriella's pursed lips.

"For god's sake," Jacob said. "You've got to go along with this. We've never been so close to the killers. Your editors are doing exactly the right thing by publishing this. They're doing what they've got to do."

Dessie shrugged free of his grip.

"Like crap, they are!" she said. "Stenwall's just thinking of the extra sales. He wants to be quoted in the *Washington Post*. It goes against every moral principle!"

The American's eyes darkened. He took a step toward her, his breath hot.

"You're talking about principles. I'm talking about saving lives. If you do this in the right way, you can get them to break their pattern, and that's exactly what we need. This'll be where they make their mistake."

She looked into his eyes, which were glittering like wild stars.

"Do you realize how much shit I'll get from my colleagues for this?" she said.

He stared at her, speechless for a few moments.

"So your career, your comfort, is more important than young people's lives?" he said.

Dessie blinked.

"No," she said, "that's not what I'm say—"

"Yes it is," Jacob interrupted. "That's *exactly* what you're saying. You just said your reputation is more important than catching Kimmy's killer and stopping the murder of others."

He ran both hands angrily through his hair and turned away from her. He looked like he was about to kick something.

She suddenly became unsure. What if he was right? Maybe her responsibility as a human being was more important than her responsibility as a reporter. Or her reputation, which wasn't worth that much, anyway.

"What's the letter going to say?" she asked. "Apart from the offer of money?"

He closed his eyes for a few moments.

"You've got to challenge them," he said. "Shake them up, provoke them into doing something irrational. I'll help you, of course. If you want my help."

"What language? English or Swedish?"

"Can you do both?"

"I'm writing my doctoral thesis in English."

They looked at each other in silence.

"I'm going to regret this," Dessie said.

"No," Jacob said, "not if we catch them, you won't."

Chapter 44

Tuesday, June 15

SYLVIA FLUFFED AND ADJUSTED THE pillows on the queen-size bed, then opened the copy of *Aftonposten*. She let out a little groan of disappointment.

"That's not very flattering at all," she said, looking at the composite picture of Mac that dominated page 6. "You're much more handsome in real life."

"Let me see what I look like," Mac said, trying to take the paper from her.

"Hang on a moment," Sylvia said, pulling the paper back. "I want to read what it says."

Mac was put out and went into the bathroom. Sylvia looked admiringly at his buttocks as he disappeared into the shower. She pushed aside the breakfast tray on her lap to read the story better.

The letter was written in both English and Swedish, and

addressed to the "Postcard Killers." The headline ran: "Accept My Challenge—If You Dare."

Sylvia ran her eyes across the page to see who had signed the letter.

"Hey," she called toward the bathroom. "Our new friend Dessie Larsson's written us a letter. How sweet of Dessie. How thoughtful she is."

The shower started up. Mac didn't answer.

Be like that, then, she thought, and started reading out loud.

"You wrote to me, and now I'm writing to you. Unlike you, I'm prepared to put my name on my correspondence. I'm not hiding, I take full responsibility for my actions. And I shall carry on doing that. So I and *Aftonposten* have chosen to reply to you with this letter..."

She skimmed through the text.

It said that the police were hot on their heels, that it was only a matter of time before they were arrested. That they had gotten too cocky, that they had started to make mistakes. That they were close to giving themselves away. That the Germans on Dalarö would be their last victims.

She looked up to see Mac standing in the doorway with the bath towel around his neck, watching her read.

"What does it say? Don't be such a controlling bitch. You know I don't like that."

"Oh, sorry, baby. Most of it's bullshit," Sylvia said, "but the end is interesting. She wants to interview us."

Mac snorted out a laugh.

"What a moron. Why would we let her interview us?"

Sylvia passed him the paper.

"They're offering us a hundred thousand dollars."

Mac's eyes opened wide.

"No way," he said, taking the paper with both hands and sinking onto the unmade bed. "Fuck. A hundred thousand dollars. That's pretty good!"

Sylvia stood up and went over to the window of the hotel room. She stretched her slender arms above her head and yawned loudly, well aware that she was fully visible in all her nakedness. "Look at me," she whispered. "Here I am. Catch me!"

On the other side of the street was a building constructed in the Swedish National Romantic style, with towers and a copper roof, its grille-covered windows glittering in the morning sun. It was Stockholm's municipal courthouse, the place where clumsy criminals were taken to atone for their pathetic misdemeanors. She stood on tiptoe. Behind the courthouse was a creamy yellow palatial building with pinnacles and a bell tower and decorative balustrades: Stockholm's police headquarters, where funny little officers were tearing their hair out in despair and thinking up lies to get them to give themselves away.

"Sylvia," Mac said, "this is actually worth considering. She's promising complete anonymity, that she will never reveal her sources. And we could really use the money. Look, there's a phone number for us to call."

She let her eyes roam across the gray-brown facade of the courthouse.

"That's not a bad idea," she said, turning to Mac. "But why stop at a hundred thousand dollars?"

"Do you think she'd pay more?"

Sylvia smiled.

"Have you got that card the Dutchman gave you?"

Mac blinked his long eyelashes.

"Why?"

She went over to the bed, got on all fours, and snaked her way slowly over to Mac. She bit him gently on the earlobe and breathed into his neck.

Then she slid down onto him, warm and wet. "First things first, sweetheart."

Chapter 45

THE BRASS DOORBELL GAVE A brittle little ring that fitted its setting perfectly.

Dessie stepped into the gallery on Österlånggatan in the Old Town, holding her breath.

"Hello?" she called cautiously.

She always felt so grubby when she came here. The floor, ceiling, and walls were all painted pristine white. Even the patrons' restroom and the staircase to the offices above were entirely white. She knew the reason why. She'd been told it was to "trap the light" and "do justice to the art."

"Christer? Are you here?"

She felt as though the illusion of purity would shatter if she called out too loudly.

"Hi, Dessie," said a surprised voice behind her. "What brings you here?"

Dessie spun around. She hadn't heard him come in.

Christer, her ex-husband, was dressed as he always was:

black polo sweater, black gabardine trousers, and soundless moccasins. He looked like a caricature of a gallery owner.

"Sorry to intrude," she said with a slightly strained smile. "I need your help."

They had been married for four years. The marriage had given Christer a wife he said he loved, and Dessie had been given a context to belong to. Parties to go to, people to talk to. Christer could be charming, but she had never been able to talk to him.

He looked at her in astonishment.

"Okay, what do you need help with?"

She felt her palms sweating. Maybe this was crazy. Maybe her idea was completely mad. But she was excited about solving these murders. She felt passionate about it.

"It's a bit complicated," she said. "It's just an idea I had..."

She took a deep breath. She was here now, after all. "It's about a particular painting," she said. "I need your help identifying a painting."

Chapter 46

CHRISTER HELD UP HIS HANDS in a gesture of curiosity.

"What painting? Have you got a picture of it?"

Dessie hesitated.

"No," she said, "not exactly. I can describe it. There's a woman sitting with a cushion on her lap, and there's a man lying on her lap with his head on the cushion."

Christer looked none the wiser.

She put her knapsack and bike helmet on the floor. Then she sat down next to them.

"A woman," she said, "sitting like this."

Then she lay down on the floor. "And a man, lying like this."

She pulled one leg up, spread the fingers of one hand, and stretched the other hand out.

Christer blinked several times.

"Dessie," he said, "what are you doing? What's this all about? Surely you're not decorating."

Dessie sat up. She had the photocopy of the dead couple

from Dalarö in her knapsack. She didn't want to show it to Christer. He was so sensitive about blood. He used to think it was unpleasant even when she had her period.

"A picture," she said. "I'm after a picture or a painting with people in the positions I just showed you."

He looked thoughtfully at her.

She lay down again, stretching her right hand across the floor.

"Like this," she said. "The man's holding something in his right hand."

"Dessie," he said quietly, "why are you here?"

Dessie felt her cheeks starting to burn. He thought the painting was a pretext.

She jerked her neck, stood up, opened the knapsack, and pulled out the photocopy.

"Maybe you should sit down," she said.

He took a step toward her.

"Just say it," he said. "Tell me why you've come to see me. It's not about art, Dessie."

Dessie showed him the photocopy. She saw his eyes open wide and his face go as white as the walls.

She caught him before he fell.

"Good god," he said. "Are those . . . are those . . . people?"

Her reply was needlessly harsh. It just came out that way.

"Not anymore. Look at the way they're positioned. Doesn't it remind you of anything? Where have I seen that before?"

"For heaven's sake," he said, shutting his eyes, shaking his head. "Take it away."

"No," Dessie said. "Take a proper look. Please. Look at the man."

She helped Christer sit down on the floor. He was breathing deeply and had to put his head between his knees for a few seconds.

"Let's see," he said, taking the picture, looking at it for a couple of seconds, then pushing it away again.

"*The Dying Dandy*," he said. "Nils Dardel, nineteen eighteen. It's in the Museum of Modern Art."

Dessie closed her eyes, seeing the painting before her. Of course! It floated up from her memory. She knew exactly which painting it was.

She leaned over and kissed her ex-husband on the cheek.

"Thank you," she whispered. "This may save lives, Christer."

Chapter 47

DESSIE CAUGHT HER BREATH AS she locked her bicycle outside the entrance to the Museum of Modern Art on the island of Skeppsholmen.

The yellow building was glowing in the sunlight, making her squint just to look up at it.

She didn't think she'd been here since her divorce from Christer.

She went into the upper entry hall, into an environment similar to her ex-husband's gallery: pristine white, harsh lighting. It looked just as she remembered it, the glass walls, the espresso bar, the chrome lamps.

She and Christer had been to a party here in the foyer just a few weeks before their marriage came to an end.

She went up to the information desk, staffed by a tall woman in an all-black outfit.

"Excuse me," Dessie said. "I'm trying to find a painting called *The Dying Dandy*."

"Eighty kronor," the woman said.

Of course, the new right-wing government had abolished free entry to Sweden's museums.

Dessie paid.

"You're on the right floor. Just follow the corridor to the left as far as you can, then take a right and then the first left again," said the woman in black.

Dessie couldn't remember the reason for the party she had attended with Christer. It was probably someone's birthday, or someone new had managed to get an exhibition at the Modern.

She suppressed the memory and headed off along the long corridor beyond the espresso bar.

The museum was almost empty at this early hour. She could hear people talking from deep within the catacombs but saw no one, not a soul. It wasn't just newspapers but also an appreciation for art that was on the decline, even here in Sweden.

Eventually she found the right room.

There it was! She recognized it immediately.

The Dying Dandy, oil on canvas, one and a half meters tall, almost two meters across. One of the most famous Swedish paintings of the last century.

Chapter 48

DESSIE STOPPED IN FRONT OF the painting, oddly moved.

It was an impressive creation, with its sweeping shapes and strong colors: the narcissistic man lies dying on his white cushion, a mirror still in his hand.

His equally affected friends are gathered around him. They're mourning, but the only one in tears is the man in the purple jacket and orange shirt up in the left-hand corner.

The woman holding him and the white cushion on her lap looks almost amused.

There was no doubt about it now: this was the model for the murders on Dalarö.

The killers must have known the painting. Maybe they'd been here.

Maybe they'd stood exactly where she was standing now, pondering Dardel's work: Was it an allegory about the act of creativity? Or was Dardel holding up a forbidden image of homosexuality?

A thought ran like fire through her brain. She took a deep breath, looking up at the ceiling, then felt the adrenaline kick in.

Up in one corner, right above the door, was a discreet surveillance camera.

Right now, her image was being captured somewhere.

She took out her mobile and called Gabriella at police headquarters.

Chapter 49

DESSIE WAS HOLDING UP THE color reproduction of Dardel's masterpiece in one hand and the photograph from Dalarö in the other.

Her hunch had to be right. Jeez, she was better at this than the police!

Gabriella's desk was covered with Jacob's postcards and the photographs of the bodies. Beside them were pictures Dessie had printed from the Internet.

Gabriella looked at the pictures one by one, her eyes opening wider and wider.

"God," she said, picking up the picture of the murdered Germans, "you're right, Dessie."

"Sorry," said Jacob, "but what are you talking about?"

Dessie looked at his unruly mop of hair. He looked like he'd been quite literally tearing it out. Suddenly she felt so sorry for him, for his pain, his terrible loss.

"The killers arrange the bodies to imitate famous works of art," she said. "Look at this one, Jacob."

Dessie picked up the photograph from Paris. Emily and Clive Spencer's bodies were sitting side by side in bed, both with their right hand over the left resting on their stomachs.

"The *Mona Lisa*," she said, putting a copy of da Vinci's masterpiece alongside the photograph.

Jacob clumsily grabbed the pictures, crumpling them slightly.

The mysteriously smiling woman on the painting was holding her right hand over her left and resting both on her stomach.

"Christ," he said finally, "you're right. That's what they've been doing."

"Karen and Billy Cowley," Dessie said.

She put down the picture of the couple murdered in Berlin, showing them in profile, the side with their uninjured eye looking toward the camera.

Beside it she laid a printout of an Egyptian statue.

"The bust of Nefertiti, probably the most imitated work of art from Ancient Egypt. It's in the Neues Museum in Berlin. The killers saw it there, I guarantee you."

Gabriella leaned forward. Her face was flushed, two red marks glowing on her cheeks. Dessie glanced at her. They had been there, too, to the Neues Museum, on their first trip away together.

Jacob picked up the picture and studied it intently.

"What do you mean?" he asked Dessie. "What do their gouged-out left eyes have to do with it?"

"The bust of Nefertiti is missing its left eye," Gabriella said. "Everyone knows that."

Chapter 50

DESSIE WASN'T PARTICULARLY INTERESTED IN art. Hell, she hadn't recognized the connection to *The Dying Dandy*. Not at first. But she was fairly knowledgeable about the theory, something she had picked up during her marriage to Christer, probably as a means of self-preservation. She hadn't wanted to come across as an ignorant country girl from Norrland at the various openings. She hadn't exactly felt any real emotion or joy from art, however.

Gabriella, on the other hand, had a genuine love of art. She'd gotten on very well with Christer, better than Dessie had actually.

"Amsterdam," Dessie said, picking out a copy of the next painting. "Vincent van Gogh. Heard of him?"

Jacob looked at her with indulgence.

"I'm an American," he said, "not a barbarian."

"One of his self-portraits," she said. "It usually belongs in London, but this spring it was on loan to the Van Gogh Museum in Amsterdam. He actually cut off his left ear, but the killers clearly didn't know that, because they cut off—"

"The right ears of their Amsterdam victims," Jacob said breathlessly. "Hell. What are they up to?"

A silence fell. Jacob drummed his fingers on the table, something he did when he was deep in thought.

Gabriella looked through the pictures of the bodies and compared them to other works of art that Dessie had printed out.

"Florence is Botticelli's *Birth of Venus*?"

"The Uffizi," Dessie confirmed.

"What about Athens, then? What's Athens meant to be?"

"I don't know that one. But Madrid has to be *The Naked Maja* by Goya—from the Prado. What do you think, Jacob?"

But Jacob wasn't listening now. He had gone very pale. He was staring vacantly out at the greenery in Kronoberg Park.

"Who was Kimmy?" he asked. "Which work of art is she? What were they imitating?"

Dessie felt her palms sweating. She looked through the printouts and held them out to him.

"The Sistine Chapel," she said softly. "The Creation of Adam is a detail from the ceiling fresco. You know, Michelangelo..."

She held the larger picture, with God lying in front of a human brain and stretching out his hand to Adam, and then a close-up of God's finger almost touching Adam's hand.

Jacob turned to look at Dessie. His eyes were an even brighter blue, radiating a sorrow she couldn't begin to understand.

This is Kimmy's dad, she thought. *Not Jacob the policeman, just Jacob the dad.*

Instinctively she put her hand on his arm, which was tensed up and very strong.

"But what does this actually tell us?" Gabriella said. "That the killers are fucked in the head? We already knew that."

Her tone was terse, almost dismissive. Dessie looked at her in surprise. She removed her hand from Jacob's arm.

"It tells us more than that," Jacob said, now a policeman again. "It tells us a lot of things. They're showing off. They're contemptuous. They're demonstrating to us how *they* have power over life and death. Maybe that death is a form of art that they can use as they please."

Dessie was surprised at the depth of the thought.

Gabriella's intercom crackled.

"The video from the Museum of Modern Art is at the Bergsgatan reception desk now," a voice said.

Jacob stood up.

"Ask for the recordings from all the museums," he said.

Gabriella's head jerked.

"Do you realize how many recordings we're talking about? Anyway, they won't have them after such a long time."

But Jacob had already left the room.

Chapter 51

THE RECORDINGS FROM THE SECURITY cameras at the Museum of Modern Art were of relatively good quality. Hopefully, they would be incriminating.

They were a bit grainy, and the colors were slightly flattened, but the people coming and going were clearly visible in the bright lighting.

The recordings had no sound.

Jacob and Gabriella had barricaded themselves into a video suite deep in the basement of police headquarters, in the middle of piles of computer disks. The files weren't in order or marked in any useful way, which meant they had to go through each of them in turn.

"Where to start with this very bad movie?" Gabriella said, a note of resignation in her voice.

Jacob flipped through the disks, thinking out loud.

"The murders took place on Saturday afternoon. So they must have visited the museum before that."

"If they were ever actually there," Gabriella said. "Don't forget that part."

Jacob chose to ignore her negative attitude.

"Saturday morning isn't very likely," he said. "They were probably busy doing other things then."

"Like what?" Gabriella said.

He looked at her in mild despair.

"Buying champagne and smoking dope with the German couple they would then murder in cold blood."

They divided the recordings between them and started their random viewing.

Chapter 52

JACOB WAS STUDYING A SCREEN where a group of schoolchildren were wandering aimlessly around the room containing Swedish art at 9:26 on Friday morning. He hit the fast-forward button, and the children suddenly started dashing about like mad things, jumping around the room like midget actors in an old silent movie.

"What do you think of Dessie?" Gabriella asked out of nowhere without turning away from her screen.

Jacob looked over at her in surprise.

She had also sped up her recording, and had reached Thursday 2:23.

"Pretty smart girl, for a journalist. Why? What do you think of Dessie?"

Gabriella got to the end of her recording and reached for a new disk from the pile. Friday 3:00 started with three old ladies who seemed more interested in one another than in the art around them.

Gabriella slowed down her recording to look more carefully at a group of Japanese visitors on a guided tour in front of Dardel's painting.

"She's got a lot of integrity, which makes her seem tougher than she is. It was probably a mistake to force her to write that letter," Gabriella said.

Jacob glanced over at Gabriella's screen and watched her hit fast-forward again after the Japanese tourists disappeared.

"Stop! Look at that," Jacob suddenly said.

At 3:27 a young couple came into the room and stood in front of *The Dying Dandy*. Only their backs were visible.

The woman had long hair, dark but not black. It was hard to judge the exact color because of the quality of the film.

Beside her was a tall, well-built man with fair hair. The man put his arm around the woman's shoulders. She stroked his back and slipped her fingers under the waistband of his jeans.

Together they went right up to the painting, like they were inspecting it thoroughly.

"Do you think that could be them?" Gabriella wondered.

Jacob didn't answer.

The couple kept standing there, looking at the painting, speaking only occasionally to each other. They paid no attention to any of the other works in the room.

Gabriella moved the video forward frame by frame so they didn't miss anything, not a single gesture.

Jacob wished he could hear what they were saying to each other.

The young couple stood in front of the canvas for almost

fifteen minutes. They had their arms around each other the whole time.

Then they abruptly turned to leave the room. The woman kept her head lowered, but just as the man reached the doorway, he threw his hair back. Suddenly his handsome features were caught in razor-sharp precision by the security camera.

Gabriella caught her breath.

"It's him!" she said. "That's the guy from the police composite."

Jacob leapt forward and paused the image. His voice was hoarse with excitement.

"I've got you now, you bastard. I've got both of you!"

Chapter 53

DESSIE SPREAD HER NOTES AND research material out across Gabriella's desk. She was starting to get excited about the possibility of solving these murders.

There was one aspect of the killers' pattern that she'd noticed several times: *they were thieves, too.* They took cameras, jewelry, electronic gadgets like iPods and mobile phones, credit cards, and other valuables that had one thing in common. They were among the easiest things to get rid of on the black market.

She leaned back in her chair, chewing the hell out of a ballpoint pen.

If she ignored the murders and the brutal artistic associations, what was left of the Postcard Killers?

Well, a couple of petty thieves.

And how did people like that behave?

She didn't need her research material in front of her to know the answer to that.

They were creatures of habit, just like everyone else, and maybe even more so.

Criminals who concentrated on break-ins, for instance, almost always started in the bedroom. That was where they could usually find jewelry and cash.

Then they did the study, with its laptops and video cameras.

Then, finally, they went through the living room, with all the expensive but bulky items, like televisions and stereos.

After the crime, the stolen items had to be gotten rid of, and that was where things started to get interesting for Dessie.

What usually happened was that the thieves passed their takings on to a fence, often at a serious discount. That was a price the thieves were willing to pay. Having an established channel to get rid of stolen property was worth its weight in gold. It took away the biggest risks.

But what did they do if they didn't have an established channel?

They used pawnbrokers, drug dealers, acquaintances, and even strangers.

So, what channels were open to the Postcard Killers in their murderous cavalcade across Europe?

They came completely fresh to each new city, which meant they lacked any form of local network. They couldn't sell to fences or acquaintances, and they would hardly take the risk of trying to sell the stolen property to strangers.

She picked up the phone, called reception, and asked to speak to Mats Duvall.

He answered in his office and she made a note of the

extension that flashed on the display. It could come in handy one of these days.

"Hello, yes, sorry, this is Dessie Larsson. I've got a quick question: have you checked the pawnbrokers?"

"The pawnbrokers? Why would we do that? We don't even know what's been stolen."

He hung up on her—the stupid bastard!

Dessie sat with the receiver in her hand.

This time they knew *exactly* what had been stolen.

Gabriella had mentioned the brand of watch, and she had even written it down.

Dessie picked up her notepad and read.

An Omega Double Eagle Chronometer in steel and gold with a mother-of-pearl case.

There couldn't have been many of those handed over to Stockholm's pawnbrokers since Saturday afternoon, certainly not one still in its original packaging.

She went over to Gabriella's computer, typed "pawnbroker Stockholm" into the yellow pages, and got eighteen hits.

She picked up the phone and dialed the first number.

"Hello, my name's Dessie Larsson, and, well, this is really embarrassing, but my boyfriend and I pawned my new Omega and a few other bits and pieces on Saturday, and, well... we'd had a few beers, and now my boyfriend's lost the receipt and I can't remember which shop we went to. I'm so sorry. The watch was an Omega Double Eagle Chronometer. In steel and gold with a mother-of-pearl case..."

No one was going to confirm that they had the watch in their shop—that would be admitting to breaking the law—but the people who worked there were only human. If they'd received a watch matching that description, they couldn't help but react.

"You can't tell me? Omega Double Eagle?"

Straight denial.

"Well, thanks, anyway."

She broke the call and dialed the next number.

Chapter 54

UNFORTUNATELY, OLGA, THE CLERK AT NK, had to resign from her job in the jewelry department. She had been very upset and apologetic because she had really enjoyed working there, but her husband had had a stroke and obviously she needed to hurry back home to look after him.

The management at NK had been understanding and let her have both the regular wages she was owed and the extra payment she had earned during tourist season. She had returned to Riga the previous evening.

Jacob slammed his fist down on the jewelry counter, making the gold rings jump.

"Fucking hell!" he shouted. "I told them. Why doesn't anybody listen to me?"

The customers around him backed away in alarm.

"Did she leave an address in Riga?" Gabriella asked, giving Jacob a look of disapproval. "*I'm* listening to you, so you don't have to shout."

"I do too have to shout. It makes me feel better."

The head of the jewelry department went over to the office to check, but Jacob couldn't be bothered to wait. The address Olga had given would be false. And there was no husband who'd had a stroke either.

He waited on the sidewalk outside, rubbing his eyes with his palms. People brushed past him on both sides. They were laughing and talking. Someone was playing a mouth organ.

It was him. It was the fair-haired man on the video. Jacob was sure of it.

Kimmy's killer, that was what he looked like. But then he looked again more closely.

The man with the mouth organ wasn't the killer.

Suddenly Gabriella came running out to the sidewalk with her cell in her hand.

"Duvall just called," she said. "Dessie's found the Omega."

Jacob spun around and stared at her.

"What! Where?"

"A pawnshop on Kungsholmstorg, a square just a couple of blocks from police headquarters."

"They've got some nerve," Jacob said, running toward their car, a Saab that had seen better days.

Gabriella unlocked the car with the infrared as she ran. She got in, stuck a blue light on the roof, and started the siren as she steered the car into heavy afternoon traffic.

Chapter 55

THE PAWNSHOP WAS AT A busy intersection and looked like pawnshops usually do, a bit messy, uncomfortable, apologetic.

They parked on a pedestrian crossing right outside the shop, then hurried inside.

On the front counter stood a digital camera, a box containing an emerald ring, a few other pieces of jewelry—and an Omega in steel and gold in a mother-of-pearl case.

Mats Duvall, impeccably dressed in a blazer and chinos, was standing with Dessie, the shop's owner, and two detectives. Duvall was leaning over a computer screen.

"Is he on video?" Jacob asked breathlessly.

"We're hoping he is," the superintendent said.

"What ID did he use?"

Duvall pushed the pawnbroker's ledger toward him without taking his eyes from the screen.

The items on the counter in the shop had been pawned by a man who had used an American driving licence as his

ID, issued in the state of New Mexico in the name Jack Bauer. He had received 16,430 kronor in total.

"Is this some sort of fucking joke?" Jacob asked. "How the hell can someone get away with calling himself Jack Bauer? Jack Bauer! The TV show? *Twenty-four?*"

"Here he is," Mats Duvall said, turning the screen to face Jacob.

A tall man in a long, dark coat, with brown hair, a cap, and sunglasses, was shown signing the agreement on the counter in the shop.

No well-built blond. No Brad Pitt. No Jack Bauer.

What had he been expecting?

"I presume you recognize him," Mats Duvall said.

Jacob gave a quick nod.

It was the same man who had been photographed taking money out of ATMs on the murder victims' credit cards throughout Europe.

Chapter 56

"OKAY, THEN," THE SUPERINTENDENT SAID a few minutes later. "We'll meet again at eight o'clock tomorrow morning. You're all working hard. We'll get these people."

He stood up and walked quickly from the shop without looking back. The two detectives on his team followed close on his heels.

Dessie was left standing by the pawnbroker's desk together with Jacob and Gabriella. On a shelf next to the computer was a copy of that day's *Aftonposten*. Her own words screamed out its battle cry: "Accept My Challenge— If You Dare."

She turned the paper over to avoid having to see it. Gabriella noticed her doing it.

"I agree that publishing the letter wasn't very smart," she said, nodding toward the paper.

Dessie took a deep breath and pulled on her knapsack.

"See you tomorrow," she said abruptly, heading for the door.

"I've got the car," Gabriella called after her. "I can give you a lift."

Dessie kept walking.

"It's okay," she said. "I've got my bike at police headquarters. It's close. I'm fine."

She opened the door and stepped out onto the sidewalk.

"I'll walk with you," Jacob Kanon called, catching up with her.

"I can put the bike in the back," Gabriella said, jogging after them.

Dessie spun around.

"It's okay," she said. "*I'll be fine*. Thanks, anyway."

It was evening. The air was damp and cool, and the sun was low in the sky.

"Whatever you want," Gabriella said, getting into the Saab and speeding off, sour as hell.

With a sense of melancholy, Dessie watched the car drive away.

"You were the one who finished it, weren't you?" Jacob said.

She gave a deep sigh.

"Hungry?" the American asked.

She thought for a moment. Then she nodded. "Strangely, I am."

Chapter 57

THEY PICKED A CHEAP ITALIAN restaurant with red-checked tablecloths and pasta and pizza on the menu. Jacob ordered a bottle of red wine from Tuscany and poured them each a glass. "This is good for whatever ails you," he said.

Dessie took a small sip, leaned back, and shut her eyes. "I doubt it very much, but thank you."

So far the letter had done no good at all. Had Gabriella's unpleasant comment been justified? Had she been completely crazy to write it?

"You did the right thing," Jacob said, reading her thoughts. "We've already ruffled their feathers. They're going to make a mistake. Cheers."

Jacob ordered Parma ham and spaghetti Bolognese. Dessie the *insalata caprese* and cannelloni.

"I heard you were the one who actually found the watch," he said. "Good thinking."

She was suddenly embarrassed.

"They aren't just killers," she said. "They're petty thieves, too."

"True, but why did you make that connection?" the American asked, pouring more wine into his glass.

Dessie laughed, not even sure why she thought it was funny.

"Remember I told you I was writing my thesis? Well, it's on the social consequences of small-scale property break-ins. Let's just say it's been an interest of mine since I was a child."

Jacob raised his eyebrows quizzically. He had a very expressive face. When he got angry, his face turned black with rage, when he was happy, he glowed like a woodstove, and when he wasn't sure of something, like now, his face looked like a big question mark.

"I grew up with my mother and her five brothers. My mother worked as home help all her life, but my uncles were villains and bandits, the whole lot of them."

She glanced at him to see how he reacted.

"'Home help'?" he said.

"Helping old people, sick people. None of my uncles married, but they had loads of kids with different women."

Jacob ate some bread. He didn't wolf down his food like some men she knew.

"What's the name of the town you grew up in?"

"I come from a farm in the forests of Ådalen," she said. "That's part of Norrland, where the military were called in to shoot workers as recently as the nineteen thirties."

The American looked at her stonily.

"I'm sure they must have had a good reason," he said.

Dessie's mozzarella caught in her throat. "What did you say?"

"The military don't usually shoot their fellow citizens for no reason," Jacob said.

Dessie couldn't believe what she was hearing.

"Are you defending state-sanctioned murder?"

Jacob stared at her, simultaneously concentrating on the chewy *ciabatta*.

"Okay," he said. "Wrong topic of conversation. Let's move on."

Dessie put her cutlery down. "Do you think it's okay to shoot people for demonstrating against their wages being cut?"

Jacob held up both hands in a disarming gesture.

"Shit, I didn't know you were a communist."

"And I didn't know you were a *fascist*," Dessie said, picking up her knife and fork again.

Chapter 58

DESSIE HONESTLY DIDN'T KNOW WHAT to make of Jacob Kanon.

He was an entirely new species to her, both shut off and extremely demonstrative at the same time. The way he moved seemed a bit clumsy and uncomfortable, as if he weren't quite house-trained.

"Tell me more about your uncles."

Dessie pushed aside the plate of cannelloni.

"Two of them drank themselves to death," she said. "Uncle Ruben was beaten to death outside the church in Piteå the night before May Day three years ago. He had just been released from a stretch in Porsön, in Luleå."

She said it to shock him, but Jacob just seemed amused.

"Were they often inside?"

"Mostly short sentences. They only managed one big thing in the whole of their miserable careers: raiding a security van where they discovered considerably more money than they'd been expecting."

The waiter came over to ask if they wanted dessert.

They both said no.

"Were they convicted?" Jacob asked. "For the security van job?"

"Of course," Dessie said, grabbing the bill. "Although some of the takings were never found."

"Let me get that," Jacob said.

"Stop being so macho," Dessie said, taking out her Amex card. "This is Sweden. Men stopped paying for dates in the sixties." She motioned the waiter over and handed him her card.

The American poured the last of the wine into their glasses with a grin.

"So this is a date, is it?" he asked, his eyes twinkling. "That's interesting."

Dessie looked at him in surprise.

"This? A date? Of course it isn't."

"You said it was. You said this was a date. 'Men stopped paying for—'"

Dessie shuddered.

"That was a figure of speech. This isn't a date. This will never be a date." She signed the credit-card slip and said, "Let's go. It's late."

They stepped out into a light blue evening that would soon be night.

"Where are you staying?" Dessie asked as they walked toward the entrance of police headquarters on Polhems-gatan.

"Långholmen," he said. "A youth hostel, actually."

"It used to be a prison," Dessie said.

"Thanks for the reminder," Jacob said. "I know."

She got her bicycle, and with Jacob walking alongside, she started slowly cycling home through the Stockholm night. A low mist hung over the waters of Riddarfjärden, thin veils sweeping in and hiding the sounds of the city: the cars, the drunken shouting, the music coming from open windows.

He kept her company all the way to her door.

She looked up at him and he was no more than a silhouette against the moon.

"See you tomorrow," he said, raising a hand in farewell as he disappeared down toward Götgatan.

Chapter 59

Wednesday, June 16

THE LETTER ARRIVED WITH THE first delivery of the morning.

Dessie recognized immediately both the envelope and the writing on it.

This time it hadn't been preceded by a warning postcard.

She opened it with her letter knife, wearing gloves on her trembling hands. She was in the presence of the police forensics team and they made her jumpy.

The envelope contained a Polaroid picture, just as the last one had.

"I'll take care of that," said one of the officers, grabbing the picture from her.

She had time to register the bodies and the blood.

She went over to her desk and sank down in the chair. An intense feeling of uneasiness started to spread from her stomach out to her limbs. "Oh, dear god, dear god," she muttered softly.

The text she'd written for the paper had evidently worked. The killers had broken their pattern. *They had carried out more murders in Stockholm instead of moving on to the next city.*

The realization made it hard to breathe.

She had caused the deaths of two more innocent people.

How could she live with herself after this?

Forsberg, the news editor, red-eyed with lack of sleep, sat down on a chair beside her.

"Feeling rough?" he asked.

She looked at him without replying.

"Maybe you should take the day off? Get some rest? You really ought to go home."

She stared at him, speechless. *Day off? Rest?!*

He drummed his fingers on her desk for a few seconds before getting up and going back to the news desk.

Dessie stayed where she was until Mats Duvall, Gabriella, and Jacob Kanon arrived at the office. They got there less than five minutes apart, Duvall and Gabriella looking white as paper.

"What have I done?" she said, looking up at Jacob. "What damage have I caused?"

He looked at her with a surprisingly calm expression.

"Aren't you crediting yourself with a bit too much? *They* did this, not you."

She quickly stood up, aiming for the restroom, but Jacob caught her with a firm grasp on her upper arm.

"Stop it," he said. "This is a blow, but it's not your fault. Instead of feeling sorry for yourself, help us."

"The conference room," Mats Duvall said, moving past them. "Right now, all of you."

Gabriella walked after the superintendent, giving Jacob a sharp look. Dessie, who was suddenly extremely conscious of Jacob's hand on her arm, shook herself free and followed the police through the sports section of the room.

Mats Duvall raised an eyebrow in surprise when she sat down with the investigating team around the table.

"Our work is covered by confidentiality laws," he said.

"First the killers dragged me into this nightmare," Dessie said. "Then you did the same. So now I'm here, whether you like it or not."

The superintendent frowned.

Jacob threw his arms out.

"So let her join in. How hard can it be? She's been useful so far. We owe her something."

Mats Duvall straightened his back.

"If you stay as an observer only. You can't write anything about what we talk about. You're clear about that?"

"Unless you order me to, right?" Dessie said sharply.

The superintendent let the subject drop. One of the detectives handed around enlarged copies of the latest photograph.

"Okay, we've got another double murder," Mats Duvall said, "but so far no bodies. So what do we have? Can anyone identify the scene of the photograph?"

Chapter 60

DESSIE TOOK A DEEP BREATH and stared hard at the photograph in front of her.

A naked young man was lying on his stomach along the back of what looked like a leather Chesterfield-style sofa. Both of his hands were stretched above his head. On the left side of the sofa sat a young woman with her hands placed demurely in her lap.

On her head she was wearing Mickey Mouse ears.

The sofa was in front of a large window. The picture had been taken from a low angle, meaning that the bodies were shot with the daylight coming from behind them.

"Millesgården," Gabriella said.

Mats Duvall looked at her.

"Do you recognize the setting?"

She nodded her head.

"The artwork they're imitating. The man is supposed to be the flying statue in the garden outside. The woman might represent one of the animal sculptures that were in an exhibition there this past winter."

"Get the security recordings from Millesgården," the superintendent said, and one of the detectives disappeared through the door. "What does this business with works of art mean in this context?"

"We don't know yet," Gabriella said. "So far it's just a theory."

Dessie squinted and held the picture closer to her face. Either she needed glasses or the picture was bad.

"I don't know, but maybe...," she said hesitantly.

"What?" Jacob said.

She pointed at a shadow next to the man's forehead.

"There," she said. "That could be a balustrade or a railing. Because it's so high up, it must be on the roof of a tall building."

"And?"

"Railings like that are unusual on residential buildings in Stockholm, unless they're to stop snow from sliding off the roof. This must be some official building."

"For instance?"

She hesitated and fiddled with her pen.

"Well, I might be wrong..."

"Jesus!" Jacob shouted. "Spit it out!"

Dessie jumped and dropped her pen.

"The Royal Palace," she said.

Jacob blinked.

"The Royal Palace? How's that? Have the killers checked in with the king?"

She shook her head.

"The palace is in the background. That's what I see. The murder scene is exactly opposite."

Mats Duvall stood up.

"The Grand Hôtel," he said on his way to the door.

Chapter 61

THE FIVE-STAR HOTEL BY THE harbor on Södra Blasie-holmshamnen had 366 rooms and 43 suites spread over eight floors. About half of them had a view of the water and the Royal Palace.

The hotel manager was calm but stern, even with the police, even with homicide.

"Naturally we're happy to cooperate," she said. "But I hope the search can be conducted with discretion."

Mats Duvall ordered all available staff on the investigation to take part in the search.

Jacob and Gabriella didn't wait for the reinforcements to arrive from headquarters.

They headed for the second floor and methodically went to room after room on the side facing the water. They were accompanied by a receptionist holding a digital hotel register.

Jacob knocked, and whenever there was an answer, he moved on at once. The killers were hardly going to be sitting with the bodies, just waiting to be discovered. That much was clear.

In the rooms where there was no reply, the majority of them, Gabriella opened the door with a master key.

The suspense was like a drug. Jacob realized that he was holding his breath every time a new door opened.

The search on the second floor gave them nothing.

They ran up the stairs to the third floor.

"What have the other hotels looked like?" Gabriella asked, slightly out of breath as she chased after Jacob along the guest corridor. "Have they been as upscale as this? The Grand Hôtel is the finest in Stockholm."

Jacob knocked on the door at the far end and got an irritated *"Oui?"* in reply.

"Sorry," he said, "wrong room," as he moved on to the next.

He knocked, no reply.

"No," he said. "Nothing in this price range. Not even close."

Gabriella put the key card in the door, and the lock clicked. Jacob opened the door and got a gruff *"What the fuck?"* from the bed in response.

"Sorry," he said again and closed it.

"There are cameras everywhere," Gabriella said, pointing at the ceiling.

"Hasn't been like that anywhere else," Jacob said, striding on. "They're breaking their pattern."

At that moment, Gabriella's cell rang. She answered with her usual grunt, listened for seven seconds, then hung up.

"Fourth floor," she said. "Two Dutch tourists."

Chapter 62

NIENKE VAN MOURIK AND PETER Visser, with separate addresses in Amsterdam, had checked into the Grand Hôtel on Saturday evening, June 11, for four nights.

They would never get to check out.

Jacob studied their dead bodies with detached concentration. There was no room for anything else, not here, not right now. Sorrow and grief for their wasted lives could come later, at night in his terrible prison cell in the hostel, when it was darkest and the alcohol in the bottle was running out.

He didn't know the works of art Gabriella had referred to, but the bodies had definitely been arranged. The dead woman's toy ears affected him particularly badly. Maybe because Kimmy had loved Mickey Mouse and had had a similar pair of ears when she was little.

He turned away.

God, these murders were so messed up, horrible in every way he could imagine, inhuman.

The 32nd District of New York police had the highest

murder stats in Manhattan, but he'd never seen anything like this. All the killings were coldly planned, and arranged with little respect. In Harlem, people murdered out of jealousy, passion, revenge, or for money. People killed because of drugs, love, or debts, not to create art exhibitions.

He rubbed his face with his hands. Mats Duvall glanced over at him and turned to one of his detectives.

"Get the recordings from the camera in the corridor," he said. "Check what the surveillance is like in the lobby and the elevators. Has the medical officer arrived yet? We need a time of death as soon as possible."

"There are two champagne bottles in the bathroom," Gabriella said. "One empty, the other half full. Four glasses, too, all with remnants of light yellow liquid in the bottom."

They would find cyclopentolate in two of the glasses, Jacob thought, looking around the hotel room.

It wasn't very big, maybe twenty by sixteen, he guessed. Several of the other hotel rooms had been bigger, but this was still a break from the norm. No other crime scene had been anywhere as elegant as this, but that was just a superficial difference. There was something else here, something that made this murder different from all the others, but he couldn't put his finger on what it was.

The medical officer arrived and Jacob stepped out into the corridor to make room for him.

He noted that there was a DO NOT DISTURB sign on the door.

Then he left the scene of the crime. There was nothing else he could do here.

Chapter 63

BY LUNCHTIME, SECURITY HAD BEEN stepped up in all public places in the Stockholm region that were frequented by tourists, and especially by young people.

All available personnel had been sent out to look for anyone resembling the composite picture from the clerk at NK, or any of the people on the security recordings from the Museum of Modern Art and the pawnbroker's on Kungsholmstorg.

When a preliminary blood test showed that the Dutch couple had smoked marijuana just before they died, sniffer dogs were brought in from around the country to join in the search.

Throughout Stockholm, young people fifteen and over were asked to empty their bags, purses, and knapsacks.

Most of them did as they were asked without protest. Those who refused were arrested.

Dessie was standing in Gabriella's office, looking out across Kronoberg Park.

Four uniformed police officers and a large Alsatian dog

had blocked one of the entrances to the park, a popular shortcut for people heading for the beach or the shops and underground station on Fridhemsplan. Picnic baskets, bags of swimming gear, and expensive attaché cases were all carefully checked without any distinction between them.

The sight ought to have made her feel more secure, but she simply felt guilty.

Jacob came into the room with three plastic wrappers containing sandwiches he had found in a vending machine somewhere.

"Where's Gabriella?"

"She went down to the video suite to get the recordings from the Grand," Dessie said, collapsing onto a chair.

Jacob tore open one of the packets and with a healthy appetite took a large bite of the bread and tuna plus mayonnaise. Dessie looked at him and cringed.

"How can you eat?" she asked. "Doesn't all the violence you see ever affect you?"

"Of course it does," Jacob said, wiping his chin with the back of his hand. "I was just thinking about how sick these murders are. But it won't help the Dutch couple if I faint from low blood sugar."

Dessie leaned her face down into her hands. "I shouldn't have written that bloody letter."

Jacob carried on chewing.

"I thought we'd gotten past that."

She had her cell phone out.

"And now it's started," she said. "Just as I thought it would."

"What has?" Jacob wondered.

"I'm getting calls from the trade press, asking why I'm doing the police's work for them."

Jacob gestured with his hand toward the pictures of the dead couple in the hotel room.

"That's your reality," he said. "What you're talking about is pretentious bullshit."

"Exactly," she said. "And what if I'm the one who made that reality happen?"

He groaned.

"It's true," she said in a low voice. "You said so yourself. They've broken their pattern—they've killed again in the same city. If I hadn't let myself be persuaded, this Dutch couple would still be alive."

"You don't know that," Jacob said. "And if they hadn't died, other young people would have, in some other city."

She took her hands away from her face.

"What do you mean? That the Dutch couple were sacrificed to a noble cause? What does your lot usually call it, *collateral damage?*"

The American wiped his fingers on his jeans. His expression had grown dark.

"I never think like that," he said. "The Dutch couple's deaths were a tragedy. But you have to lay the blame where it belongs. You didn't kill them, and neither did I. Those bastards on the recordings did that, and we're soon going to catch them. Right here in Stockholm. It ends here."

Chapter 64

THE SUSPECTS FROM THE MUSEUM of Modern Art were identified almost immediately on the security recordings from the Grand Hôtel. They appeared on four different film files: two from the lobby and two from the corridor on the fourth floor.

The fair-haired man and the dark-haired woman were caught on camera in the hotel lobby at 2:17 on the afternoon of June 15.

They were with a couple who were quickly identified as Peter Visser and Nienke van Mourik.

The four of them disappeared together into an elevator.

Two minutes later all four reappeared on another recording, in the corridor outside the Dutch couple's room on the fourth floor. They all went into room 418 and the door closed.

Forty-three minutes later, the fair-haired man and the dark-haired woman came out into the corridor again.

After another two minutes, they passed the reception desk and left the hotel.

The detectives who had been out to Millesgården came back with results as well.

A woman who worked as a gardener thought she recognized the fair-haired man. She had noticed him as he walked around with a woman in the sculpture garden. At first glance she thought it was the actor Leonardo DiCaprio.

The recordings from the exhibit rooms at Millesgården were requisitioned and were now being checked down in the basement.

Prosecutor Evert Ridderwall had signed an arrest warrant in the pair's absence.

"This is completely incredible," Gabriella said excitedly. She was walking up and down in Mats Duvall's office, two red spots flushing her cheeks.

Jacob was staring at prints made from the recordings from the Grand Hôtel, tearing at his hair.

Something was fundamentally wrong here. Was he the only one who saw it?

Why had the killers suddenly dropped all safety precautions?

Why were they showing themselves so openly?

It was too easy.

"We've got them now," Evert Ridderwall said happily. "They'll never get away. I don't see how they can."

Even Mats Duvall looked pleased.

"It's just a matter of time before they're arrested," he agreed.

Jacob looked through the pictures again. Both the fair-haired man and the dark-haired woman were clearly visible in all the pictures. There was no doubt that they would be recognized. A national alert had been put out for the couple.

Interpol would be releasing these same pictures internationally within half an hour. Every police patrol in the Stockholm region had already received the printouts.

Sara Höglund came into the room.

"We've released their pictures to the media. They ought to be up on their websites in a few minutes."

Mats Duvall turned to his computer and quickly logged into *Aftonposten*'s website.

"Sometimes they're really quick," he said, turning the screen toward the others.

The headline was in a size usually reserved for world wars and Swedish victories in the ice hockey world championships.

"Police Suspects: These Are the POSTCARD KILLERS."

Underneath was a picture of the fair-haired man and the dark-haired woman.

Chapter 65

THE SQUARE OUTSIDE STOCKHOLM'S CENTRAL Station was filled with police, their dogs, and cordons.

Mac was walking slowly toward the train terminal's main entrance with his arm around Sylvia's shoulders. They could hear the beeping and crackling voices of police radios wherever they went.

Two long-haired boys were picked up with their back pockets full of grass just a few meters ahead of them. What idiots!

"Sorry, guys," Sylvia said.

No one thought to stop the couple.

No one asked to look in their bags, because they didn't have any.

They had been walking around the streets, looking at their reflections in plate-glass windows, admiring their work. Mac tried on a new leather jacket at Emporio Armani. Sylvia sampled different perfumes in Kicks. She smelled nice now. Fresh and sexy for her man.

A police car glided slowly past them. Sylvia took off her

sunglasses and smiled at the officer in the car. He smiled back and drove on.

An elderly woman started yelling when two officers asked to go through her handbag. Three teenage boys ran past like the hounds of hell were after them, followed by two plain-clothes policemen.

"Come on, let's go in," Sylvia said. "These people, the police, are so stupid."

Mac hesitated at the entrance.

Sylvia gave him a quick kiss on the cheek. "You're such a star, Mac."

With their fingers laced together, they walked into the lion's den.

Children were crying, dogs barking, adults complaining. Loudspeaker announcements about delays and canceled trains followed one after another. The crowd got thicker and more agitated with every step they took. Some people had already missed trains because of the mindless searches.

After just ten meters or so they reached the first police checkpoint.

Mac stiffened when he caught sight of his own portrait in the hands of a well-built policeman with a big Alsatian panting at his side, but Sylvia pushed her way through to the policeman and tapped him on the shoulder.

"Excuse me," she said, "but what's going on?"

The policeman turned around, looked right at her, and quite literally jumped.

"I see you've got my picture there," she said, wide-eyed, pointing to it. "What's this all about?"

Chapter 66

THEY WERE AMERICAN CITIZENS, THEIR names Sylvia and Malcolm Rudolph, from Santa Barbara, California.

Their arrest was entirely undramatic.

They went right along to the police station without protest to clear up what was obviously a misunderstanding. They were both very calm, if a little curious and perhaps a little anxious, but no more than might be expected.

Naturally, they wanted to cooperate in any way they could to sort out the *mix-up.*

The premises of the Stockholm police had no rooms equipped with one-way mirrors. Instead, Jacob and Dessie, together with Gabriella and the rest of the investigative team, were shown into a control room where the recorded interview was being shown live.

Jacob's hands were trembling, his mouth completely dry. *There they were.* After all the months spent searching, all the cities he'd been in.

He stood at the back of the room, worried that he might otherwise attack the television screens with his fists.

The fair-haired male, Malcolm Rudolph, was already sitting down, nervously rubbing his hands. He was stunningly handsome, no doubt about that.

Jacob couldn't take his eyes off this man.

It was him, Jacob was sure of it. There he was: the bastard who had killed Kimmy.

The door of the interrogation room opened and Mats Duvall and Sara Höglund entered and sat down opposite the man.

Mats Duvall jabbered his way through the formalities about time and location. Then Sara Höglund leaned across the table and began the first interview.

"Malcolm," she said calmly, "do you understand why you're here?"

The young man bit his lip.

"The police at the Central Station had our pictures," he said. "I guess you've been looking for us, that you think we've done something."

"Do you know what?"

He shook his head. "No, not at all."

"It's about Nienke van Mourik and Peter Visser," the head of the unit said. "They were found dead in their room in the Grand Hôtel this morning."

Malcolm Rudolph's face registered shock and alarm.

"That can't be true," he protested. "Nienke and Peter? But we just saw them, what, yesterday afternoon! We're all going on a cruise to Finland together this weekend!"

Jacob let out a noise that sounded like a purr.

"So you maintain you don't know anything about their deaths?" Höglund asked.

"Are they really dead?"

Malcolm Rudolph began to cry.

Chapter 67

THE YOUNG AMERICAN WAS SOBBING as if his heart were about to break, as if he had just lost his best friends in the world.

"And you think *we* had something to do with it? That *we* could have harmed Peter and Nienke? How could you even *think* that?"

Sara Höglund and Mats Duvall let him cry for a few minutes.

Then they asked if he wanted a lawyer present. They had to do this. He had the right to one under Swedish law, the same as in America.

The murder suspect merely shook his head. He didn't need legal representation. He hadn't done anything wrong. He couldn't understand how anyone could suspect him of anything so terrible. The Dutch couple had been happy and full of life when he and Sylvia had left them in their hotel room the previous day.

What were they doing in the hotel room? Did they eat or drink anything?

"No," Malcolm Rudolph said with a sniff. "Well, actually we did. Peter had a Coke that I drank a bit of."

"No champagne?"

"Champagne? In the middle of the afternoon?" The question seemed to strike him as absurd.

"Did you smoke anything in their room? Marijuana, for instance?"

"Marijuana is illegal here, isn't it? And Sylvia and I don't smoke, anyway."

He slumped down on the table and started crying again. The questions kept coming.

When did you arrive in Sweden?

How long have you been traveling in Europe?

Can you tell us about Peter and Nienke?

"They were so much fun, so nice. We were really looking forward to the trip to Finland with them. We had a great lunch at that place in the Old Town..."

The detectives' questions bounced off him, many unanswered, then into the control room.

Where were you on November twenty-seventh last year?

December thirtieth?

January twenty-sixth this year? February ninth? March fourth?

The interrogation was stopped after just forty-three minutes. To be humane, and to be lawful.

Malcolm Rudolph was led away to a cell in Kronoberg Prison.

Chapter 68

JACOB HAD TO STOP HIMSELF from smashing his fist through the cement wall. He was forced to take a quick walk out in the corridor to calm himself down, if that was even possible.

He came back into the control room just as the young woman was taking her place in the interrogation room.

Sylvia.

She seemed more collected than her husband and answered the questions calmly and clearly.

When she heard that the Dutch couple had been murdered, she put her hands to her face and wept quietly for a moment.

Then she confirmed Malcolm's story: they'd eaten lunch with Nienke and Peter and were planning a joint trip to Helsinki next weekend.

"How did you arrange it?"

"We booked the tickets on the Internet—from a Seven-Eleven shop," she said.

"Which company?"

"Silja."

She smiled.

"I remember that because it sounds a bit like my name, Sylvia."

"Where was the shop?"

"On the long pedestrian street that runs right through the Old Town, Vasterlang—?"

"Västerlånggatan?"

"Yes, that's it."

One of the detectives got up at once and left the room to check out her story.

"Who actually purchased the tickets?" Sara Höglund asked. "Do you remember?"

Jacob slapped his forehead.

"Good God!" he said. "What sort of performance is this? Question time in Sunday school? Jesus, ask her some tough questions, for fuck's sake!"

Gabriella came over and stood right next to Jacob. Her eyes were red and her breath smelled of coffee.

"Pull yourself together," she said. "You're behaving like a kid. Let Sara and Mats do their jobs."

"That's precisely what I mean!" Jacob yelled. "They're not doing their jobs! They're sitting there making nice with her! She's a cold-blooded murderer. Look at her. She's so calm."

"Take it easy, Jacob," Dessie said, putting her hand on his arm.

He ran his hands through his hair and swallowed audibly.

On the television screen the interrogation slowly continued. No big ups or downs.

"Where were you on November twenty-seventh last
year?"

Sylvia Rudolph played thoughtfully with a curl of hair.
She was very pretty, though not as striking as her husband.

"I can't remember offhand. Can I check in my diary? I
might have something there."

Mats Duvall switched on his electronic notepad.

"Let's take something more recent," he said. "Where were
you on February ninth this year?"

Jacob leaned forward to hear better. That was the date of
the killings in Athens. He knew every murder date by heart.

"February?" the woman said with a frown. "In Spain, I
think. Yes, that's right. We were in Madrid in early February, because Mac had a stomach bug and we had to go to a
doctor."

"Can you remember the name of the doctor?"

She pulled a face.

"No," she said, "but I've still got the receipt. It was really
expensive, and the doctor was useless."

Jacob gave a groan.

The questions meandered on, and Sylvia answered them
all in the same calm, matter-of-fact manner.

"What's the reason for the trip to Europe? Why did you
come here?"

"We're art students," Sylvia said.

Dessie and Jacob exchanged a quick glance. Finally there
was something.

"We're at UCLA and have taken a year off. It's been really educational. Super. Until today, anyway."

"How long have you been married?"

The young woman opened her eyes wide, then burst out laughing. Dessie and Jacob looked at each other again.

"Married! We're not married. Mac's my twin brother."

Part Two

Chapter 69

DESSIE PHONED FORSBERG AT THE paper once Sylvia Rudolph had been taken back to her cell.

"How's it going?" the news editor asked. "Have they confessed yet?"

"You know I can't answer that. I'm not here as a reporter," Dessie said. "What's the reaction at the paper?"

"We've got extra pages in all of tomorrow's editions. This is huge. Everyone's totally focused. We've got newspapers around the world contacting us. There's even a guy from the *New York Times* sitting at your desk. I hope you don't mind him borrowing it…"

"I meant the reaction to my letter and the two murders. I can see I'm getting a whole load of crap on the Net."

"Oh, that. Well, no one's bothered about that."

"Come on," Dessie said. "What are people really saying?"

Forsberg hesitated.

"Alexander Andersson is upset and going around talking a load of rubbish. He's saying that you're 'unethical' and 'desperate for headlines' and quite a lot of other stuff, but that's nothing to worry about. He's just jealous of the attention you're getting."

Dessie closed her eyes.

She *knew* it would turn out like this. She told them it would.

"Are they saying anything in the proper media?"

Forsberg sighed.

"Forget about all this, Dessie. The killers have been caught. Everyone's happy. Go have a beer or something."

He hung up.

The killers have been caught. Everyone's happy.

Dessie desperately wished it were that simple.

Chapter 70

AT 8.30 THAT EVENING, SYLVIA Rudolph volunteered that she had new information for the police. The interrogation resumed at her own request.

Her face was paler now, and she had obviously been crying.

"I don't really want to say this," she said, "because I don't like gossip. But I can see we're in a serious situation here, and I can no longer protect..."

She fell quiet, hesitating about whatever she was going to say next.

"Who are you protecting?" Sara Höglund said gently. "You have to tell us now."

Sylvia Rudolph discreetly wiped away a tear. Then she took a deep breath.

"I didn't tell you the whole truth earlier," she said, and Jacob and all the others in the control room leaned toward the screen at the same time.

"We didn't set out for Europe just to look at art. I had

to get away from Los Angeles, and Mac offered to come with me."

Mats Duvall and Sara Höglund waited in silence for her to go on.

"There's someone who wants to hurt me," she said in a very quiet voice. "He's an old boyfriend, although if you ask him, he'll say we're still together. He just can't accept the fact that I am finished with him. He...used to hit me. He can't stay away from me."

Sylvia Rudolph started to cry softly.

Sara Höglund put a reassuring hand on her arm.

"It feels awful to say something so bad about another person," the young woman went on, taking the police chief's hand and squeezing it.

"But I really think Billy is capable of doing anything if it would hurt me. He might have followed me to Europe."

Chapter 71

THE INVESTIGATING TEAM WAS GATHERED in Mats Duvall's office.

They made a hollow-eyed, determined crowd as they settled on the sofas and chairs.

"We've gone through their hotel room in the Amaranten," the superintendent said. "A preliminary search hasn't revealed anything that can help our case. Quite the reverse, in fact..."

He looked through his papers.

"Malcolm Rudolph really was tested for salmonella on February ninth in Madrid, *the same day the murders in Athens were committed.* Here's the receipt."

Jacob shut his eyes, covering them with his hand. He almost couldn't bear to hear any more.

Mats Duvall went on to summarize the state of the investigation: No drugs had been found in the hotel room, neither marijuana nor any muscle relaxant containing cyclopentolate. No weapons had been found. No knives or scalpels.

Inquiries at the 7-Eleven shop on Västerlånggatan confirmed that one of their computers had been used at lunchtime on Tuesday to book a Helsinki cruise with Silja Line for four people. The four passengers were Peter Visser, Nienke van Mourik, Sylvia Rudolph, and Malcolm Rudolph.

No stolen property, neither that of the victims in Sweden nor from anywhere else in Europe, had been found, and no champagne. In fact, there was nothing to suggest that Sylvia or Malcolm Rudolph had ever been in contact with any of the other murder victims.

A response from Berlin indicated that no trace of the Rudolph siblings had been found at any of the European crime scenes.

On the other hand, their fingerprints were found in various places in the room in the Grand Hôtel.

There was complete silence after the superintendent finished with his list.

"Reactions?"

"It's them," Jacob said. "I know it is. I don't know how they've done it, or what the purpose of this little charade of theirs is, but they're guilty as fuck."

"And how do we prove that, sir?" Sara Höglund said. "They've looked at paintings, which isn't a crime, at least not here in Europe. They've been traveling around and they visited friends in their hotel room. What can we possibly charge them with? And based on what evidence?"

Jacob recalled the reassuring hand she had laid on Sylvia Rudolph's arm.

"We have to go through the confiscated material more

thoroughly," he said. "There's something there, something we've missed. Let me help you. Please."

"They turned themselves in," Sara Höglund said. "They're being very cooperative. They've declined legal representation. They're horrified by the deaths of their friends. And they've got an alibi for the murders in Athens."

There was an oppressive silence when she stopped talking.

"This won't hold," Evert Ridderwall said. "We have to have something more than this. I can hold them until lunchtime on Saturday. Then I'll have to let them go."

Chapter 72

JACOB STEPPED ONTO THE STREET. His whole body was numb and felt hollowed out.

He couldn't imagine a worse scenario than these two killers walking free.

As if it weren't bad enough that they had killed and humiliated their victims, they'd be able to stand there laughing at everyone afterward.

He had to stop himself from kicking over a motorcycle leaning against the wall.

"See you tomorrow," Dessie said, walking past him with her bike helmet in her hand.

"Wait up," Jacob said instinctively, holding his hand out toward her. "Hold on..."

She stopped, surprised.

He looked at her, his mouth open, apparently not knowing what to say next.

Don't go, I can't stand being alone anymore?

I can't go back to my prison cell at the hostel. Not tonight?

They're laughing at me, can't you hear them laughing at me?

"Jacob," the journalist said, walking over to him. "What's wrong? I mean, I know what's wrong in a particular sense, but *what's wrong?*"

He made an effort to breathe normally.

"There are…a few things I've been wondering about. Have you got a couple of minutes?"

She hesitated.

"It won't take long," he said. "You've got to eat anyway, haven't you? I'll pay tonight. I'll even make an effort to be civil."

"I'm so exhausted. I need to go home. We can get something along the way."

Chapter 73

THEY HEADED OFF DOWN TOWARD the Central Station side by side.

"What does it mean that the Rudolphs are *being held* according to Swedish law?" Jacob asked.

"The prosecutor can hold them for up to three days."

"Can they post bail?"

"No, we don't have that sort of system here. Have you ever eaten a flatbread roll?"

"A what?"

They stopped at a little kiosk selling hot dogs and hamburgers. Dessie ordered something in her incomprehensible language and let him pay for whatever it was.

Gradually the solid panic inside him started to let go and open up some.

"Here you are," Dessie said.

She handed him a sort of pancake filled with mashed potato, hamburger dressing, grilled hot dog, chopped dill pickle, onion, mustard, ketchup, and prawn mayonnaise, and all wrapped in foil.

"Jeezuz," he said.

"Just eat," Dessie said. "It's really good."

"I thought you didn't eat meat," Jacob said.

She looked at him in surprise.

"How'd you know that?"

He took a deep breath and tried to relax his shoulders.

"Just something I noticed, I guess. What do you think of the Rudolphs? Are they our Postcard Killers?"

"Probably," she said. "Mine's vegetarian, by the way."

They sat on the bench inside a bus shelter and ate the sticky rolls. Jacob, who considered himself an expert in junk food, had to admit she was right: it was really good.

He wolfed it down and thought he might even have another hot-dog-with-mashed-potatoes thing.

Dessie Larsson had a calming effect on him. He'd known that almost from the beginning, but he'd never felt it more than he did right now.

He looked at this woman next to him in the yellow glow of the streetlights.

She was actually very beautiful without being conspicuously pretty. Her profile was classically clean and simple. She didn't seem to wear any makeup at all, not even mascara.

"What makes you think they're guilty?" he asked, studying her reaction.

She glanced at him and wiped her mouth with a napkin.

"The bodies," she said. "We know they're arranged as works of art, and the Rudolphs are art students. I don't know, but there's something there, in that mix of art and reality. Also, I don't believe them, especially her."

He threw the foil wrapping and the small remains of mashed potato into the bus shelter's trash bin.

"What do you mean, 'that mix of art and reality'? Either it's art or it's reality, right?"

Dessie gave him a serious look.

"It's not unusual for art students to blend them together. We had several cases like that a year or so ago.

"First there was a girl who faked a nervous breakdown in a psychiatric ward as part of her degree show for the Art School. She had the resources of a whole ward focused on her for an entire night. Anyone who was sick or really suicidal had to wait because of her act."

"You're kidding," Jacob said.

"Nope. Then we had a guy who smashed up a car on the subway. He covered it in black graffiti and broke several windows. He filmed the whole thing and called it 'Territorial Pissing.' Believe it or not, it was exhibited in an art show. The cost to repair the car was one hundred thousand kronor."

"And I thought we had a monopoly on crazies in the States," Jacob said, looking at his watch. "Speaking of the States, there are a few things I have to check on there. Do you know where I can get hold of a computer?"

She looked at him, her eyes large and green.

"I've got one at home," she said.

Chapter 74

IT WAS THE FIRST TIME in nearly six months that he'd been in somebody's home.

It felt odd, almost a bit ceremonial. He took off his shoes by the door because that's what Dessie did.

She lived in a minimally furnished four-room apartment with very high ceilings, a lot of mirrored doors, ornate plasterwork, and a wood-burning stove in every room.

Jacob couldn't help whistling out loud when he entered the living room. Three large windows opened onto an enormous balcony with a fantastic view over the entrance to Stockholm harbor.

"How did you get hold of a place like this? It's great."

"Long story," she said. "The computer's in the maid's room. There's no maid, of course."

She gestured toward a little room beyond the kitchen.

"Have you got any wine around here?" he asked.

"Nope," she said. "I don't drink that much. Maybe I will after this."

She turned the computer on for him. He noticed she smelled of fruit. Citrus. Very nice.

He sent two e-mails on the same subject: one to Jill Stevens, his closest colleague on the NYPD, and one to Lyndon Crebbs, the retired FBI agent who had been his mentor once upon a time, and maybe still was.

He asked them rather bluntly for information about Sylvia and Malcolm Rudolph, residents of Santa Barbara, California, and about Billy Hamilton, Sylvia Rudolph's former boyfriend, reportedly living somewhere in western Los Angeles. Everything, no matter what it was, was of interest to him, absolutely everything they could find.

Then he went back out to the kitchen, where Dessie was rummaging around.

"I found a bottle of red," she said. "Gabriella must have left it. I don't know if it's still good."

"Yeah, of course it is," Jacob said.

She seemed unfamiliar with how to extract a cork, so he helped her.

They sat down on the sofas in the living room, leaving the lights off, admiring the stunning view.

Jacob leaned back, sinking into her cushions.

A white boat plowed toward the center of Stockholm out on the water.

"A view like this makes coming home worthwhile," he said. "What's the long story you mentioned?"

Chapter 75

DESSIE FINGERED HER WINEGLASS. SHE'D never told anyone the whole truth about how she bought the apartment, not even Christer or Gabriella. So why should she tell Jacob Kanon?

He was a cop on top of everything.

"I inherited a large sum of money a while back," she said. "From my mother."

Jacob raised an eyebrow.

"I thought you said she worked with the elderly and the sick?"

"That's right, she did."

"So you're upper class," he said. "I hadn't guessed that."

She knew exactly what he was thinking. He thought her mother was the sort who jangled their jewelry in front of the poor at charity galas.

"You're wrong," she said. "Do you really want to know this story? I don't do chitchat very well."

"I really want to know."

She put her glass down on the coffee table.

"That security van raid I mentioned yesterday—you remember?"

He nodded and emptied his glass, then filled it again.

"Three of my uncles were involved," she said. "They got hold of almost nine million kronor, which was something like eight and a half million more than they were expecting, and they panicked. They didn't know what to do with all the money. They buried some of it, but they put most of it in my mother's savings account."

"*What!*" Jacob exclaimed, almost choking on his wine. "You're kidding me."

"It was pretty smart of them, as it turned out. All the money they buried was found, but no one thought to check my mother's account."

She watched carefully for his reaction. Was he about to turn his back on her? Dismiss her as the daughter of a scheming criminal?

"Your uncles can't have been the sharpest knives in the drawer," he said.

She avoided his gaze as she went on with the story.

"They all got the same punishment, five and a half years for aggravated robbery. They were due to be released in May four years ago. That winter had been unusually snowy in Ådalen, and my mother helped the old folks clear the snow, which she wasn't supposed to do because the doctor told her...But she was stubborn. And proud."

Dessie picked up her glass and turned it slowly in her hand.

"She died on Hilding Olsson's drive with a snow shovel in her hand."

She took a careful sip. "The amount in her savings account was completely untouched, and I was her only heir."

Chapter 76

"SHIT," JACOB SAID. "THAT'S A *hell* of a story."

He didn't seem horrified, more like impressed.

"Didn't your uncles come and ask for their money when they got out?"

She sighed.

"Of course. They were pretty persistent until I called my cousin Robert in Kalix and asked him for a favor. For two hundred thousand and a bottle of Absolut every Christmas, he's promised to make sure the rest of the family leaves me alone. Which they pretty much do."

Jacob was staring at her, wide-eyed.

"Wow," he said.

"Robert's two meters tall and weighs a hundred and thirty kilos," Dessie said. "He's very persuasive."

"I might have guessed," Jacob said.

She looked at him.

The story of how she had been able to afford the apartment had gnawed away at her for almost four years now. She had been terrified that someone would find out what had really happened. Now she had dragged her secret out, and Jacob didn't seem the least bit bothered. Instead, he seemed amused.

All of a sudden she realized she was weak with tiredness from all the tension of the day.

She stood up, clutching her glass like someone's hand.

"I really have to go to bed," she said.

Jacob took the almost empty bottle back to the kitchen. He pulled on his shoes by the door and stood up straight again. He hesitated by the door.

"You're pretty cool," he said in a quiet voice.

"You're pretty weird," she said. "Do you know that?"

He shut the door soundlessly behind him.

She leaned her forehead against the door and listened to the sound of his footsteps as they disappeared down the marble staircase.

"Plus, I'm stubborn. And proud," said Dessie.

Chapter 77

Thursday, June 17

MALCOLM RUDOLPH HAD DRAPED HIS body so that he was half lying in his chair in the interrogation room. His legs were wide apart and one arm was hooked around the back of the chair.

His tousled hair had fallen across his forehead, and the top two buttons of his shirt were undone.

"It was cool. We were traveling around, studying art and life," he said over the sound coming from the television monitor.

And death, Jacob thought as he sat in the control room, listening to the murderer talk.

Above all, you studied death, you bastard.

"It was really great to begin with," the fair-haired man said and yawned. "Although it's gotten a bit boring in recent weeks, actually."

So, to start with, they thought it was fun killing people,

Jacob thought. Then that became routine as well. How would you like an axe through your skull? Would that be cool, or just half cool?

Mats Duvall and Sara Höglund were going through the log of the Rudolphs' movements in Europe over the past six months.

Their passports showed that Malcolm and Sylvia Rudolph had landed at Frankfurt airport eight and a half months ago, October 1.

Since then, according to Malcolm, they had been traveling around, looking at paintings and enjoying life. They had kept within the part of the European Union governed by the Schengen Agreement—in other words the countries that no longer insisted you show a passport when you crossed between them. So they had no stamps to show where they had been.

The investigating team therefore had to look for that information elsewhere, which was more easily said than done.

Apparently neither of them owned a cell phone, so there were no calls that could be traced.

They each had a credit card, both Visa, which they very rarely used.

They had withdrawn cash with a credit card on two occasions—in Brussels on December 3, and in Oslo on May 6. A credit card had also been used to pay for Malcolm's medical treatment in Madrid in February. On March 14 a hotel bill in Marbella in the south of Spain had been paid with Sylvia's card, and on May 2 Malcolm had bought four theater tickets in Berlin with his. The cruise to Finland over the coming weekend was the last time the cards had been used.

Jacob followed the questioning out in the control room with his jaw clenched. Dessie was sitting next to him, just as absorbed in the interrogation as he was.

"The murders in Berlin took place on May second. Did they really go to the theater afterward?" she whispered, but he shushed her.

"To go back to our discussion about Stockholm," Sara Höglund said on the screen. "Why did you decide to come here?"

Malcolm Rudolph gave a nonchalant shrug.

"It was Sylvia who insisted we come," he said. "She's interested in form and design, in the whole Scandinavian simplicity thing. Personally, I think it's seriously overrated. I find it cold and impersonal and rather a bore."

He yawned again. His grief at the death of his Dutch friends had evidently faded.

Mats Duvall adjusted his tie.

"You have to take this more seriously," he said. "You were the last people to see Peter Visser and Nienke van Mourik alive. You were caught on the security cameras in the corridor. Don't you realize what that means?"

Jacob leaned forward, inspecting the bored young man: Was the little shit just sitting there *smiling*? What did he know that the police clearly didn't?

"We can't have been the last people to see them alive," Malcolm Rudolph said. "Because they were still alive when we left. Someone else killed them. Obviously. You can't have looked at the recordings long enough."

Sara and Mats glanced at each other, and their faces showed signs of alarm.

Had anyone actually watched the security recordings in their entirety? One would hope so, but it had been so chaotic. Sometimes things were missed or got messed up when a case was really hot.

They broke off the interrogation and ordered all of the security recordings from the Grand Hôtel to be taken out once more.

Chapter 78

NO ONE HAD WATCHED THE entire tapes. Or paid proper attention. It was a terrible mistake.

Now they were watching the tapes, though.

Tuesday afternoons in the middle of June weren't exactly rush hour in the corridor on the fourth floor of the Grand Hôtel.

During the forty-three minutes that Sylvia and Malcolm Rudolph were inside room 418, two cleaners and a plumber went along the corridor outside.

A woman who had evidently forgotten something in her room ran in and then out again and back to the elevators.

At 3:02 the door to room 418 opened.

A triangle of light from inside the room fell on the floor and the wall opposite. The door stood open for a few seconds before Malcolm Rudolph stepped out onto the thick carpet.

He turned and smiled back into the room, said something, laughed.

Then Sylvia Rudolph came out into the corridor. She

stopped, half hidden by the open door, and seemed to be talking to someone as well.

The brother and sister stood by the door for another fourteen seconds, facing back at the room, talking and laughing.

Finally they leaned through the door to exchange kisses with someone. The door closed and they headed for the elevators.

"The Dutch couple were alive when they left the room," Sara Höglund said. "It's obvious. *How could this happen?*" She stared daggers at Mats Duvall.

"And they didn't hang a sign on the door," Gabriella said.

"What?" Dessie asked.

"'Do not disturb,'" Jacob said through clenched teeth. "The sign was hanging on the door when the bodies were found."

The hotel corridor shown on the recording lay empty and dark once more.

Jacob could feel the adrenaline tearing through his veins.

"Can we fast-forward a bit?" he asked.

Gabriella sped up the playback.

At 3:21 an elderly couple came out of the lift, walked slowly along the corridor, and opened a door on the rear side of the hotel.

A few minutes later a cleaner passed through the whole length of the corridor with her trolley and disappeared into a stairwell.

"Will it play any faster?"

Jacob couldn't hide the impatience in his voice. Or the anger at whoever was responsible for this bungle.

A middle-aged couple went past.

A man in a suit carrying a briefcase.

A family with three children, a tired mother, and a very irritated-looking father.

And then he came.

Midlength coat, light shoes, brown hair, cap, and sunglasses.

"Shit," Jacob said.

The man knocked on the door of the Dutch couple's room, waited a few seconds, stepped into the room, and shut the door behind him.

"They let him in," Sara Höglund said. "At least it looks that way. Impossible to tell from this angle."

"Make a note of the time," said Mats Duvall.

4:35.

The corridor was deserted once more.

The seconds crept past.

Jacob had to make an effort to stop himself from screaming.

Twenty-one minutes later the goddamn door opened.

The man in the coat stepped into the corridor. He hung the DO NOT DISTURB sign on the handle, closed the door after him, and walked quickly toward the lifts. He kept his eyes on the floor, his face hidden from the camera.

"I've been holding the wrong people," Evert Ridderwall said with despair in his voice.

Chapter 79

THEY WERE SITTING IN MATS Duvall's room when the press spokesman of the Criminal Investigation Department contacted them and confirmed that the situation with the media was chaotic, almost completely out of control. This sort of thing just didn't happen in Sweden. And imagine if they discovered the police had made mistakes.

Stockholm was besieged by foreign newspapers and television crews—especially American ones. The Postcard Killers saga had all the ingredients of a really juicy criminal scandal. *Good grief*—two young Americans with Hollywood good looks who were either notorious serial killers or the victims of a terrible miscarriage of justice. It didn't matter which of these it was, they were both "Breaking News."

"We'll have to hold a press conference," Sara Höglund said. "We have no choice."

"And say what?" Jacob wondered. "That we haven't found a thing that connects them to the crime? That the prosecutor thinks we've been holding the wrong people?"

"Well," Mats Duvall said. "We've got something. They've been traveling throughout Europe all the while these murders have been going on."

"And can come up with alibis for several of them," Jacob said. "When the Athens murders were committed, they were definitely in Madrid. They were in the south of Spain when the couple was found in Salzburg. And in the countries where they withdrew cash, Norway and Belgium, there haven't been any murders at all."

"So, now you think they're innocent?" Gabriella said.

"Not for a second," Jacob said. "We just haven't got the evidence yet, that's all. They're clever and they've covered their tracks pretty good."

"We've still got to handle the press," Sara Höglund said. "Several of the main channels have already done their own vignettes on the Rudolphs, with music and everything."

Jacob stood up.

"We've got to knock a hole in their defense," he said. "We've got to continue to provoke them into making mistakes."

He stopped in front of Sara Höglund.

"Let me question them," he said. "Let Dessie interview them. Let us talk to them both together."

Sara Höglund got to her feet.

"You're not exactly the shy, retiring type, are you? What makes you think that a reporter on the evening paper and a desperate father would be better at breaking down criminals than experienced murder investigators?"

"With all due respect," Jacob said, forcing himself to

sound calm and collected, "you aren't the only murder cops in this room. And I'm American. You don't pick up the nuances in the language."

"And Dessie Larsson can?"

"She's written a doctoral thesis on criminology. In English. Have you?"

Dessie stood up as well.

"I've done it before," she said in a quiet voice.

Jacob and Sara Höglund looked at her in surprise.

"I've interviewed criminals during ongoing investigations," she said. "Without pen and paper, or a tape recorder, of course, and under police supervision, but it wouldn't be the first time."

"What do we stand to gain from it?" Mats Duvall asked. "Please tell me that."

"What do you stand to lose?" asked Jacob.

Chapter 80

THE PRESS CONFERENCE WAS OUT of control from the very start.

Several American television channels were broadcasting live and had no desire to sit through Evert Ridderwall's painstaking details of the progress of the investigation.

Their reporters started shouting questions almost at once, which revealed yet another complication: Evert Ridderwall was extremely bad at English.

He was also rather hard of hearing. He just about managed to read out the details that the investigating team had jointly put together for him, but he could neither hear nor understand what the reporters were asking him.

"A sufficient lack of self-doubt can get you anywhere," Dessie muttered as she stood next to Jacob at the back of the room.

"And we have a stunning example of that in front of us," Jacob agreed bitterly.

Evert Ridderwall had insisted on holding the press conference himself because he was, after all, the head of the investigating team.

Sara Höglund, who was standing on the podium next to him, eventually leaned purposefully across the table, picked up the prosecutor's script and started reading.

Her English bore traces of the East Coast of the United States, and Jacob recalled that she had a good knowledge of the NYPD. Maybe she'd trained there, or worked with them once upon a time.

In actual fact, she said very little other than that the investigation was continuing, and that certain evidence had been obtained but she couldn't go into details because of the significance of the material to the investigation.

"Fuck it, they haven't got anything," said a reporter from one of the Swedish news agencies to his colleague. They were sitting right in front of Dessie and Jacob.

"Shall we go?" Jacob whispered.

"Yes. Please. *Now*."

They got to the exit before the reporter from *Dagens Eko* caught sight of Dessie.

"Dessie," he called after her. "Dessie Larsson?"

She turned around, surprised that he had recognized her.

"Yes?" she said, and the next moment she had a huge microphone pressed up under her nose.

"What do you think of the unpleasant criticism that's being directed at you?"

Dessie stared at the man. He was unshaven and had bad teeth.

Don't blow up, she thought. Don't get angry, don't rush off, that's exactly what he wants.

"Criticism directed at me?" she said. "What do you mean specifically?"

"What do you think of the fact that you've introduced to Scandinavia the Anglo-Saxon tradition of paying large amounts of money to brutal serial killers?"

"I think you've completely misunderstood that," she replied, trying to sound calm and confident. "I haven't paid any money to—"

"But you *tried to!*" the reporter cried indignantly. "You *wanted* to buy interviews with brutal serial killers. Do you really think it's morally defensible to pay for their violent deeds?"

Dessie swallowed before she spoke again.

"Well, firstly, not a single penny has been paid, and secondly, it wasn't my decision to—"

"Do you think you've made yourself complicit in the crime itself?" the reporter yelled. "What's the difference between paying for a murder and paying for the *details* of a murder?"

Dessie finally pushed the microphone aside and walked away from the rude, stupid man.

"Let it go," Jacob said in her ear.

He was right beside her, struggling to keep up. He hadn't understood the exchange, but the content and spirit of it were all too clear to him.

"After this disaster, Duvall will be clutching at straws. In less than ten minutes' time he'll be asking us to interview the Rudolphs," Jacob continued.

Dessie took a deep breath and pushed the *Eko* reporter from her mind.

It turned out that Jacob was right.

It took seven minutes.

Chapter 81

IT WAS ALREADY AFTERNOON WHEN Malcolm and Sylvia were led *separately* into the interrogation room where
Dessie and Jacob sat waiting for them.

Sylvia gave a small squeal of delight when she saw her
brother.

They gave each other an emotional hug before the officers escorting them pulled them apart.

Dessie had expected to be nervous before the meeting,
but her anger and determination had pushed aside most feelings of that sort. She was quite convinced that the Rudolphs
were the Postcard Killers.

Now she and Jacob had to pull the rug out from under
them. Somehow. But where to begin?

She studied each of them. They really were strikingly
attractive. Malcolm was trim but also muscular, and in all
the right places. Dessie guessed that he must have swallowed
a good number of anabolic steroids. Sylvia was extremely

thin, but her breasts were plump and round. Silicone, of course.

The man had much fairer skin and hair than his sister, but they had the same eyes: the same shade of light gray, with long eyelashes that only added to their allure and magnetism.

They were clearly overjoyed to see each other again. They settled down side by side on the other side of the table and seemed relaxed and happy to be there.

Dessie realized immediately that they hadn't recognized her.

They'd never seen a picture byline of her in the paper, and they evidently hadn't Googled her picture before they sent the postcard to her at *Aftonposten*.

Dessie and Jacob let the pair settle in, and they did not introduce themselves. Their expressions were completely neutral and they didn't take the initiative.

The siblings smiled contentedly and looked around the room. They were considerably more alert now than they had been during their questioning that morning. The change of questioners had evidently livened them up.

"So," Sylvia said, "what shall we talk about now?"

Dessie didn't change her expression.

"I've got a few questions about your interest in art," she said, and the brother and sister stretched their backs and smiled even more confidently.

"How nice," Sylvia said. "What are you wondering about? How can we help?"

"Your attitude toward art and reality," Dessie said. "I'm thinking about the murders in Amsterdam and Berlin, for instance. The killers mimicked two real people, Nefertiti and Vincent van Gogh."

Both Sylvia and Malcolm looked at her, a little wide-eyed. Their contented expressions were replaced by one of watchful interest.

"I'll explain," Dessie said. "It isn't at all clear that the Egyptian queen Nefertiti was missing her left eye. It's just that the bust of her in the Neues Museum is. Yet you still took out Karen's and Billy's eyes. I suppose you chose to imitate the art and not the person, didn't you?"

Sylvia laughed.

"This might even be exciting, your theory, this line of questioning," she said, "if it wasn't so crazy and absurd."

"Do you know how I realized it?" Dessie said. "Lindsay and Jeffrey — you remember them? — the British couple you killed in Amsterdam. You cut off their right ears, even though van Gogh cut off his left. But in the painting, his self-portrait, the bandage is on the right-hand side, of course, because he was painting his reflection. So you chose to re-create the artworks, rather than the people themselves."

"This is obviously going nowhere," Sylvia said. "I thought you were going to ask us some questions that might help catch the killers."

"We are," Jacob said, turning to Malcolm. "Where have you hidden your disguise?"

Chapter 82

THE SIBLINGS REMAINED COOL AND controlled, but their supercilious attitude had vanished. Dessie noted how they unconsciously leaned closer to each other as the questions suddenly got tougher. They were a very tight-knit team, weren't they?

Malcolm manufactured a laugh.

"Disguise? I don't understand…"

Dessie looked at Jacob. He was clenching his teeth. He was presumably having to strain every muscle to overcome the desire to smash the killer's head in.

"The brown wig," Jacob said. "The cap, the sunglasses, the coat you wear when you go around emptying your victims' accounts. The outfit you wore when you pawned Claudia's Omega watch? And that you were wearing when you pretended to kill Nienke and Peter?"

Malcolm held his arms out, a questioning expression on his face.

"What are you talking about?"

"And the eyedrops," Jacob said. "They weren't in your hotel room. So you must have hidden them in the same place as the disguise."

Malcolm looked over at his sister.

"Do you understand what he's talking about?"

"The recording from the Grand Hôtel was good," Jacob went on, "but not good enough."

He turned to Sylvia.

"It's obvious that you were kissing thin air when you pretended to kiss their cheeks, and that you were faking a conversation. And you forgot about the shadow."

Sylvia shook her head, but her smile seemed far less certain now.

"Sorry," she said, "but where are you going with this? I'm completely lost."

"I'm telling you about your mistakes," Jacob said. "I'm talking about the shadow, the one formed when a dead body got in the way of the daylight coming through a window."

Sylvia's eyes had narrowed and turned quite dark and small.

"This is harassment," she said.

"The statue from Millesgården," Dessie said. "The one clearly visible on the floor of the corridor when you opened the door to Peter and Nienke's room. That's the shadow he's talking about."

"We want a lawyer," Sylvia said.

Chapter 83

THE PAIR CLAMMED UP. THEY refused to say another word without a lawyer present.

The interrogation was stopped. The two of them were taken back to their cells, and Dessie and Jacob headed off to Mats Duvall's office, where the investigating team had gathered.

Sara Höglund looked distinctly pleased.

"That business with the shadow worked very well," she said.

"A shame we made it up," Jacob said. "Otherwise we really would have a case. Anyway, it's a start."

"Now we just have to hope that they get tangled up in their various lies and explanations," the head of the crime unit said.

The theme music to the 4:45 *Eko* news bulletin came over the radio, and Mats Duvall turned up the volume.

The lead story was the "questionable arrest" of the two American art students traveling through Sweden.

The newsreader's voice sounded stuffy and pompous.

"According to reports received by *Dagens Eko,* the

suspects have solid alibis for several of the murders in Europe. Video recordings from security cameras in the Grand Hôtel show that the Dutch couple were *still alive* when the brother and sister left them on Wednesday afternoon…"

The air in the room had turned to ice.

Obviously, someone in, or very close to, the investigation had talked to the press.

No one looked at anyone else. They all just stared straight ahead or down at the table.

Dessie felt a sense of unease creeping up her spine.

She was the one whom these detectives would suspect of leaking information. And because it was against the law for the authorities to investigate the media's sources, no one would ask her straight out, but she knew what they were thinking. She was the journalist, the outsider, the one who was the most likely to be disloyal.

From now on, she wouldn't be welcome here, that much was clear to her.

The superintendent's face stiffened into a mask that grew more rigid the longer the broadcast went on.

The chair of the Swedish Bar Association gave a statement, seriously criticizing the fact that "the two American youngsters" hadn't been given a lawyer until late this afternoon, a whole day after they were taken into custody.

Sara Höglund was quoted saying in an irritated voice that the investigation was proceeding—a sound bite that was probably taken from the very last minutes of the press conference, when she had already answered the same question umpteen times.

Then the *Dagens Eko* bulletin turned its attention to criticism of the media.

The newsreader's voice was full of indignation as he trumpeted the next item.

"In a letter that has received harsh criticism, a newspaper reporter at *Aftonposten*, Dessie Larsson, attempted to buy an interview with the suspected killers.

"For one hundred thousand dollars, almost a million kronor, she wanted to secure an exclusive interview with the American youths. The chair of the Journalists Federation, Anita Persson, considers the development a scandal that should be investigated."

Dessie felt the floor sway beneath her. Her mouth went dry and her pulse was racing.

"Dessie Larsson has brought shame on the entire profession," Anita Persson said over the radio. "She should be expelled from the Journalists Federation right away."

The author and journalist Hugo Bergman was next to be interviewed. He added to the criticism, saying that Dessie Larsson was "a lightweight" and "a useless journalist."

Everyone in the room turned to look at Dessie.

Hugo Bergman clearly didn't like being spurned when he had paid for wine and dinner at a fancy restaurant, she thought. It was a hell of a price to pay for mashed potatoes.

Dessie stood up and went toward the door.

"I'm not even a member of the Journalists Federation," she said.

Jacob followed her out through the door.

Chapter 84

DESSIE COULD SEE THE SATELLITE dishes on the television crews' vans, some of which had come all the way from Götgatan. What a waste of time, money, and gas.

The media storm had settled right outside her door, blocking the whole of Urvädersgränd. She stopped, her bicycle beside her, and stared at the crowd.

Jacob caught up with her and let out a quiet whistle.

There were unfamiliar figures with huge microphones and colleagues she had met at the Association of Professional Newspapermen, photographers with long lenses, and radio reporters who looked like giant beetles with their broadcast antennas mounted on their backs.

"Impressive," Jacob said drily. "You must be the hottest date in town."

"I can't go in there," she said.

"They'll go home when they get hungry," Jacob said. "Come on, let's go and get something to eat in the meantime."

They headed toward Mariatorget. The sky was full of dark clouds; there was rain in the air.

They stopped at a steak house on Sankt Paulsgatan, where Jacob ordered barbecue ribs and Dessie corn on the cob.

"Is that all you're having?" Jacob said when the food arrived.

"I don't think I can even get this down," she said in a quiet voice.

He looked at her with something in his eyes she hadn't seen before. If she didn't know better, she'd say he was actually worried about her.

"I know you're finding this unpleasant and unfair," he said, "but you should know that you did the right thing. You've probably already prevented some murders."

She finished her glass of wine and poured some more.

He put his hand on hers.

"Dessie," he said, "listen to me, please. Kimmy was killed by these monsters, and you're one of the reasons they've been caught. I thank you for that. I owe you my life."

Chapter 85

JACOB'S HAND WAS DRY and warm, burning on her skin. She looked up and met his gaze.

"You must have loved her very much," Dessie said before she could stop herself.

He shut his eyes tightly and squeezed her hand. For a few moments she thought he was going to start crying. She felt terrible for making him suffer like this.

"Yes," he whispered, weaving his fingers through hers. "Yes, I did. It was just her and me..."

Dessie kept hold of his hand.

He stared out through the window, seemingly losing himself in his memories.

She looked at him and wondered what he was thinking.

"What happened to her mother?"

"Lucy? Yes, I've often wondered that, too."

He pulled back his hand. The air in the restaurant suddenly felt cold on her skin.

He met her eyes and gave a little smile.

"I wasn't the one who leaked that stuff to the *Dagens Eko*," she said.

"I know that perfectly well," he said, emptying his glass. "It was Evert Ridderwall."

She blinked.

"What makes you say that?"

"He'll change with the wind," Jacob said. "He doesn't have any principles, he just wants to avoid criticism. That leak was a test. He wanted to see what the media think of the Rudolphs."

His knee ended up between hers under the table.

Neither of them changed position.

"Did you hear who they want as their lawyer?" Dessie said, emptying her second glass of wine. "Andrea Friederichs."

"And?" Jacob said, filling her glass.

Dessie took a deep sip.

"She isn't an expert on criminal law. She's a copyright lawyer. Doesn't that seem a bit strange to you?"

Chapter 86

THE MEDIA CROWD OUTSIDE Dessie's front door hadn't gotten any smaller. It actually seemed bigger. It was starting to resemble the mob that gathers outside courtrooms for notable court cases in New York. Jacob knew all about them. He'd had to fight his way through a phalanx of reporters and microphones on numerous occasions.

"Okay," she said with a sigh. "I take it they aren't hungry yet. Nobody's leaving."

She was standing close to Jacob, hiding behind him so as not to be seen from the top of the narrow street.

He resisted an impulse to push a strand of hair away from her face.

"I don't know that I want to see myself darting into a doorway in all the papers and newscasts tomorrow," she said in a low voice.

"No need," he said.

She looked at him with her big eyes. He took a deep breath before going on.

"My roommate has gone back to Finland. You can have the lower bunk in my cell on Långholmen. It's not a problem."

He said it in a light, joking way, careful not to show any feeling. *It's not a problem.*

She hesitated a few seconds before answering, her eyes still on his.

Then she made up her mind. "Okay," she said and turned her bicycle around.

It started to rain as they passed the Zinkensdamm metro station, almost halfway to the hostel.

They started walking quickly. Jacob turned up the collar of his suede jacket, but the water still trickled down his back. He shivered in the cold.

"I can give you a ride if you like," she said. "If you have the guts to get on."

"On the bike?"

She nodded. "Of course. Only if you dare."

He sat on the narrow luggage carrier at the back, holding on to her hips with both hands. She set a good pace, and they flew past a large church with two identical spires. Her thighs moved rhythmically and methodically. She was strong and obviously in good shape.

He was suddenly overwhelmed with a memory of Lucy. She had once given him a ride like this in Brooklyn, a hundred years ago, a thousand years ago, before Kimmy, before the drugs and adulthood with all its complications came into the picture and shattered a perfect life for all of them.

He jumped off as Dessie rolled into the parking lot in front of the youth hostel.

"What are the rules?" she asked, taking off her helmet. "Are you allowed lady visitors in your room?"

"I'm not about to ask for permission or about any rules," Jacob said. "I'm a big boy now."

"Are you?"

He pulled her to him, her body shaping itself to his. Her hair smelled fresh, like fruit again. He closed his eyes and felt her warmth through his jacket. She breathed lightly against his neck.

Then he kissed her.

She tasted of rain and corn on the cob.

Chapter 87

THEIR CLOTHES ENDED UP in a heap just inside the door of the former prison cell.

They didn't even make it to the Finn's lower bunk before she drew him to her. They landed on the floor and he slid into her with no resistance, his eyes catching hers.

He could feel the room starting to spin and had time to think *no, no, no, not yet* before he came inside her with a hoarse roar.

He sank down on top of her, hiding his face in her hair.

Damn, what a failure. Coming after ten seconds. What must she think?

But she kissed his hair as he lay there panting and trying to pull himself together. Then her hips started to move beneath him.

At first he thought she wanted to get up, but when he went to move, she took a firm grip on his buttocks and held him to her, held him right there.

"Relax and go with it," she whispered in his ear as the swaying beneath him started up again. "Stay with me."

To his surprise he felt himself getting hard again almost immediately.

He did as she said and allowed himself to be swayed by her rhythmic movements. Her whole body was sucking and pulling him into her, harder and deeper.

He noticed he was starting to breathe heavily and join in, his pulse speeding up and throbbing in his head, and when he felt the dizziness come, he stopped and looked into her eyes. Her gaze was completely unfocused. She wasn't far off now.

"Come here," he said in a gravelly voice, pulling out of her and lifting her up onto the bed.

"What are you doing?" she asked.

"Relax and go with it."

She stretched out on the lower bunk, her legs hard and sinewy, her stomach soft as velvet and her breasts firm and well shaped. He let his hand glide up along her thighs as he leaned forward to suck one of her nipples. Dessie groaned and her whole body shuddered.

He sucked and licked her entire body, and when he finally pushed inside her again she leaned her head back and yelled. While the contractions were still convulsing her lower body, he felt the rushing noise in his head grow into an explosion that made all sound and vision disappear for him.

When he came to his senses again, he realized he was freezing.

He rolled to one side, sliding out of her. He fumbled for the covers beneath them and pulled them over their bodies.

She looked at him, wide-eyed and surprised.

"Wow," she said.

Chapter 88

DESSIE WAS STILL ASTONISHED at what had happened.

When she accepted his invitation to stay at his place, she had made up her mind that nothing like *this* was going to happen. Her life was so turbulent just now that a messy affaire was the last thing she needed. Probably the last thing Jacob needed, too.

"Wow?" he replied, and smiled.

Now his eyes were warm again, that crazy blue, completely focused on her.

This really wasn't good at all. How could it be?

She ought to get up at once and leave and face the damn reporters at her house.

Instead she smiled back.

"Dessie," he whispered. "Dessie, Dessie, you're pretty amazing, you know that?"

She felt a warmth spread inside her, out from her stomach, her core.

"Dessie," he said again, this time in a questioning tone. "What sort of name is that anyway? *Dessie?*"

She cuddled up next to him. He pulled her closer so that she could rest her head on his chest. She let her fingers play on his skin, small, featherlike strokes.

"I was christened Désirée," she said, "the least known of the Swedish princesses."

She could see her mother in front of her, Eivor, her dear, sweet mom, born in 1938, the same year as Désirée Elizabeth Sibylla, the second-youngest of the Haga princesses, the "Hagacesses," daughter of Crown Prince Gustaf Adolf and his wife, Sibylla av Sachsen-Coburg-Gotha. Princess Désirée was Eivor's great role model, so it was obvious that that was what her daughter would be called.

"It's a beautiful name," Jacob said.

She laughed.

"You can imagine how much fun it was being called Désirée when you're ten years old and living in Ådalen. 'Désirée, have you got diarrhea?'"

"Poor Désirée," said Jacob, stroking her hair, then her face, his fingers lingering.

"It was lucky my cousin Robert from Kalix came to visit sometimes," Dessie said, lifting her face to look at Jacob's. "Robert was big and strong, and he protected me."

He kissed her, and she felt an immediate little shiver between her legs.

She felt him react the same way.

She rolled over to sit on top of him and nibbled gently at his earlobe, then his cheek.

If this was wrong, how come it felt so right?

Dessie kissed Jacob's eyes one at a time.

Chapter 89

Friday, June 18

SHE WAS WOKEN BY a muffled electronic noise. It was coming from somewhere beneath them, and she waited quietly until the annoying sound stopped.

Carefully she laid her head back on Jacob's chest and breathed in his smell, a combination of sweat and aftershave. Everything was quiet. The sun was already high in the sky, drowning the little room in white light.

Dessie wondered how long she had been asleep.

An hour, maybe two.

She wanted to lie here forever. Never have to get up from this bed or leave this man, never do anything else for the rest of her life but make love to him until the day they died, or possibly until the lack of caffeine made her change her mind.

It would soon be unbearably hot in here. In his cell. That much was a certainty.

She wriggled her way out of his embrace, pulled herself up on one elbow, and looked at his sleeping face.

He looked so young when his face was relaxed and all his worries were far away.

His hair curled over his forehead and spread out on the pillow. He couldn't have had it cut for at least six months.

Not since Kimmy. She thought about Jacob's daughter now, picturing her face. How unbearably sad to lose her like that... to outlive your own child.

The electronic noise started up again, longer and more persistent this time.

It was her cell phone.

Damn, it was in her knapsack, which had slid under the bed the night before, during their somewhat chaotic entry into the little room.

She waited until it stopped buzzing. Jacob stirred in his sleep beside her.

She leaned over the edge of the bed, pulled out the knapsack, and fished out her phone.

One missed call.

One new message.

She clicked on the message.

It was a news flash from the main Swedish news agency, short and concise as usual.

She gasped, "Oh, no."

Jacob's heavy breathing stopped and she realized he was awake. She'd woken him. She felt his warm hand on her back, a caress that carried the promise of something more.

She turned to face him, meeting his radiant eyes.

His smile faded when he saw the look on her face.

"What is it?" he said. "What's happened?"

Oh god, oh god, how was she going to tell him?

He sat up so abruptly that he hit his head on the top bunk. "Just say it, for god's sake!"

She shrank from his words.

"They're out," she said. "Ridderwall has let the Postcard Killers go free."

Chapter 90

DESSIE HELD HER ARMS out to him, wanting to catch him as he fell into despair at the news. She wanted to hold his face in her hands and reassure him that everything would sort itself out, that this was just a mad, stupid mistake, that Kimmy would get justice and he would be able to move on with his life, and that the rest of his life started right here in this bed with her.

But Jacob leapt up from the bunk, making his way across her and stumbling onto the floor.

He grabbed his jeans, pulling them on without bothering with his underwear.

"You can't change the decision," Dessie said, forcing herself to sound calm and collected. "There's nothing you can do about it."

His hair was a mess, still damp with sweat. His face was almost completely drained of color.

"No," he said, pulling his black T-shirt over his head.

"But I can follow them. So that's what I'm going to do, right to the ends of the damn earth, if I'm not there already..."

Dessie sat up in bed now, lifting the covers over her breasts, suddenly very conscious of her nakedness. She felt incredibly vulnerable, too. A little sad.

"They were let out at six this morning, to avoid the media. They could be halfway across the Atlantic by now. They could be anywhere."

He pushed his feet into his shoes without bothering to untie them and tugged his suede jacket on. Then he stopped by the door, hesitating.

"Sorry," he said. "I didn't mean...I'm just sorry!"

The door frame shook as he slammed the door shut behind him.

Jacob is gone, Dessie thought. *The policeman is back.*

Chapter 91

THE NEWSROOM WAS EMPTY, deserted as though a bomb had gone off inside. Forsberg was sitting on his own behind his desk, half asleep, his eyes rimmed with red, watching a TV screen. His jowls seemed to have grown larger overnight.

"Where is everyone?" Dessie asked, sitting down next to him.

The news editor nodded toward the television.

"The Grand Hôtel," he said. "Our favorite killers have booked into the honeymoon suite, if you can believe that. The whole of the world's press is there, including all our esteemed colleagues."

Dessie stared at him.

"Are you serious?"

"They're giving a press conference at two p.m."

"The Grand?"

Forsberg rubbed his hedgerow of stubble. He hadn't shaved for three days or more.

"The Rudolphs have decided to speak. They want to tell the world how innocent they are."

Dessie leaned back in her chair. This had to be a very bad dream. Soon she'd wake up with Jacob's arms around her and the Postcard Killers safely locked back away in Kronoberg Prison.

"This is surreal. What in hell are they up to?" she said. "Those bastards are guilty as hell. Now they're holding press conferences?"

Forsberg gave a long yawn.

"So anyway, how are we doing with our journalist's objectivity these days?"

Dessie stood up.

"Shouldn't you go home and get some sleep?"

The phone on the desk rang. Forsberg grabbed it.

"What is it?"

He gestured that Dessie should stay, then listened carefully for more than a minute.

Dessie shook her head to say that she wasn't there and pulled her knapsack on.

"Just a moment..."

He put his hand over the mouthpiece.

"It's a Danish journalist. He wants to talk to you specifically. Says it's important."

"I'm not giving any interviews," she said, fastening her helmet strap under her chin.

"I think you should talk to him. He says he received a postcard in this morning's mail—*postmarked yesterday in Copenhagen*. He thinks it's from the Postcard Killers."

Chapter 92

JACOB CAME TOWARD HER in the departure hall of the Central Station and something fluttered in Dessie's chest, something that made her catch her breath and break into a broad, genuine smile. Even here, even now.

But then she saw his eyes and clenched jaw, and the smile froze on her lips.

"Have you got the copies?" he asked in a monotone.

Dumbly she handed over the faxed copies of the Danish postcard, front and back. He put his duffel bag down beside him, clutching the sheets of paper, staring at them.

The card was a picture of the Tivoli pleasure gardens. She knew the place well.

Apart from the name of the city, the back of the postcard had exactly the same capital letters and layout as Dessie's.

TO BE OR NOT TO BE
IN COPENHAGEN

THAT IS THE QUESTION

WE'LL BE IN TOUCH

"I'll be damned," he said, studying the copies. "It's quicker to get hold of evidence through the media than through useless bloody Interpol. That's unbelievable."

She swallowed hard. So that was why he'd agreed to meet her, because she had access to information that the police hadn't yet gotten hold of.

"What do you think about the handwriting?" she asked, trying to sound neutral. "Is it the same person?"

He shook his head and ran his fingers through his hair. She thought of last night, couldn't help it. What had she been thinking?

"It's impossible to tell with this lettering. Looks like it. Can I keep this?"

She nodded, unsure if she would be able to control her voice if she tried to say anything.

"You've heard about the Grand Hôtel?" she finally managed to say.

"The press conference at two o'clock, yeah."

He heaved his duffel bag onto his shoulder again.

She tried to smile.

"So at least you know where they are," she said. "You don't have to go to the ends of the earth after all."

He stopped in the middle of what he was doing and looked at her, and she suddenly wanted the floor to swallow her up.

How could she be so clingy? She wasn't that way—not ever—not even as a kid, especially not then.

"I've had a reply from the States," he said. "From my contacts, those e-mails I sent from your computer."

"That's good," she said.

"I'm on my way to Los Angeles right now," he said, looking at his watch. "My plane leaves in two hours."

She felt like someone had just poured a bucket of ice cold water over her.

"You're—Los Angeles? But..." She'd been about to say, "But what about me?"

She bit her cheek so hard she could taste blood.

She was acting like an idiot. She wanted to shrivel up, to be anywhere but here.

He looked at his watch again, hesitating. Then he took a step toward her and gave her a clumsy hug. The duffel bag was in the way and she got no contact with his body. How very fitting, she thought. The perfect ending for them.

"See you," he said, turning around and walking quickly toward the express train to Arlanda.

She watched him go until he was swallowed up by the mass of people and disappeared in the crowd.

"See you."

Chapter 93

CNN, SKY NEWS, AND BBC World were all broadcasting live from the Hall of Mirrors in the Grand Hôtel. The overblown decor with its gold pillars, mirrored doors, and crystal chandeliers made Dessie think of Versailles or some other wedding-cake château. Journalists and photographers and cameramen and radio reporters were all pushing and shoving to get the best places.

It was so crowded that the television people were standing shoulder to shoulder as they spoke to the cameras.

Usually she did all she could to avoid press conferences.

There was something humiliating in all the pushing and shoving to get close, packed in with other reporters and turned into a babbling crowd.

The hierarchy was ridiculously strict as well.

The television people always got to sit at the front. The bigger and noisier the channel, the closer their reporter got to the center of the action.

Then came the radio reporters with their antennas, the

news agencies, the national press, and then the specialist and local press. Researchers and editorial staff like her were let in only if there was room.

Today she decided to behave like Jacob, storming through everybody like an express train, quickly showing her press pass at the door and forcing her way into the back of the room, not taking no for an answer, not caring what anybody thought of her.

The room could hold five hundred, but the hotel management had limited the number to three hundred because of all the equipment needed for live television broadcasts.

She leaned back against the wall, craning her neck to see. What an absurd circus.

At the front of the room was a small, important-looking podium with metal steps on both sides.

The jungle of microphones shouted out the fact that this was where the siblings were going to proclaim their innocence to all the world.

The level of sound in the room was rising steadily, like the tension in a stadium during the World Cup final.

Dessie closed her eyes.

She felt almost completely paralyzed inside. Events in the room were reaching her through a thick, toughened, glass-like material. It felt like that, anyway.

How could everything have gone so wrong? And so quickly.

Her cell rang and she only noticed it because she was holding it in her hand.

It was Forsberg.

"How does it look? Did you manage to get inside? How close are you?"

"I thought this whole spectacle was going out live on seventeen channels," Dessie said. "Can't you see for yourself?"

"They're just showing a forest of microphones. I can't tell anything. Have you seen Alexander Andersson?"

"I don't think we're in quite the same place," Dessie said. "I'm standing right at the back."

Forsberg took a deep breath.

"Is it true that you interviewed them?" he said. "While they were being held?"

She kept her eyes fixed on the podium. Something was happening in the front.

"Don't believe everything you hear. They're coming in now!"

The Hall of Mirrors exploded in a storm of flashbulbs and spotlights. From a door on the left Malcolm Rudolph walked into the room. He was wearing a light blue shirt unbuttoned at the neck and a pair of fashionably torn jeans.

His sister, Sylvia, was walking behind him, her billowing chestnut brown hair glittering in the flashing lights. She was dressed entirely in white.

"Shit," Forsberg said in her ear. "She's beautiful! How does she look in person?"

"I'll call you later," Dessie said, ending the call.

After Sylvia came a tall, thin woman whom Dessie recognized as Andrea Friederichs, their lawyer—their *copyright* lawyer.

The central characters stopped in front of the jungle of microphones and stood there for three long minutes so that they could be photographed properly.

Then the lawyer leaned forward and said in the queen's English: "If we could get started with this press conference..."

Chapter 94

THE RUDOLPHS' MESSAGE TO the world was crystal clear: a miscarriage of justice had narrowly been avoided today.

This was repeated time after time during the forty-five-minute live broadcast.

The emcee for the performance was Andrea Friederichs, and Dessie had to admit that she performed her duties with aplomb.

She said that thanks to the civic-minded courage of Prosecutor Evert Ridderwall, these innocent young people had been spared yet another day of stressful interrogation, and another night in a Swedish prison cell.

Obviously, the Rudolph siblings had nothing to do with the Postcard Killers.

The very idea was preposterous.

The lawyer systematically went through all the points that proved they were innocent. She reeled them off from memory, no notes:

They were in Madrid when the killings took place in Athens.

They were in the south of Spain at the time of the Salzburg murders.

They were buying theater tickets when the murders in Berlin were carried out.

The Dutch couple, Nienke van Mourik and Peter Visser, were clearly still alive when the Rudolphs left their hotel room.

The Swedish police had arrested and held them *because they were looking at art.*

"I have never seen such an extreme case of high-handed policing," Andrea Friederichs said.

Dessie looked around the room, noting her colleagues' sympathetic demeanors. They clearly shared the lawyer's righteous indignation.

Maybe she was wrong?

Had she let herself be misled by Jacob, a man who clearly wasn't able to be objective in this case? How could he be? He had lost a daughter.

Were the Rudolphs innocent?

She swallowed nervously and was forced to consider the possibility.

Then it was the siblings' turn to speak for themselves. Malcolm went first.

He was in tears again as he described his sorrow when he was told of the deaths of their Dutch friends. The photographers' flashes reached a crescendo as he hugged himself around the chest and the tears ran down his handsome face.

Sylvia was more collected—but at the same time extremely humble and likable.

The Postcard Killers were the worst murderers ever seen on the European continent. She appreciated that the police had to investigate every lead, she really did. The fact that she and her brother had coincidentally and innocently been drawn into it all was a great shame. She at least was grateful that the Swedish judicial system more or less worked, and that two innocent suspects were no longer being held, even though there were some reactionary police officers who were happy to ignore such things as motives and evidence.

"Would we really have carried out a brutal double murder and then gone to buy tickets to *A Streetcar Named Desire*?" she asked, her eyes filling with tears.

"What do they think we are? A couple of callous monsters? No. We came to Europe on vacation. To see museums. To visit your great cities. Is that a crime?"

A cascade of flashes exploded everywhere in the room. There was even some applause.

Dessie pushed her way to the door, took out her cell phone, and rang Forsberg.

"What a show!" the news editor exclaimed. "We're the lead on CNN!"

She noted his empathy toward the Rudolphs.

"I'm going away for a few days," Dessie said. "Just so you know."

"What do you mean, 'away'? Where to?"

"Copenhagen," Dessie said, closing her phone.

Chapter 95

Saturday, June 19
Los Angeles, USA

THE LANDING GEAR HIT the ground with a thud at LAX, Los Angeles International Airport.

Jacob was back on American soil for the first time in six months.

This wasn't how he had imagined his return, if he had actually come back at all. But he'd had to come back. This was where the Rudolphs had lived and created their scheme.

The air outside the terminal building was thick with exhaust fumes. He stood for a moment looking at his surroundings from the parking lot outside the rental-car office. It was such a familiar scene: the sea of private cars spreading out around him, the advertising billboards, the voices, the sound of traffic in the streets.

The U.S. was just as he remembered it, just a bit more…
unsubtle.

He rented a Chrysler with GPS. He didn't know his way
around L.A. and had no desire to learn right now, not on
this trip.

Programming Citrus Avenue into the wretched machine
turned out to be tougher than finding the address on a map,
so he gave up and drove north along Sepulveda Boulevard in
heavy city traffic. God, the traffic. It was even worse than in
New York.

He would never come to grips with Los Angeles, he was
thinking to himself.

A sort of romantic shimmer lay over the whole city. Here
was Hollywood and the dream factory and a glamorous life
in the sun. For some people, anyway.

Personally, he could see only the crass advertisements,
the elevated freeways, and the endless blocks of ugly single-
story villas.

California wasn't exactly his bag of potato chips.

He ignored the freeways and followed Sepulveda for
miles, until he reached Santa Monica Boulevard.

He swung off right and drove on until he nearly fell asleep
at a streetlight. He'd been warned that jet lag from Scandinavia
was no joke. It sure wasn't. The time difference was nine hours.
Here it was only seven in the evening, but after six months in
Europe, his body thought it was four in the morning.

Exactly one day before, he had been lying in a narrow
bunk in an old prison cell, feeling more alive than he had
since Kimmy died.

He hadn't showered since he left her, and he could still make out the smell of fruit from her body on his...

He pushed the confusing thought aside and parked the car near a loading bay on Beverly Drive.

Two quick coffees and a parking ticket later, he was more or less ready to go on.

Number 1338 Citrus Avenue was a fairly rundown two-story rental with a flat roof and a walkway, just a few blocks from Grauman's Chinese Theatre on Hollywood Boulevard.

Lyndon Crebbs opened the door before Jacob had time to even ring the bell.

Chapter 96

"YOU OLD BASTARD!" THE FBI agent said with feeling, hugging him. "Come in, for god's sake!"

Jacob stepped into a sparsely furnished room with a deep-pile beige carpet that had seen better decades.

His mentor had aged. His hair was white and his sun-tanned face was covered in a network of wrinkles. But his eyes were the same, dark brown and crackling with intelligence. And suspicion.

"God, Lyndon, you look like an old man."

The FBI agent laughed hard and closed the door behind him.

"Prostate trouble, Jacob. The cancer's eating me up, slowly but surely."

Jacob let his duffel bag fall to the floor and sank down on a chair at Lyndon's round dining-room table. "So—what have you heard? Anything?"

"I got a message from Jill in New York," Lyndon said, taking out two Budweisers. "They're wondering when you're going to stop running round Europe chasing murderers. They say they've got enough of those in the Thirty-second and could do with your help. Today, if not sooner."

Jacob laughed so loud and long that the noise almost shocked him.

"Well," he said, "I'm certainly not planning to settle in *this* dump of a city."

Lyndon smiled.

"You know what they say: L.A. isn't a cat that jumps into your lap and licks your face. But with a little time and patience, it just might."

And Jacob replied the same way he had for the past twenty years whenever pets were mentioned.

"No cats for me, Kimmy's allergic."

Lyndon Crebbs suddenly became very serious and looked much more like himself, which meant even more suspicious.

"I've got a whole lot to tell you," he said.

Chapter 97

Copenhagen, Denmark

IT WAS REALLY STILL night, but the sun was already up.

The pretty American girl named Anna took a careful sip from the last of her margarita. She didn't usually drink this late, but they had decided to do "crazy things" while they were traveling and "break all the rules."

She looked up at Eric and moved closer to him. Sometimes it felt like she could never get close enough.

The hip club was throbbing with music, but it was almost possible to talk in the upstairs bar. Not that anything sensible ever got said at this time of day, not in bars like this one.

"One more, then, eh?"

The guy who had bought their drinks was panting against her neck again. He was cute, but still...

She pressed herself against Eric, away from the other man.

"No, thanks," she said. "I've had enough."

"Go on," Eric whispered in her ear. "Just one more. We're all having fun."

Anna gulped and said, "Okay, then. To fun!"

The other guy ordered her another margarita.

Anna looked at her watch. It was late.

"Whereabouts in the States are you from?" the guy asked as he handed her the drink. The salt around the rim rained down on her fingers.

"Tucson, Arizona," Eric said. He was always so polite to everyone.

"'Jojo left his home in Tucson, Arizona, for some California grass...,'" the guy's pretty girlfriend sang, waving her glass.

"There's nothing but desert there, am I correct?"

"Not quite," Eric said.

Anna tugged at his shirtsleeve, even though she knew he didn't like it when she did that.

"I want to go back to the hotel now," she said. "Please, Eric."

"Have you been traveling long?" the girl asked, sucking on the straw in her empty glass.

"Two and a half weeks," Eric said. "We really like Scandinavia. It's totally awesome!"

"Yeah, isn't it?" the girl said.

She moved closer to Eric and kicked off one of her sandals. Anna watched her toes climb up Eric's sneaker.

"You know what they say about men with big feet?" she said, looking up at Eric from behind her hair.

Eric smiled in that way that made his eyes twinkle.

Anna blinked. What the hell were they doing? Flirting with each other? While she was standing here, right next to them?

"Eric," she said, "I really am tired. And we're going to Tivoli tomorrow..."

Eric gave a shrill laugh, as if she'd said something really childish. The girl laughed along with him.

"I think this feels like a magical evening," the girl said. "I'd really like a souvenir of tonight, wouldn't you, Anna?"

She draped herself against her boyfriend and kissed him softly on the lips.

The guy buying the margaritas gave a slightly forced laugh.

"This could get expensive," he said. It was almost as if he was reading a script.

"There can't be any shops open at this time of day," Eric said.

The guy stiffened. "Hell!" he said. "You're right! So let's get a bottle of champagne!"

He signaled to the bartender again.

The girl tilted her head and smiled at Eric.

"I'd really like to drink it with the two of you," she said, "in your hotel room."

Anna felt herself tense up, but Eric raised his glass in a toast. He had drunk too much, and nothing could stop him when that happened. She'd known that before she married him. He pulled her tight to him.

"Come on," he whispered right in her ear, his breath hitting her eardrum. "We wanted to meet new people on our trip, didn't we? These two are great."

Anna felt like she wanted to cry.

Eric was quite right.

She really had to stop being such a deadhead. They should go back to the hotel and party.

Chapter 98

LYNDON PUT TWO MORE bottles of beer on the table. Jacob grabbed one of them.

"I didn't think my sources would have much to say about Sylvia and Malcolm Rudolph, but I was wrong," he said, sitting down heavily at the table.

"Are they really twins?" Jacob asked, opening the bottle. The time difference was helping him feel a little high. He didn't mind.

"Oh yeah, they really are. Born fifteen minutes apart. Why do you ask that?"

Jacob thought back to the video from the Museum of Modern Art in Stockholm, how the couple had held on to each other, her hand sneaking inside the waistband of his trousers.

"Don't know," he said, taking a deep swig of beer.

"The really interesting thing happened when the twins were thirteen."

Lyndon raised his bottle and drank, and Jacob could see

his hand trembling. How ill was he exactly? He looked bad, which upset Jacob. He didn't have a lot of friends like Lyndon.

"Their parents, Helen and Simon Rudolph, were murdered in their bed eleven years ago."

Jacob blinked.

"Don't tell me," he said. "Let me guess. They were naked and their throats had been cut?"

The FBI agent chuckled. "Precisely. The bedroom evidently looked like a slaughterhouse. Blood everywhere."

"Who did it?"

Lyndon Crebbs shook his head.

"The case was never solved. The father was an art dealer. There was talk that he was transporting more than just Renaissance paintings in the containers he shipped between South America and the U.S., but nothing was ever proved."

The ingenuity of the drug cartels knew no limits. Cocaine and Renaissance art?

"What happened to the kids?"

"Some relative looked after them. My contact thought it was a cousin of the mother's, but he didn't have a name."

Jacob drank some more.

"Sounds like they were pretty well-off," Jacob said.

"You're not wrong there," Lyndon said. "Their home was evidently some sort of manor house, slightly smaller than the Pentagon. It's empty these days, owned by some bankruptcy agency."

"Is it far from here?"

"Not really. Just east of Santa Barbara. Why? You thinking of going there?"

"Possibly. Did you get anything on the boyfriend, William Hamilton?"

Lyndon snorted.

"He was hardly in Rome last Christmas. He's never even had a passport. He's never been out of the States."

Jacob groaned.

"I've got an address in Westwood," Lyndon said, "but I don't know if it's current. The Rudolphs used to hang out around that area, too. Looks like they studied art at UCLA, started some sort of group called the Society of Limitless Art..."

All of a sudden Jacob realized that he could no longer sit upright without a lot of concentration. He looked at his watch.

She's just woken up, he thought. The boats are gliding to and from the quays of Gamla Stan beneath her living-room windows, the sun has been up for hours and she's sitting on her sofa watching the sails flap in the wind, drinking coffee and eating a flatbread roll...

"Come on, I'll help you to the sofa," Lyndon Crebbs said. "You don't look so terrific yourself."

Chapter 99

Sunday, June 20
Copenhagen, Denmark

IT WAS RAINING.

Dessie was sitting at a table by the window of a packed café on Strøget, a long pedestrian street, watching people hurry past with umbrellas and raincoats. She was surrounded by families with young kids out for the weekend, the youngsters sleeping in buggies or sitting in kids' seats and gurgling while their mothers drank lattes and their dads had a Sunday beer.

"Is this seat taken?"

She looked up.

A young father with tousled blond hair and a little girl in one arm had already taken hold of the chair opposite her.

"Yes," she said quickly. "I'm waiting for someone. Sorry. He'll be here shortly."

The father let go of the chair and gave her a sympathetic look. "Sure. No problem."

She had been sitting at the table on her own for over an hour now. But she actually was waiting for somebody.

Nils Thorsen, a crime reporter on the Danish paper *Extra-Avisen* had been chosen as the Postcard Killers' Danish contact: a position he was as enthusiastic about as she had been in Sweden.

During the past twenty-four hours, the two of them had gone through all the details, pictures, and evidence that Jacob had left behind when he disappeared.

About an hour ago Thorsen had been called back to the office: a letter had arrived in the afternoon mail, addressed to him. White, rectangular, capital letters.

Dessie watched the father go back to the mother. He said something and nodded in her direction. The woman snickered, and they both laughed.

She looked down at the table again and pretended she hadn't seen them.

The fact was, she had a lot in common with Nils Thorsen. They had the same profession, the same interests, and even the same moral principles. He wasn't bad-looking either. A bit thin on top, maybe...

Why couldn't she feel the same way about him as she did about Jacob Kanon? God, she was starting to get loony, wasn't she? It was pretty pathetic, but it was out of her control now.

Slowly she wound her hair up, fastening it with a ballpoint pen, and went back to looking at the postcard in front of her.

Tivoli. The amusement park in the middle of Copenhagen. *Posted while the Rudolphs were being held in Stockholm.*

She had to face facts here.

However much she wanted to believe Jacob, his theory just didn't make sense.

Sylvia and Malcolm Rudolph weren't guilty.

Not of sending this card, and not of sending the letter that Nils and the police here in Copenhagen had presumably opened by now.

Why had she let herself believe it?

People will let themselves be convinced of anything, she supposed. Anything was better than a life without meaning. That was why religion existed, and football team fan clubs, and volunteer torturers in the service of dictators.

As both a researcher and a journalist, she had regarded questioning everything as her guiding principle. Investigating. Thinking critically. Not taking anything for granted.

All at once a longing burned her like a hot iron.

Oh, Jacob, why aren't you here? How did you get into my head this way? How did you get into my heart?

Chapter 100

"SORRY, DESSIE, SO SORRY," Nils Thorsen said, shaking the rain from his oilskin coat and sitting down opposite her. "That took ages, didn't it. I apologize."

He ordered a fresh beer at once, sneaking a look to see how she was taking his absence.

"Was it a Polaroid picture?" Dessie asked.

The reporter wiped his glasses on his sweater and put a copy of a blurry photograph in front of her.

The setting was unclear, and the focus all wrong. It was difficult to see what the picture was of, actually.

Dessie squinted and looked closely at the shot.

It had been taken from a very low angle. She could make out the foot of a bed, but whatever was on top of it was unclear to her.

"Have they found the location where this was taken?" she asked.

"It's only a matter of time," Nils said. "It has to be a hotel room. Look at the painting in the background. No one would have anything that ugly in their own home."

"Are there... people on the bed?" Dessie asked.

Nils Thorsen put his glasses back on. His hands were trembling. The man was clearly frightened, and she understood that better than anyone.

"I don't know," he said.

She held the picture up to her face, shifted it around in the light. Bedding, some items of clothing, a handbag, and—

Suddenly a foot came into focus. Then another. And another.

Instinctively she thrust the picture away from her eyes.

There were people there, two of them.

The evidence seemed to suggest that they were no longer alive.

"Do you really think that's an imitation of a work of art?" the Dane asked.

"Impossible to say," Dessie muttered.

She pushed the terrible picture away and began to run through Denmark's most famous works of art in her mind.

The Little Mermaid, the statue in Copenhagen's harbor, was obviously the best known. But there were the artists of the Skagen School, the cubist Vilhelm Lundstrøm, and plenty more.

She pushed the stray hairs away from her brow. A lot of the other photographs had been very easy to trace back to various artworks, usually well-known ones.

This wasn't one of them, was it? Something had changed.

"I don't think it was the same photographer," she said to Nils Thorsen. "So who took this picture?"

Chapter 101

Los Angeles, USA

"HEY, SLEEPYHEAD, YOU STILL alive?"

Jacob slowly opened his eyes without the faintest idea of where he was. He examined the clues.

A ceiling with a large damp stain.

The rattle of an exhausted air-conditioning unit.

A sharp smell of coffee, a smell he hadn't woken up to for the past six months.

"Ah, there you are. It lives. It snores. I've got some more information for you."

Jacob sat up on Lyndon Crebbs's lumpy living-room sofa. It had been insignificantly more comfortable than the recliner on the flight across the Atlantic.

The FBI agent held out a mug of steaming coffee.

"I've got the name of the guardian who took care of the Rudolph kids after their parents died," he said. "Jonathan

Blython, a cousin of the mother's, also a resident of Santa Barbara."

Jacob took the mug, had a sip, and immediately scalded himself.

"Excellent job," he said. "Do you think he'd appreciate an informal visit?"

"Hardly," Lyndon said. "He's been dead three years."

Jacob snapped awake.

"A sudden and violent death?"

Lyndon nodded.

"He was found with his throat cut. Parking lot over on Vista del Mar Street. He'd been with a prostitute. It was written off as a violent mugging. No arrest."

"Three years ago, you say?"

"The twins had just turned twenty-one. They were living here in L.A. No one connected them to the murder. Why would they?"

Jacob drank the bitter liquid and fumbled for his trousers. They'd slid beneath the sofa. Suddenly he remembered his night with Dessie. He put it out of his mind.

"I think I'm going to head out to Montecito," he said, pulling his jeans on. "How far is it?"

"A hundred miles or so, a bit less. You'll be there in two hours if you miss rush hour. But—"

Lyndon Crebbs placed a heavy hand on his shoulder.

"First you're going to take a shower," he said.

Chapter 102

Copenhagen, Denmark

THE CRIME SCENE WAS A hotel close to the Central Station.

The hotel looked like it had been built in the 1930s. It was three stories and pretty basic, not to say shabby. It fit the pattern for the killers—*before* the Grand Hôtel murders, anyway.

Dessie and Nils Thorsen arrived at the same time as one of the officers from the forensics team.

"We'll help you carry your equipment up," Thorsen said to them. This was met with wide eyes but no word of protest. Dessie was impressed with Thorsen's sly move.

They were waved past the cordon by the uniforms whose job it was to keep the press and public away.

The murders had been committed in a double room on the top floor.

There were no security cameras in the corridors, Dessie noted. *The killers' old pattern.*

Two of the forensics officer's colleagues had already started examining the room. It was harshly lit by various lamps, and Dessie could tell from the smell that the bodies were still there. Several detectives were walking around the room with notepads or cameras in their hands.

Dessie came to a halt just outside the door. She stood on tiptoe to see past one of the plainclothes officers, and when he leaned over, she got a clear view of the bed.

She gasped, couldn't help herself. The scene was beyond horrifying.

The man's genitals had been cut off and stuffed in his mouth.

The woman's stomach had been cut open and her guts laid out between her legs. She had an empty champagne bottle rammed down her throat.

Dessie turned away and grabbed at the wall for support.

"What is it?" Nils Thorsen asked.

"See for yourself," she said, stepping aside to let him through. "Although I advise against it."

Thorsen gulped for air and let out a noise that sounded like he was retching. He staggered back along the corridor.

Dessie moved to the door. She vividly recalled the scene in the house on Dalarö.

The similarities were striking.

Two dead bodies, a man and a woman, their throats cut.

But there were differences, too.

She hadn't thought it possible, but this scene was even more revolting. It was rougher and more graphic.

"What nationality are they?" someone from the forensics team asked.

"American," the senior detective said. "From Tucson, Arizona. Anna and Eric Heller, newlyweds. Here on their honeymoon."

Dessie's desire to throw up grew stronger. Her mind was working very fast. The similarities were undeniable, but there was also something different about this scene.

Nothing suggested that the bodies had been arranged in a particular way. The couple lay splayed on the bed without any apparent attention to their position, as if they had been thrown there, or had even just fallen asleep that way.

This was no *Little Mermaid*. Nothing from the Skagen school either. No famous art.

She took out her mobile and called Gabriella.

The detective grunted in answer.

"Are Sylvia and Malcolm still at the Grand Hôtel?" Dessie asked.

"They haven't left their suite."

"You're quite sure?"

"The entire hotel is besieged by the press. The Rudolphs can't move without the whole world knowing about it. Andrea Friederichs is busy selling the rights to the whole circus to the highest bidder. You know, 'Based on a true story...'"

Dessie closed her eyes. She massaged her forehead with one hand. "You've heard about Copenhagen?" she said.

"Grisly from what I've heard," Gabriella said.

"This is different," Dessie said. "Even more disgusting. I

don't think it was the same killers. *This was someone different.*"

There were a few moments of silence from the other end.

"Or else it was never actually the Rudolphs," Gabriella said.

Dessie couldn't think of a response.

"You have to consider that Jacob might be wrong," Gabriella said. "Everything we find is pointing to the fact that Sylvia and Malcolm are innocent."

Yes, she was perfectly aware of that.

"They might just have been incredibly unlucky," Gabriella went on. "They might have been in the wrong place at the wrong time. Or else someone really is trying to set them up."

Dessie moved to one side to let the ambulance crew through with their stretchers.

"Or else they're guilty," Dessie said, "and now someone else is mimicking their murders in almost the same way, just not as well thought through."

"And this 'someone else,'" Gabriella said. "Who might that be?"

Chapter 103

Montecito, USA

THE DIRECTIONS JACOB HAD been given led him to a huge gate at the end of a paved private road.

A tarnished bronze sign revealed that this was THE MANSION, with a very definite capital M.

No false modesty here.

Jacob sat in his car for a moment studying the surroundings.

While he had been cruising the streets of Montecito, he realized that this whole area was a playground for the wealthy and famous. Many of the houses were showy mansions built in a faux Mediterranean-style, with ornate gates and colorful bougainvillea.

This one was different, though.

The walls were several feet high, unwelcoming, granite gray. They stretched as far as he could see up toward the hills. They protected the house and grounds so well that he had no idea what might be on the other side.

The Mansion, my ass. More like the Fortress. To protect what secrets?

He got out of the car and went up to the phone to the left of the gate.

"*Sí?*" a crackling voice said.

So it wasn't entirely uninhabited.

"*Hola,*" Jacob said. "Speak English?" He had many good qualities, but a talent for languages wasn't one of them.

"*Sí.* Yes."

"Jacob Kanon, NYPD. New York City police. I'd like to ask a few questions about the Rudolph family. It's important that I speak to someone."

"Can you hold your ID up to the camera beside the phone?"

Opening his wallet, Jacob pulled out his badge and held it up to the camera.

"Come in!" the crackling voice said, and the tall gates started to glide apart.

A small Tudor-style gatekeeper's lodge was situated some fifty yards in on the left. The door opened and an elderly man limped out onto the drive.

Jacob stopped the car again and climbed out.

"You've no idea how long I've been waiting," the man said, holding his hand out and saying that he was Carlos Rodríguez.

"What for?" Jacob said, surprised.

The man hastily crossed himself. "The killing of Mr.

Simon and Mrs. Helen has been unsolved for too long! It is like a heavy weight I carry."

"So you knew the Rudolphs?" Jacob asked.

"Knew?" Carlos Rodríguez exclaimed. "I've been the gardener here for more than thirty years. I was here the night it happened. I called the police."

Chapter 104

CARLOS RODRÍGUEZ AND HIS wife, Carmela, had lived in the small gatekeeper's lodge at the Mansion ever since he returned from the Vietnam War in the spring of 1975. Both of their children had grown up there.

"Children are the future," Rodríguez said. "Do you have children?"

"No," Jacob said, putting his ID back in his wallet. "But I'm interested in the Rudolphs' children. What happened to them after the murder?"

The gardener sucked his teeth.

"The twins were looked after by Señor Blython," he said. "He took them down to Los Angeles, to the big house he bought in Beverly Hills."

The man moved closer to Jacob and lowered his voice, as if someone might overhear him.

"Señorita and Junior didn't really want to move," he said. "They wanted to stay in their house here, but it was up to Señor Blython to decide. He was their legal guardian, after all."

"Who owns this place these days?" Jacob asked.

He remembered that Lyndon said it had been in the hands of a bankruptcy agency.

Rodríguez's face darkened.

"The children inherited it, along with everything else: paintings, jewelry, stock shares, and small businesses. Señor Blython was charged with managing these assets until the children were twenty-one. But when that day came, the money was gone."

Jacob raised an eyebrow. "Their guardian defrauded them?"

"He took every last penny. The house was sold at an executive auction. The company that bought it was going to turn it into a conference center. But they went bankrupt in the financial crisis."

"What did Sylvia and Malcolm Rudolph say about what happened?"

The man's gaze wavered.

"They couldn't stay on at UCLA. There was no money, not even for the fees. So they had to get jobs. But they managed," he said. "They're very resourceful."

Jacob's jaw tightened. If the old man only knew.

"When did you last see them?" he asked.

Carlos Rodríguez didn't need to think about the answer. "The weekend before the house was sold at auction," he said. "They came to collect a few mementos, photo albums and things like that."

"They were both here?"

"And Sandra," the gardener said. "Sandra Schulman,

Sylvia's best friend. They only stayed a few hours on that last visit, and then they left, in the middle of the night..."

"And then Señor Blython was murdered," Jacob said.

Carlos Rodríguez snorted.

"If you hang around with *putas* in Los Angeles...," he said.

Jacob nodded and let the subject drop. The gardener had told him more than he had expected.

"The main building," he said, "is it still here?"

Carlos Rodríguez's face broke into a smile again.

"*Pero claro que sí!* I'm not formally employed anymore, of course. I get a little from the bank. Mostly we live on my pension. But I look after the Mansion."

"Could you show me around?" Jacob asked.

"*Sí, claro!* Of course I can."

Chapter 105

LYNDON WAS RIGHT.

The house was enormous, and it looked like something from a horror film set in the English countryside. Señor Rodríguez may have done his best to keep the building in good condition, but his lame old body had no chance against the wind, the damp, the weeds, and the ivy. One window frame had slipped its hinge and was squeaking in the wind.

This was where it all began, wasn't it? The murders — the mystery of the Rudolphs.

"The electricity has been cut off in the main house," the gardener said apologetically as he unlocked the oak door.

Jacob's footsteps echoed in the grand stone hallway. Doors stood half open, leading into high-ceilinged rooms and down long, dark corridors.

He took a quick look into the various rooms where Sylvia and Malcolm had once lived.

The whole building seemed to have been emptied of its

contents. Jacob noticed a single curtain in a library that was empty of books.

"The master bedroom is on the second floor. Follow me."

A magnificent curved staircase led up to the more private parts of the mansion.

Pale rectangles on the walls revealed where paintings had once hung. A battered rococo sofa, its stuffing hanging out, stood alone and dusty on the first landing.

"Straight ahead," Carlos Rodríguez said.

The bed was still there, an ornate four-poster without curtains or bedclothes. Otherwise the room was empty.

"So this was where it happened?" Jacob said.

The gardener nodded.

"And you were here that night?"

He nodded again.

"What did you see? Tell me anything you remember. Please. It's important."

The man swallowed.

"Terrible things," he said. "Blood all over this room. Mr. and Mrs. were lying dead in that bed. They must have been asleep when it happened."

"Did you see their injuries close up?"

The man ran his index finger like a knife across his throat.

"Deep cuts," he said. "Almost through to the bone at the back of the neck."

He gave an involuntary shudder as Jacob watched him closely.

"How did you come to be here, in your employers' room in the middle of the night? I don't understand."

The man took a deep breath, then spoke.

"I was asleep with my family when Señorita rang. I hurried here straightaway."

"It wasn't you who found them?"

"No, no. It was little Sylvia."

Chapter 106

Monday, June 21
Copenhagen, Denmark

THERE WAS STILL A pattern here. It had just changed slightly.

Dessie kept thinking she could see it clearly, just for a few seconds. Then it would slide out of her reach again.

She was sitting on the unmade bed in her hotel room with all the pictures and postcards around her, all of Jacob's crumpled copies. She picked them up, even though she had seen them a hundred times, maybe more. All the buildings and people and details were already imprinted in her memory.

The postcard from Amsterdam of the plain building on Prinsengracht 267: the house where Anne Frank was hidden during the war, where she wrote her famous diary.

Then Rome and Madrid: the Coliseum and Las Ventas, gladiatorial combat and bullfights. Arenas for theater based on killing.

The Paris card was of La Conciergerie, the legendary antechamber of the guillotine.

Berlin was a view of the bunker built by Hitler, the most famous failed artist in history.

Stockholm showed the main square, Stortorget, the site of the Stockholm Bloodbath.

But she couldn't make three of the cards fit the pattern of the others.

The Tivoli pleasure gardens in Copenhagen.

The Olympic stadium from the Athens games of 2004.

And that anonymous shopping street in Salzburg.

What did they have to do with death?

Dessie let the pictures fall to the bed again.

Was she imagining this pattern?

Was it foolish to try to give any sort of order to the way these sick bastards thought?

She stood up and went over to the window. The rain had given way to mist and fog. Cars and bicycles were crossing Kongens Nytorv below her.

Why was she really bothering? Jacob had left her. The newspaper hadn't been in touch for days now. No one missed her.

To be or not to be.

As if you could choose to live or die.

Could you? And in that case, what sort of life would it be?

She knew she could do just as she liked, continue digging around in this story or go home: get involved or let go. Quite regardless of what other people thought, and what they thought about her, what did *she* actually want to do now?

She turned around and looked at the mess on the bed.

Jacob hadn't managed to contact the Austrian reporter. He had never gotten hold of a copy of the picture of the bodies in Salzburg either.

She walked toward her mobile phone, then picked it up and held it to her chest for a few seconds before dialing International Directory Inquiries.

A minute later the phone rang at the reception desk of the *Kronen Zeitung*.

"*Ich suche Charlotta Bruckmoser, bitte,*" Dessie said.

Chapter 107

THERE WERE SEVERAL CLICKS on the line, then the Austrian reporter was there.

Dessie introduced herself as a fellow reporter from Stockholm.

"Before I start, I want to apologize for phoning and disturbing you," she said in her rusty schoolgirl German.

"I was the one who received the postcard and picture in Sweden," she explained. "I wonder if I could ask you a couple of questions."

"I haven't got anything to say," the reporter said, but she didn't sound angry. Just watchful.

"I completely understand," Dessie said. "I know what you've been through."

"I read about the killings in Sweden," Charlotta Bruckmoser said, sounding slightly less guarded.

"Well, here's something you might not know," Dessie said, and she told her story. About the photographs mimicking famous works of art, with a few exceptions; about the postcards of places where death and art mixed together, again with a few exceptions; about Jacob Kanon and his murdered daughter; about Sylvia and Malcolm Rudolph, their alibis and Jacob's conviction that, in spite of everything, they were the Postcard Killers.

The only thing she left out was the night in Jacob's room in the hostel.

Two sharp beeping sounds told her that someone was trying to call her, but she ignored them.

Charlotta Bruckmoser was silent for a few moments after Dessie had finished speaking. "I haven't read any of this in the papers," she eventually said.

"No," Dessie said, "and I doubt you could get confirmation of it from any official sources."

"What about you, what do you think?" the reporter asked cautiously. "Are the Rudolphs guilty?"

Dessie took a moment to reply.

"I really don't know anymore."

Silence again.

"Why are you telling me this?" the Austrian woman asked.

Two more beeping sounds. Someone was keen to get hold of her.

"The pictures you received," Dessie said. "I'd really like to see the pictures you received."

"I'll e-mail you the card and the letter and everything," Charlotta Bruckmoser said.

Ten seconds later there was a ping from Dessie's mailbox. The pictures were here!

There was blood all over the room, as if the victims had been crawling about while they bled to death. Two lamps had been broken. The bodies had fallen forward onto their sides and lay about a meter apart on the floor.

"Is there any Austrian work of art that looks like this?" Dessie asked. "Famous art?"

The reporter took her time replying.

"I don't think so," she said, "but I'm no expert. *Famous art*, though? I really don't think so."

Dessie clicked open the PDF of the envelope and looked at the address. It was written in the same block letters as the others. But on the back was something she hadn't seen before: nine numbers, hastily written down.

"That number on the back," Dessie said, "what does that mean?"

"It's a phone number," Charlotta Bruckmoser said. "I tried calling it. It's for a pizzeria in Vienna. The police decided it had nothing to do with the case."

At that moment Dessie's inbox pinged again. She felt her stomach lurch.

It's Jacob, ran the thought going through her head. He's e-mailed me because he misses me.

It was from Gabriella.

Tried to call you. Another double murder in Oslo.

"I've got to go," Dessie said and hung up on Charlotta Bruckmoser.

Chapter 108

Los Angeles, USA

UCLA WAS AS BIG as a decent-size town in California. More than thirty thousand students, some two hundred buildings, more than fifty thousand applicants to be freshmen every year.

Jacob had punched Charles E. Young Drive into the GPS, an address that was supposed to be in the university's northern campus, where the School of the Arts and Architecture was based.

His contact, Nicky Everett, was waiting for him outside room 140, on the first floor of the building. The young man was wearing chinos, a golfing shirt, boat shoes, and frameless glasses. Jacob had never met anyone studying for a PhD in conceptual art, but he'd been expecting something more bearded and absentminded.

"Thanks for taking the time to see me," Jacob said.

"I believe in art that communicates," Nicky Everett said seriously, looking at him through the sparkling clean lenses.

"Er....," Jacob said, "you knew Malcolm and Sylvia Rudolph?"

"I wouldn't use the past tense," Everett said. "Even if we no longer have a physical relationship, there are other forms of contact, correct?"

Jacob nodded. Okay.

"Could we sit down outside perhaps?" he said, gesturing toward some benches just outside the main entrance.

They went out and sat in the shade of a few spindly trees.

"If I've understood this right, you studied here at the same time as the Rudolph twins—until they left—correct?"

"Absolutely," Everett said. "Sylvia and Mac were leaders in their field."

"Which was?"

"Let me quote Sol LeWitt: 'In conceptual art the idea or concept is the most important aspect of the work. The idea becomes a machine that makes the art.'"

Jacob made an effort to understand, and also to keep his emotions in check. "So an event, or a series of events, can be a work of art?" he asked.

"Of course. Both Mac and Sylvia were determined to take their work to its ultimate limits."

Jacob remembered Dessie's stories of the art student who faked a psychotic attack for her examination piece, and the guy who smashed up a car on the subway and called his art-work *Territorial Pissing*. He described these cases to Everett.

"Could the Rudolphs ever do anything like that?"

Nicky Everett pressed his glasses firmly onto his nose. "The Rudolphs were more meticulous in their expression. That all sounds rather superficial. '*Territorial Pissing*'?"

Jacob ran his fingers through his hair. "So," he said, "explain it to me: how can that be *art?* I want to hear this and understand it as best I can."

The student looked at him with complete indifference in his face.

"You think a work of art should be hung on a wall and sold on the commercial market?"

Jacob realized the futility of going any further down this road and changed the subject. "They started an art group, the Society of Limitless Art..."

"It was more of a web project. I don't think anything ever came of it."

"What was their social life like otherwise? Family, friends, boyfriends, girlfriends."

Nicky Everett seemed not to understand, as though the very idea that he might possess such insignificant facts was completely ridiculous.

"Do you know if they were upset when their guardian died here in L.A.?"

"Their *what?*"

Jacob gave up.

"Okay, I think we're good," he said, standing up. "It's a shame the Rudolphs couldn't afford to stay on here. Imagine all the incredible art they could have created..."

He turned to go back to his car.

Nicky Everett had also stood up, and for the first time, a genuine expression showed on his face. "'Couldn't afford to stay on here'? Sylvia and Mac were exceptional talents. They both had scholarships. There was no problem with fees."

Jacob stopped short.

"No problem? So why did they leave, then?"

Everett blinked a few times, a sure sign that he was agitated.

"They created the work *Taboo* and were expelled. They showed up the bourgeois limitations and the hypocrisy of our society, and of this institution, of course."

Jacob stared at the student.

"What did they do? What was *Taboo*? What was it that got them expelled?"

Nicky Everett's mouth curved into a smile.

"They committed an act that was entirely relevant within the frame of their art. They had intercourse in a case in the exhibition hall."

Chapter 109

JACOB SAT IN THE car with the GPS switched off and his duffel bag beside him on the passenger seat. The more he found out about the Rudolphs' background, the weirder they became. *Taboo* went way beyond *Territorial Pissing.*

If he started with this latest piece of information, the signals he had picked up on from the recording at the Museum of Modern Art had been correct. The siblings had an erotic relationship. It was possible that people had different preferences within the world of conceptual art, but in Jacob's reality, you didn't have intercourse with your twin in public, not unless you had a whole toolbox full of loose screws.

The long trail of slashed throats they had left behind them couldn't be a coincidence either. The question was, What came first, the chicken or the egg?

Had Sylvia discovered her murdered parents and been traumatized for life? Was she trying to get over the experience by repeating it, again and again, in the form of macabre works of art? Or was she the one who had killed her mother and father at the age of thirteen? Was that even physically possible? Would she have had the strength to do it? The neck was tough. It was full of muscles, sinews, and ligaments. But above all, why would she have killed her parents?

He took it for granted that the twins had murdered the guardian who had embezzled the whole of their inheritance.

And who was Sandra Schulman, the friend mentioned by the gardener? He would have to track her down, too. And the boyfriend, William Hamilton.

For some reason he suddenly saw Dessie Larsson before him, her long hair and graceful profile, her slender fingers, her vigilant green eyes.

Had the mob of journalists finally given up waiting outside Dessie's door? Had she gone back to her old routine?

Was she thinking of him? Was she all right?

Irritated, he shrugged off the thought. He had more work to do in L.A.

Chapter 110

WILLIAM HAMILTON, OR BILLY as his friends called him, opened the door with his long, dirty blond hair standing on end and wearing nothing but a pink bath towel.

"What?" he said abruptly, blinking in the dim light from the stairwell. "What now?"

"Police," Jacob Kanon said, holding up his badge, obscuring the NYPD. "Can I come in? Of course I can."

"Shit," Billy said, frowning, but letting the door swing open.

Jacob took that as a yes and stepped into the apartment.

It wasn't bad, the apartment. It was on Barrington Avenue, just a few miles from Westwood Village and the UCLA campus. It was at the top of the building, with a large terrace overlooking the pool and a garden.

There was a fashionable kitchen/bar and an open gas fire.

"What the hell's the matter this time? What do you people want now?"

Billy sank into a white corner sofa facing the artificial fire. The towel slid open, revealing well-muscled, suntanned thighs.

"Honey, who is it?" a woman's voice called from one of the bedrooms.

"Mind your own business," he muttered under his breath.

"I'm here about Sylvia and Malcolm Rudolph," Jacob said, sitting down on the sofa without being asked. Billy let out a low groan.

"What the fuck? I've already answered a load of dumb questions! When am I supposed to have found the time to slum around Europe? I *still* don't have a passport. I've got a job here."

"Doing what?" Jacob asked, fighting an instinctive dislike of the guy on the sofa.

Billy straightened his shoulders. "Actor," he said.

"Wow," Jacob said. "What have you been in?"

Billy's shoulders sank a bit. He wiped his nose. "I'm a musician, too. And I'm working on a script for television."

Jacob tried to look impressed. He wasn't, not in the least. He thought that a baboon could probably write a script for television.

"You met Sylvia when you were studying performance drama at UCLA..."

Hamilton spread his arms.

"Okay, this is how it is: I tried to save Sylvia from her crazy brother. Their relationship got seriously fucked up when Sandy disappeared. Malcolm was totally obsessed with her. You following me, taking notes?"

Jacob interrupted him.

"Disappeared? Who disappeared? Sandra Schulman?"

Irritated, Billy Hamilton got up and walked up and down in front of the fire.

"They were going up to the Mansion to get the last of their stuff, but I had an audition and couldn't go. They waited for her, but Sandy never showed up for the car trip. No one knows what happened to her. Mac took it real bad. We all did."

Jacob sat there without moving, trying to fit the information together in his head.

"Malcolm Rudolph and Sandra Schulman were a couple?"

"Well, *yeah*. Ever since high school. She came from Montecito. They were neighbors."

"Darling, who are you talking to?" called the woman in the bedroom. "I'm lying here waiting for you."

"Shut the fuck up!" Billy shouted. "I'm busy!"

He sniffed and wiped his nose again. "I don't know what else to tell you, dude."

Jacob took that as a signal to move on and started toward the door.

"Where was Sandra Schulman living when she disappeared?" he asked.

"Same place as Sylvia and Mac. Apartment on Wilshire and Veteran. Ask me, they might have been a threesome.

Except that Sylvia was jealous of Sandy. *Very.*...Hey, are you going? *Already?* What a shame."

"What was the number? The apartment on Wilshire?"

Hamilton looked scornfully at him.

"What do I look like, fucking Google?"

Chapter 111

JACOB WENT BACK TO his car and made a phone call.

Carlos Rodríguez answered with the same crackling *sí* as he had at the gate of the Rudolphs' mansion in Montecito.

"Jacob Kanon here," Jacob said. "NYPD? We spoke yesterday."

"*Sí, señor. ¿Qué pasa?* How can I help you, Detective?"

"Just one more question. It's about Sandra Schulman. You said she was with them at the Mansion that last weekend before the auction? Is that correct?"

"*Sí.* Why?"

"You're quite sure?"

"Sandra used to play here since she was a little *chiquitita.* Of course I recognized her. She and Malcolm were boyfriend and girlfriend."

"How did Sylvia feel about her?"

"Oh, I don't know. She liked having Malcolm to herself. They were very close, brother and sister."

"Did you speak to Sandra that evening at the house?"

"*Sí, claro!* She kissed me on the cheek."

Jacob pushed the hair from his forehead.

"You said the twins left in the middle of the night. Did you see them drive away?"

"*Pero claro que sí.* They woke me up. The gate can only be opened manually, from inside the lodge."

"Did you notice if Sandra Schulman was in the car?"

There was silence at the other end.

"It was late at night," he said. "You couldn't see anything inside the car."

"But you spoke to the Rudolphs?"

"With the *señorita.* She was driving."

"But you didn't actually see Sandra Schulman leave the property?"

There was a moment's silence.

"She must have gone with them, because they didn't leave her behind."

Jacob covered his eyes with his hand.

"Thanks," he said. "That's all I needed to know."

He ended the call and quickly made another.

Chapter 112

LYNDON CREBBS ANSWERED AFTER the first ring.

"How's it going, you amateur? Are you getting anywhere?" Lyndon asked.

"Can you check on a Sandra Schulman? Last known address Wilshire Avenue, corner of Veteran Avenue."

"Anything special about her?"

"She may have disappeared, permanently. Take this as a tip from an anonymous source: she could be buried in the hills above Montecito. Sylvia was jealous of her. Enough said."

Jacob could hear the FBI agent's pen scratch.

"What about William Hamilton?" Lyndon Crebbs asked as he wrote. "Is he still alive, I hope?"

"If the LAPD takes a look there, they'll find a heap of snow in the bedroom. He's alive. But he's an obnoxious little prick."

Lyndon chuckled.

"By the way," he said, "I was reading the report on the

search of the Rudolphs' hotel room in Stockholm. What did that key belong to?"

"What key?" Jacob said.

"The little key that's mentioned at the bottom of page three."

"How the hell could you read that, Lyndon? *It's in Swedish.*"

"Haven't you ever used the site www.tyda.se?" Lyndon Crebbs said. "Just an old man wondering."

The police in Stockholm must have checked it out, Jacob thought. "Christ, this is mad," he said. "Do you know why the twins were thrown out of UCLA? They had sex with each other in public."

"Ah, today's youth," the FBI agent said. "Something else occurred to me: what if there are other killers? What if the Rudolphs have inspired copycats?"

"The thought has occurred to me, too," Jacob said. "But it doesn't fit. The content of the postcards has never been made public, for instance. If there are more killers, they have to be working together."

"Sicker things have been known to happen," Lyndon Crebbs said. "When do you think you'll be back at Citrus Avenue?"

Jacob grew serious. "I won't be back this visit," he said. "I'm heading off now."

Lyndon Crebbs was silent, a silence that only grew. Jacob was treading water. He couldn't bring himself to ask the only relevant question: exactly how bad was the prostate cancer?

Jacob spoke again. "Just one more thing. Could you pull a

few strings and see if you can find out anything about Lucy? My ex? I should tell her about Kimmy."

The old man let out a sigh.

"I thought you'd never ask."

"Thanks for everything," Jacob said.

"Well, *adios, amigo,* then," Lyndon Crebbs replied.

"*Hasta la vista,*" Jacob said. "Till next time."

But the line was already dead, and Jacob wondered if he'd ever hear his friend's voice again.

Chapter 113

Tuesday, June 22
Oslo, Norway

THE MOTOR HOME WAS in a campsite just outside the city. The police cordon had been lifted from the entrance to the site but was still in place around the vehicle.

Dessie pulled the zipper on her Windbreaker up snug and tight under her chin.

The campsite was almost empty, and not just because of the weather. The Italians' motor home was all alone in its section of the site, like a leprous metal box whose neighbors had fled in panic.

She went closer.

Drifts of dead insects were still littering the insides of the windows. They covered the bottom third of the screens.

She pulled the hood over her head. A stiff gale was blowing in from the Oslo fjord just below, sharp as needles.

It was the flies that had let on that something was wrong

inside the Italians' motor home. The people in the neighboring tents had complained about the buzzing, and eventually also about the smell.

The owner of the site, a man named Olsen, hadn't been too bothered. The Italians were paying for their patch on account, and he wasn't fussy. If people wanted to keep flies as pets, he wasn't about to stop them.

When the police eventually arrived, the windows were completely covered in swarms of black insects. They were as thick as curtains.

It was estimated that the bodies had been there for over a month.

Dessie pulled out the copy of the Polaroid picture, taken before the flies had started to lay eggs.

The wind tore at the sheet of paper, and she had to hold it with both hands.

The letter and postcard had only been found the previous morning. The reporter the killers had chosen had gone away on vacation the day the card was posted. No one had been checking his mail.

When he returned to work at the paper, he found both the postcard, TO BE OR NOT TO BE, and the photograph Dessie now had before her.

Antonio Bonino and Emma Vendola had been on a driving tour of Europe, and had arrived in Oslo on the morning of May 17. They wanted to experience Norway's national day, the celebrations when the Norwegians mark the anniversary of their country's independence.

Emma worked as a secretary at a PR agency. Antonio was

studying to be a dentist. They had been married for two years.

She looked at the victims' picture again.

Their hands had been placed close to their faces, the palms to their ears.

The killers had stuffed two pairs of black tights in their mouths, giving the faces a grotesque expression of pain and horror.

She had recognized the work of art immediately, and it *was* famous.

Edvard Munch's *The Scream,* a painting that had become world-famous to a new generation as the logo for the horror movie *Scream.*

Dessie could feel her eyes welling up. She didn't know if it was because of the wind or the thought of the dead couple.

They had been saving up to buy this vehicle ever since they got married. Six bunks, so there would be room for the children when they came along.

Did they have time to feel afraid?

Did they feel any pain?

She turned away from the motor home and walked toward the exit, not wanting to think about the dead anymore.

Instead she conjured up Jacob's image. His messy hair, the crumpled suede jacket, the sparkling blue eyes. He hadn't been in touch.

He'd disappeared from her life as though he'd never been there.

This past week could have been a dream, or, rather, a

nightmare, in which her whole life had been turned upside down by forces she had no control over.

Dessie shivered.

She stopped by the exit and turned around to look back at the abandoned campsite.

Willowy birch trees bent beneath the wind; the water down below was gray with geese. The cordon around the motor home flapped in the wind.

The Rudolphs could have been responsible for these murders.

They hadn't been arrested yet in the middle of May.

Chapter 114

Stockholm, Sweden

SYLVIA LET MALCOLM GO in first.

She enjoyed watching the effect he had on poor, dull Andrea Friederichs: the lawyer clearly became positively moist the moment he walked into a room.

"Dear Malcolm," the lawyer said, standing up and grasping his hand with both of hers. Her cheeks glowed bright red. Her eyes swept from his biceps down toward the curve of his backside.

Sylvia sat down opposite her and smiled.

"It's great that we're getting close to a financial agreement," she said.

The lawyer's smile faded as she glanced at Sylvia. She put on her ugly-duckling reading glasses and started to leaf through the papers on the table.

They were in one of the smaller conference rooms of the

Grand Hôtel, the room the lawyer had reserved to conduct negotiations for the global rights to Sylvia and Malcolm's story.

"Well, I've had final bids for both the book and the film rights," she said, putting the documents in two piles in front of her.

"There are four parties bidding for both packages, six who want only the book, and three, possibly four, who just want to make the film. I thought we might go through them together so that you—"

"Who's offering the biggest advance?" Sylvia asked.

The lawyer blinked at her over the thick black frame of her glasses.

"There are a number of different conditions attached to the various bids," she said. "Nielsen and Berner in New York, for instance, have a very interesting proposal including a television series, a computer game, a lecture tour...for the two of you."

"Excuse me," Sylvia interrupted, *"but how much are they offering as an advance?"*

Dear Andrea took a theatrical deep breath.

"Not much at all. Their package is the largest in total, but it's conditional upon your full participation in the marketing campaign."

Malcolm stretched, making his T-shirt ride up. He scratched his stomach.

"The advance?" he said, smiling toward Andrea.

Her angular face broke into a foolish smile and she fumbled with the papers again.

"The largest advance is offered by Yokokoz, a Japanese company that really wants only the digital rights. They will make a manga series, with all the spin-offs that entails—collectable cards, clothing, and so on. They want to sell the book and film rights, without you having any say in where they end up..."

"How much?" Malcolm asked.

"Three million dollars," Andrea said.

Sylvia stretched her back.

"That sounds pretty good," she said. "Sign up with Yokokoz."

The lawyer blinked.

"But," she said, "the agreement has to be refined. We can't leave the question of subsidiary sales open. You have to have control over the finished product..."

"Try to get them up to three and a half million," Sylvia said, "although that's not a deal breaker. But they have to pay us now. Anything else and the deal's off with them. Right? We're clear?"

Andrea Friederichs shifted uncomfortably in her chair. Clearly, she *wasn't* clear.

"If I could just remind you about my fee," she said. "I can't take a percentage because I'm a member of the Association of Swedish Lawyers, but I presume we're following usual practice?"

Sylvia raised her eyebrows in surprise.

"Are we? I don't remember signing an agreement like that. Nor does Malcolm."

"No, I don't."

Andrea Friederichs clicked her ballpoint pen in irritation.

"A quarter of the total is usual in cases like this. We discussed it the first time we spoke. I must tell you that some agents take considerably more."

Sylvia nodded.

"I know twenty-five percent is the norm," she said, "but in our case I think five percent is more appropriate."

The lawyer looked as though she couldn't believe what she'd just heard.

"What do you mean? A hundred and fifty thousand dollars? That's quite absurd!"

Sylvia smiled again.

"You're getting five percent."

Andrea Friederichs started to get up from her chair. Her blushes had grown into fiery blotches covering her whole neck.

"Almost a million and a half Swedish kronor for a few days' work," Sylvia said. "You think that's absurd? I suppose that it is."

"There's such a thing as legal precedent...," the lawyer began.

Sylvia leaned over and lowered her voice to an almost inaudible whisper.

"Have you forgotten who we are?" she breathed, and she saw how Andrea Friederichs sank back in her chair, her face drained of color.

Part Three

Chapter 115

Wednesday, June 23
Stockholm, Sweden

URVÄDERSGRÄND WAS DESERTED AND doing its best to show why it had been named after bad weather.

Gusts of rain tore and tugged at the street lamps and signs, the shutters and gables.

The reporters had finally given up and gone the hell home. That was the good news.

Dessie paid the taxi driver and hurried in through the doorway. Her steps echoed in the empty stairwell. She felt like she'd been away for ages.

Her apartment welcomed her with gray light and complete silence and a certain unappealing mustiness.

She pulled off her clothes, letting them fall in a heap on the hall floor. Then she sank down and sat on the telephone table in the hall, staring at the wall opposite. Suddenly she

was far too exhausted to take the shower she had been looking forward to all day.

For some reason her mother came to her mind.

They hadn't been in regular contact during the last years
she was alive, but right now Dessie would have liked to call
her and tell her what had been written about her, about the
terrible murders, about her own loneliness.

And about Jacob.

She would have liked to tell her about the unusual American with the sapphire blue eyes. Her mother would have
understood. If there was one thing she had experience in, it
was doomed relationships.

At that moment the phone rang right next to her. It star-
tled her so much that she jumped.

"Dessie? The phone didn't even ring on my end. You must
have been sitting on it."

It was Gabriella.

"Actually, I was," Dessie said, standing up.

She got hold of a towel and grappled with it to pull it
around her with one hand, then took the cordless phone out
through the kitchen and into the living room.

"How are things with you? You sounded so down when I
last spoke to you."

Dessie slumped onto the sofa and looked out at the harbor. It was still gorgeous; at least that never changed.

"Everything got a bit much in the end," she muttered.

"Is it Jacob?"

Unable to stop herself any longer, Dessie started to cry.

"Sorry," she sniffled into the phone. "Sorry, I..."

"You fell for him hard, didn't you?"

Gabriella sounded neither angry nor disappointed, but more like a good friend now.

Dessie took a deep breath.

"I suppose so," she said.

There was a moment's silence.

"Things don't always work out as you hope," Gabriella said, so quietly that her words were almost inaudible.

"I know," Dessie whispered. "Sorry."

Gabriella laughed.

"That took its time," she said.

"I know," Dessie repeated.

Silence again.

"What's happening today?" Dessie asked, to break the silence more than anything else.

"The Rudolphs have announced that they're checking out of the Grand at lunchtime. Not a moment too soon, if you ask me."

Dessie bit her lip. "Do you really think they're innocent?" she asked.

"There's nothing to link them to the murders," Gabriella said. "No forensic evidence, no witnesses, no confessions, no murder weapons..."

"So who did it? Sell me on a new explanation," Dessie said. "Who are the real Postcard Killers, then?"

Before Gabriella could answer, the doorbell rang.

What the—?

Who could it be now? A reporter who still hadn't given up?

She had no peephole and no safety chain.

"Hang on a moment while I get the door," Dessie said, going out to the hall and unlocking the door.

She opened it cautiously, then suddenly she couldn't breathe.

"I'll call you later," she said into the phone and hung up on Gabriella.

Chapter 116

JACOB WAS ALMOST AS crumpled-looking and unshaven as he had been the first time he stood outside Dessie's door.

She took a great leap into his arms, holding him *tight, tight, tight,* as though she never meant to let go, kissing him hard and letting her hands roam inside his checkered flannel shirt.

"Dessie," Jacob whispered into her hair. "We're standing in the stairwell and you're not wearing any clothes."

Her towel had fallen to the floor. She kicked it into the apartment and pulled him into the front hallway. The dirty duffel bag ended up under the telephone table, his jeans by the door, his shirt and T-shirt by the radiator.

They made it as far as the door to the living room before they collapsed to the floor. She fell into his bright blue eyes and felt him pushing inside her. The world spun and she closed her eyes, straining her head back against the wooden floor when she came.

"Jeezuz," Jacob said. "I guess that means you're happy to see me!"

"Just you wait," she said, nipping his earlobe with her teeth.

They stumbled into the bedroom. Dessie pushed him onto the bed and began to explore every inch of his body. She used her fingers, hair, and tongue, tasting and licking and caressing.

"Oh, god!" he panted. "What are you doing to me?"

"I'm just happy to see you," Dessie said. "What are you doing *to me*?"

Then she sat astride him.

She moved gently above him, deep and intense, forcing him to calm down, slow down. It gave her a chance to catch up, and when she felt the rush coming, she let go completely. He seemed to lose several seconds when he came, but she forced him to continue for another minute or so until she came as well.

Then she fell into his arms and passed out.

Chapter 117

DESSIE OPENED HER EYES and looked deep into his bright blue ones. They crackled with a warmth that left her breathless. And more confused than ever.

"You're here," she whispered. "It wasn't a dream. I'm so glad. I'm happy."

He laughed. His teeth were white, a bit crooked. His hair was sweaty, sticking out in every direction. He sank back down on the bed and pulled her to him.

"Why did you come back?" she asked.

He kissed her and then grew suddenly serious.

"Several reasons," he said. "You were the most important one."

She hit him playfully on the shoulder with her fist.

"Liar," she said.

"How did you make out in Denmark and Norway?" he asked.

She told him about the grotesque murders in the hotel in Copenhagen, about the mutilation of the bodies and the fact that the woman had probably been raped. They had found bruises and scratches on the inside of her thighs, and the semen in her vagina wasn't her husband's. It didn't seem to her like the Rudolphs' work.

She went on to tell him about the motor home death scene at the campsite outside Oslo, how neither the bodies nor the letters had been discovered because the reporter had been on vacation, and how the bodies had been arranged to look like Munch's *The Scream*.

"How did you get on in America?" she asked.

He gave her a summary of his investigations, telling her that the Rudolphs came from an extremely privileged background. That Sylvia had found their parents murdered when she was thirteen years old. That their guardian, Jonathan Blython, had embezzled their inheritance and been found dead with his throat cut. That Mac's girlfriend Sandra Schulman—whom Sylvia was jealous of—had disappeared after a visit to the Rudolphs' home. That the twins had set up an experimental art group, the Society of Limitless Art, and been expelled from UCLA because of a public act of incest.

"A public act of incest?" Dessie said.

"They called the work *Taboo*. The two of them made love in an exhibition hall."

"They really are mad," Dessie said, pulling him to her once more.

Chapter 118

AFTERWARD, THEY SAT IN bed and ate an improvised lunch. Jacob was finishing one of her microwaved vegetarian lasagnas.

Dessie had taken her laptop back to bed and was reading *Aftonposten*'s report of the deal that the lawyer, Andrea Friederichs, had negotiated for the rights to Sylvia and Malcolm's story.

"An advance of three and a half million dollars," she read, "plus royalties and even more money for the subsidiary sale of the book rights. And get this — the lawyer has decided not to charge for her services. She only represented them because it was the right thing to do, she says."

"Are they still at the Grand?"

She clicked further on the site and looked at her watch.

"According to Alexander Andersson's blog, they checked out half an hour ago. They left through the back door to avoid the media scrum outside the main entrance."

Jacob threw off the covers, leapt out of bed, and disappeared into the kitchen.

Dessie looked after him in surprise.

"There's nothing that links them to the murders," she called into the kitchen. "Jacob? They're free to come and go as they like."

She heard the kettle boil.

The next minute he was standing in the doorway with a mug of coffee in each hand. His face was as dark as a thundercloud.

"It was them," he said. "I know it was. We can't let them go free."

"But there's still no evidence," Dessie said glumly. "We can't prove a damn thing."

He handed her a mug.

"Their gear must be somewhere. The eyedrops, the outfit he was wearing when he emptied those accounts, the things they've stolen and not managed to get rid of. And the murder weapon..."

"Exactly," Dessie said. "That could be in any rubbish bin, and do you know why? Because I told them in that bloody letter that they were about to get caught. I gave them time to clean up."

Jacob stopped beside the bed and looked at her.

"There was nothing wrong with that letter. You were doing the right thing when you wrote it. You were very brave."

"Was I?" Dessie said. "What did it actually achieve? Apart from warning the Rudolphs and making a fool of me in front of every proper journalist in Sweden."

He walked angrily across the bedroom floor, turned, and came back.

"They didn't throw their stuff away," he said, "not all of it, anyway. Most serial killers keep trophies. They would have chosen a hiding place as soon as they got to Stockholm. It's entirely possible that it's all still there. I think that it's even likely."

He stopped midstride.

"The little key!" he said.

Dessie blinked.

"What?"

He reached across Dessie and her computer to grab her cell phone from the bedside table.

"What's going on?"

"At the bottom of page three of the official report, there's something about a key. My FBI friend noticed it. I can't help hoping it belongs to some left-luggage locker in Stockholm."

Chapter 119

GABRIELLA SIGHED HEAVILY INTO the phone.

"Of course we looked at the key," she said. "There was nothing to indicate that it actually belonged to the Rudolphs."

Jacob realized he was grinding his teeth again. This could be the *second* big error by the police in Stockholm. "What do you base that on?"

"It was in the toilet cistern in the hotel room. It could have been there for weeks. Who knows for how long?"

Jacob had to stop himself from slamming the phone against the bedroom wall. You didn't have to be an expert to know that water cisterns were a favorite hiding place for lots of people, and especially criminals in a new city. Christ!

"The key belongs to them!" he said. "It fits a locker, a postal box, or some other form of lockable space. And I hope that's where you'll find all the evidence. Please get on it immediately."

"The Rudolphs have been ruled out of the investigation," Gabriella said curtly, then hung up.

Dessie took her cell phone away from him before he smashed it against the head of the bed.

Jacob collapsed onto the bed, all his energy gone, his patience, too. He'd flown across the Atlantic twice within a week, and by now his body clock had practically lost track of what century it was.

"What was the name of that art group at UCLA?" Dessie asked, pulling the laptop over.

He had shut his eyes and was massaging his own neck. "The Society of Limitless Art," he muttered.

What could he do to persuade the police to open the investigation again? Or even to act like real cops?

He couldn't just let the Rudolphs disappear.

"Here's something," Dessie said. "Look at this! You don't even have to move. Just open your eyes."

She turned the laptop to face him.

Welcome to the Society of Limitless Art
You are visitor no. 4824

"The address is www.sola.nu," she said. "That's a domain registered on Niue, an island in the South Pacific. They let anyone register any sort of address in just a couple of minutes."

Jacob took a look at the screen.

"They set this up when they were at UCLA," he said.

Dessie tried clicking on the first tab, Introduction.

"And here we have the background of conceptual art," she said. "Marcel Duchamp tried to exhibit a *urinal* in New York in nineteen seventeen. He was refused."

"I wonder why," Jacob said.

"Look here," Dessie said.

Jacob sighed and sat up.

The gallery included a long sequence of strange photographs that he would hardly have associated with art: motorways, trash, an unhappy cow, and a few shaky home movies of—what a surprise!—motorways, trash, and presumably the *same* unhappy cow. It was hard to tell for certain.

"This is ridiculous," Jacob said. "I feel like that cow, though. Does that make me a work of art?"

"Their ridiculous art project got them thrown out of school," Dessie said. "This sort of thing matters to them."

Jacob stood up now, looking for his jeans.

He found them out in the hall. He stopped there, trousers in one hand, and stared back into Dessie's living room.

So this was where it all ended, in an apartment halfway to the North Pole. He'd done his best, but it wasn't enough. Kimmy's killers were going to walk free. Could he live with that? Who cared? What was the alternative?

"Hey!" Dessie called. "Look here!"

"What?"

He went back toward the bed.

"Sections of the site are locked. It's a puzzle to be solved. We need a password."

Chapter 120

A BOX HAD APPEARED against a gray background, with the message *Log in!*

Dessie typed "sola" for Society of Limitless Art in the box and pressed Enter. The screen flickered.

Sorry — wrong password.

"I didn't think it would be that easy," she said.

Suddenly an idea came into Jacob's head. There was a key with no lock in the report. Here was a lock but no key.

"We could be onto something here," he said. "Try 'Rudolph.' Maybe it *is* that easy."

Sorry — wrong password.

Jacob stared at Dessie. He remembered the last conversation

he'd had with Lyndon Crebbs: *What if there are other killers? What if the Rudolphs have inspired copycats?*

He heard his own reply echo in his head: *If there are more killers, they have to be working together.*

"If the Rudolphs have got an accomplice," Jacob said slowly, "then they need some way of contacting him, them, whoever it is. Could they be using this site to communicate with one another?"

Dessie tried a hundred other possibilities. Again and again:

Sorry — wrong password.

"We're lucky the site is still letting us try new ones. Most sites will block you after three tries," Dessie said.

"Where are the postcards?" Jacob asked.

Dessie reached for her knapsack on the floor beside the bed. She tipped out the copies, letting them fan across the bed.

"What are you thinking?" she asked.

"Let's try all the words on the cards," Jacob said. "What's this one here?"

He picked up a photograph he hadn't seen before. It was of two dead or seriously wounded people in a room that showed clear evidence of a struggle.

"That's the picture from Salzburg," she said. "I spoke to the reporter. She mailed it to me."

Dessie tried word after word: "Rome," "Paris," "Madrid," "Athens."

Sorry — wrong password.

"What are these numbers?" Jacob asked, pointing at the back of the Salzburg envelope.

"The phone number of a pizzeria in Vienna. The reporter already checked it. Nothing to do with the case," Dessie said.

Next she went through all the sites on the postcards: "Tivoli," "Coliseum," Las Ventas."

Jacob picked out the pictures from Copenhagen and Oslo.

Oslo was done by the Rudolphs.

Copenhagen was the copycat.

"What if they've got a password that isn't a word but something else?" he said.

Dessie looked at him intently.

"When would you need that information?" Jacob asked. "When are you most in need of instructions? The moment you're about to carry out your task, wouldn't you say?"

Dessie stared at him. "I don't know, I've never been a murderer. I've been tempted a couple of times."

"Where would you write the password you need to get your instructions for the kills? On the nearest thing available maybe?"

He picked up the copy of the back of the envelope from Salzburg.

"The Rudolphs had an alibi for the murders in Austria," he said. "So that must have been carried out by their accomplice. Try these numbers."

Dessie picked up the laptop again and carefully typed in the nine numbers.

She pressed Enter.

The screen flickered.

A new image appeared.

"Holy fucking Christ," Dessie said.

Chapter 121

THE INVESTIGATING TEAM HAD gathered in Mats Duvall's office. Their faces were pale and drawn.

"Do we have any idea where the hell the Rudolphs have gone?" Jacob asked, sitting down opposite Sara Höglund.

The head of the unit shook her head. She looked to be in utter despair. As she ought to be.

"They were let out the back door of the Grand Hôtel this morning. No one's seen them since then."

"And the key? The key that no one on the team paid much attention to?"

"We know it belongs to a left-luggage locker."

Jacob slammed his fist on the table so hard that the coffee cups jumped.

"We've put out a national alert and informed Interpol," Mats Duvall added quickly. "Arlanda, Skavsta, Landvetter, Västerås, Sturup, and every other airport with international connections is on increased alert. The Öresund Bridge to Denmark is blocked and every vehicle is being searched.

The ports have been informed. The border posts are on the alert. Surveillance of all highways and European routes has been intensified. They won't get out of Sweden."

Jacob stood up.

"For fuck's sake, they've just gotten hold of three and a half million dollars! They can buy their own *plane!*"

"The whole amount is in an account in the Cayman Islands," Gabriella said, reading from a document in front of her. "The transfer has been confirmed by the bank they used here in Stockholm."

Jacob was close to upending the table and all the useless paperwork on it.

"So they haven't got much cash at the moment," Dessie said, just to be clear.

Jacob leaned back in his chair, pressing the palms of his hands to his forehead.

Dessie had already given him the hopeless details. The Rudolphs were free and had vanished, in a country with fewer inhabitants than New York and an area almost as big as Texas. There were thousands of miles of unguarded borders with both Norway and Finland, and just as much coastline. A couple of hours in a fast boat would get them to Estonia, Latvia, Lithuania, Poland, Russia, Denmark, or Germany.

Silence fell around the table.

Gabriella Oscarsson was concentrating on a bundle of papers, Mats Duvall was fiddling with his BlackBerry. Evert Ridderwall, the hotshot prosecutor, was staring blankly out the window.

Jacob clenched his fists at the sight of the fat little man.

He was the one who had let the bastards out in the first place.

"What does the analysis of the website tell us?" Dessie eventually asked.

Sara Höglund leaned forward.

"Your first assumption turned out to be correct," she said. "The Rudolphs have set themselves up as masters of their own universe. Their project aims to integrate life, death, and art, to find the ultimate form of expression. The Society of Limitless Art is their own university. As far as we can make out, they've got about thirty-five followers around the world. There could be more. Other art students who share their worldview and admire their ambitions."

Dessie looked down at her hands. "Three other couples have taken the 'exam' that the Rudolphs provide. Hard to believe, isn't it? So many crazies out there."

The pages of the website contained detailed instructions on how to pass the exam, or "graduate," as the Rudolphs called it, in the special project of the Society of Limitless Art. By causing death in a particularly artistic way, humankind could become a creating divinity, and thus immortal.

The procedure of "the Work" was described in detail, from the dialogue to be spoken when the victims were seduced, to how the champagne, eyedrops, and knife were to be used. All the postcards and Polaroid pictures had been uploaded as JPEG files onto the site. Links and PDFs of the media coverage in each of the countries were also cataloged.

It seemed that the press clippings were an important part of the artwork.

"But none of the so-called graduates have actually passed the exam," Jacob said, aware of how hoarse his voice sounded. "The amateurs always messed up the murders somehow. Sometimes there was no symbolism in their choice of postcard. Or they didn't manage to imitate famous works of art with their Polaroids."

No one responded; they just listened to the American now.

"It isn't easy to kill, no matter how motivated or focused you are," Jacob said in a low voice. "The others have all panicked and lost their grip on the situation."

"Athens, Salzburg, and Copenhagen were probably carried out by different members of the group," Sara Höglund confirmed. "The police in each country are tracing the IP addresses of computers that accessed the site. We'll have located them by this evening."

Mats Duvall stood up, holding his electronic gadget. "The perpetrator in Copenhagen has just been identified," he said. "He's a repeat sex offender. His DNA was on file."

"He's a member," Dessie said softly. "His user ID is *Batman*."

"How do you know that?" Gabriella asked.

"He *graduated* on Sunday," she said. "They had a ceremony on line."

Chapter 122

THE MEETING BROKE UP and the members of the investigating team went back to their respective rooms. Everyone was excited about the new leads but also shocked about the Rudolphs being on the loose.

Jacob and Dessie ended up sitting beside the coffee machine in the unofficial staff room on the fourth floor. On the table in front of them was a map of northern Europe.

"They never go back to where a murder was committed," Jacob said. "They keep moving on to new places, new countries."

Dessie ran her hand over the map.

"So we can probably discount Denmark, Norway, and Germany," she said.

"They know things are heating up," Jacob said. "They'll want to lie low for a while now. So they'll avoid any transport that involves passenger lists. They won't pay with credit cards or anything that means they have to provide ID. So where the hell are they going, and how?"

Dessie put both hands over the Stockholm district on the map.

"They're pretty much broke," she said, "and they're on the run."

"So?" Jacob said.

"They'll steal a car," Dessie said. "If you're right, they're heading for Finland."

Jacob looked at the map, his finger landing on the Baltic Sea.

"Why not a boat? It's only a couple of inches to the Baltic states."

"In this country we guard our leisure craft like they were gold reserves. It's much easier to steal a car. Then they'll have to get up to Haparanda."

She indicated a point on the map where the two countries met. "That's over a thousand kilometers from here."

"So they're behaving like petty criminals again," Jacob said.

"There are no motorways north of Uppsala. The E-four isn't bad, but there are speed cameras the whole way. They'll have to drive up inland, past Ockelbo, Bollnäs, Ljusdal, Ånge…"

Jacob followed her finger as it moved along the narrow, winding roads leading up the oblong country.

"Your home territory," he said. "When will they get to the border? How long?"

Dessie bit her lip.

"They'll have to stick to the speed limit—they can't risk getting stopped for speeding. And there's a lot of wildlife out on those roads. Elk, deer, maybe reindeer farther north…"

"Are there self-serve gas pumps where they can pay cash to refuel without being seen?"

"They're everywhere," Dessie said.

Jacob ran his hands through his hair.

"We've got to check all cars stolen in Stockholm this morning, and any that are stolen in the north of Sweden over the next few hours."

He put his index finger on the map and screwed his eyes shut. *Postcard Killers*, he thought, *where the hell are you?*

Chapter 123

THE STOLEN MERCEDES WAS speeding over a bridge with glittering bright blue water on both sides.

Small, wooded islands strewn with light gray rocks rose on the left and right.

"Do I turn off up here?" Mac asked, leaning in toward the windshield. "What do you think?"

Sylvia looked down at the road atlas and started to feel sick. She always got carsick when she tried to read on a car trip.

"Left onto the two-seven-two," she said grouchily. "Somewhere on the other side of this lake."

She fixed her eyes on the horizon, the point where the road disappeared in the distance, just as her mother had taught her.

Mac slowed down.

"There's no need to be so miserable about it," he said. "This was your idea, after all. I'm doing the best I can."

She swallowed and glanced at him, leaning close and giving him a quick kiss on the ear.

"Sorry, darling," she cooed. "You're driving brilliantly."

She ran her hand lazily along the dashboard. There was no longer any reason to hide their fingerprints or DNA. On the contrary, it was time to let the world know their message.

Soon they would be able to sit back and enjoy what they had achieved.

Mac braked, signaled, and turned off to the left. They drove past fields with sheep and cattle, past thick groves of trees.

"It's kind of beautiful in its own way, don't you think?" Sylvia said, putting the atlas away. She wasn't planning to look at it again. They were almost there now.

Mac didn't answer.

The landscape opened up around them as they drove through a small town. To the left were a few houses, to the right a farm. They passed a row of what was once laborers' housing, a school, and an apartment block. Then they were out the other side. So much for civilization on this road trip.

They drove on in silence.

Mac was looking intently through the windshield.

"What do you think about that one?" he said, pointing to a farm on the edge of the forest.

Sylvia leaned forward to check the place out. "Could be. Maybe."

Mac slowed down, then stopped the car. "Yes or no?"

The farmyard seemed quiet and deserted. All the windows and doors were shut. They could see an old Volvo behind a barn, a sedan that must have been the height of style in the early 1980s.

"This'll do," Sylvia said, taking a quick look behind her.

No cars in sight.

"Quickly, now," she said. "We need to be really careful from here on. No mistakes."

Chapter 124

MAC JUMPED OUT OF the car. Sylvia took her seat belt off and slid over to the driver's seat.

With a certain amount of effort she put the car in gear. She wasn't used to driving cars with gears and a clutch. Then she sped off to the far side of the next bend.

There she stopped.

She wound down the window and listened over the sound of the engine. The trees sighed; some sort of animal was bleating in the forest. The sound of a car rose and fell in the distance, but nothing came past.

She would have to wait here for a while.

Her eyes settled on some sort of construction in the trees. Planks, a ladder. A tree house, or maybe a hunting post.

Suddenly she was filled with a feeling of intense hatred and disgust.

Imagine, there were people who lived the whole of their pointless lives in godforsaken places like this, working and drinking and fucking and building hunting posts without any awareness that there was anything else, that a higher level of human consciousness even existed. People out here abandoned their lives to meaningless banality, never bothering about *brilliance,* about *aesthetics.*

She tore her eyes from the hunting post and concentrated on the rearview mirror.

Mac was driving the red Volvo now. He didn't slow down as he passed her, just carried on at the same carefully precise speed: not too slow, but not too fast either.

She put the car in gear and followed at a safe distance. Careful. No mistakes.

Now they had to find a good spot to dump the car from Stockholm, somewhere it would be found relatively quickly, but not immediately.

She licked her thumb and pressed it against the wheel. A lovely print.

Suck on that, dear police!

It made her giddy to think of what they'd already achieved, and that was only the start.

The next part could be even more impressive, their next act. She and Mac were maturing as artists.

Chapter 125

THE WHOLE CASE WAS breaking open now—*and quickly.*

The killers from Athens lived in Thessaloniki. They weren't a couple, just two art student friends at the Aristotle University of Thessaloniki, the largest university in Greece. They were arrested on the campus, given away by the electronic trail left on their computers.

They were both deeply religious, and both claimed that they were in direct contact with "the creating God, the unknowable ruler of all the universe." They admitted to what had happened in Athens, but denied it was murder. Their work was part of a global conceptual artwork intended to reveal humankind's divinity.

The murders in Salzburg were traced to a young British couple from London. They were enrolled at a fashionable art college in the middle of London. They hadn't attended any classes for the past four months.

Their fingerprints and DNA were found at the scene of

the crime, and the murder weapon was discovered under a loose floorboard in the couple's apartment.

They didn't comment on the accusations. They didn't respond to any of the authorities' questions, and they even refused to talk to their own lawyer. On their blogs they had written that *every individual was responsible for creating their own morals and their own laws, and that everything else was an affront to the rights of the individual.*

The killers in Copenhagen were arrested that evening, both the repeat offender whose details had been in the DNA register and his accomplice, a younger woman who was deeply remorseful once she was captured. The woman confessed at once, in floods of tears, and said that she had changed her mind and tried to stop the killings. Her change of heart had occurred when her colleague had raped the young American woman, which hadn't been part of the "artwork" design.

Dessie looked at Jacob and saw how his eyes registered everything that was reported about the murderers, how his jaw clenched every time new information was received.

The other police officers exhibited the sort of relief that comes after an arrest and a confession, but not Jacob. The others' shoulders relaxed, became less tense, and the way they walked seemed somehow freer, but Jacob's face remained carved from stone.

She knew why.

Kimmy's killers were still out there somewhere, probably on their way to Finland.

Chapter 126

DURING THE DAY, THREE cars had been stolen in the Stockholm region.

An almost-new Toyota from the suburb of Vikingshill. A Range Rover out in Hässelby garden suburb, at the end of the underground network. An old Mercedes from a parking garage beneath the Gallerian shopping center in the middle of the city.

"The Merc makes sense, right?" Jacob said. "They wouldn't take the underground all the way out to the suburbs just to get a car."

He picked up the map again.

"So now they're driving north. That's how Dessie and I figure it," he said. "They might even have changed cars by now. I would have. They're traveling on minor roads and heading for Haparanda. They're sticking close to the speed limit. So they should get there early tomorrow morning, at the latest."

Mats Duvall looked skeptical. "That's just speculation," he said. "There's nothing to *prove* that they'd choose that particular route, or even that mode of transport. We don't know anything for certain."

Dessie watched Jacob stand up. He was making an effort not to attack anything, or anyone.

"You've got to reinforce the border crossings in the north," he said. "What's the name of that river right on the border? The Torne River?"

"We can't allocate manpower simply on the strength of guesswork," Mats Duvall said, closing up his electronic gadget, a sign that the conversation was over.

At that, Jacob stormed out of the room, closely followed by Dessie.

"*Jacob*...," she began, taking hold of his arm. "Stop. Look at me."

He spun around, standing right next to her.

"The Swedish police are never going to catch them," he said in a low voice. "I can't let them get away again. I can't do that!"

Dessie looked into his eyes.

"No," she said. "You can't."

"When's the next flight to Haparanda?" Jacob asked.

She took out her cell and called the twenty-four-hour travel desk at *Aftonposten*.

The closest airport was in Luleå, and the last flight that evening was an SAS plane, leaving Arlanda at 9:10.

She looked at her watch.

It was nine o'clock exactly.

The airport was forty-five kilometers away.

The first plane the next morning was a Norwegian Air Shuttle, due to leave at 6:55.

"We can be in Luleå at 8:20," Dessie said. "Then we have to rent a car and drive up to the border. It's another hundred and thirty kilometers away."

Jacob stared at her.

"Do you know any police up there? Or some customs officer who can keep an eye on things until we get there?"

"No," she said, "but I can call Robert. He lives in Kalix. It's a forty-five-minute drive from the border."

"Robert?"

She smiled, a smile that was almost a grimace.

"My criminal cousin. The big one who protected me when I was a kid. And even now."

Jacob ran his fingers through his hair and paced quickly around the coffee machine.

"How long would it take to drive up there?" he asked. "If we leave now."

She looked at her watch again.

"If we go for it, and the road isn't full of trailers and lumber trucks, we'll be there by six."

He slapped the wall with his hand, nearly putting a hole in it.

"That's not good enough," he said.

"If Robert keeps an eye on things, they won't get through," she said. "A blue Mercedes, registration TKG two-nine-seven, wasn't it?"

He looked at her, fire in his eyes.
"Have you got access to a car?"
"No," she said, "but I've got a bicycle."
She waved her American Express card.
"We'll rent one, you idiot."

Chapter 127

Thursday, June 24
Norrland, Sweden

IT WAS PAST ONE o'clock in the morning when Dessie sailed past the town of Utansjö. She had driven almost five hundred kilometers and needed to get petrol, drink coffee, and go to the bathroom. Not in that order actually.

She glanced at Jacob in the reclined seat next to her as he slept the comatose sleep of the jet-lagged. The diesel would last until they got to the twenty-four-hour truck stop in Docksta, but she had a much better idea.

It would mean a slight detour, but it might be worth the trouble.

She reached the turning to Lunde, hesitated just for a second, and then headed left along Route 90.

The car's rhythm changed and the very poor road surface made Jacob stir.

"What the hell…?" he said, confused, as he sat up straight. "Are we there?"

He looked around, astonished, at the early dawn light. Mist was lying in thin veils on the water, black fir trees reached up to the heavens, several deer fled across the fields.

"We're exactly halfway to Haparanda," Dessie said. "Those are reindeer, by the way."

He looked at his watch.

"This whole midnight sun thing is pretty fucked up," he said, shaking his watch. "And the reindeer, too. Where's Santa?"

Dessie slowed the car and pointed ahead.

"See that?" she said. "Wästerlunds Bakery. I lost my virginity in the parking lot around the back."

This nugget of information woke him up properly.

"So these are your old stomping grounds? Interesting. You're really a hick."

"Until I was seventeen. I spent a year at Ådal high school in Kramfors, then went to New Zealand as an exchange student. I ended up staying there nine years."

Jacob looked at her.

"Your weird English accent," he said. "I've been trying to place it. Why New Zealand?"

She glanced over at him.

"It was as far away as I could get…from being a hick. See that? There's the memorial to the workers who were shot by the military in nineteen thirty-one. Remember our talk, *fascist?*"

She pointed to a sculpture of a horse and a running man that was just visible down by the water.

They drove up onto Sandö Bridge, and Jacob peered down at the river below.

"When it was built, this was the longest single-span concrete bridge in the world. I had to cross it every day to get to school."

"Lucky you," Jacob said.

"It scared me every single time, every day, twice a day. The bridge collapsed once, killing eighteen people. The most forgotten tragedy of the last century, because it happened on the afternoon of August thirty-first, nineteen thirty-nine."

"The day before the Second World War broke out," Jacob said. "I have a good memory for history, too. Where are we actually going?"

"Past Klockestrand," she said. "It's not far now."

She slowed down and turned off to the right, onto a narrow dirt road.

"I thought we might need some expert help," she said, driving up to a huge wooden building in a state of more or less complete ruin.

"What the hell is this place? The House on Haunted Hill?"

"Welcome to my childhood home," Dessie said, switching the engine off.

Chapter 128

THERE WAS A FAINT light coming from a window on the ground floor, the sort of blue light that an old television set gives off.

Dessie wondered how many of her family were there. The house was a base for her uncles, the few who were still alive, and for a number of her cousins.

"Will anyone be awake at this time of day?" Jacob asked.

"Granddad," Dessie said. "He usually sleeps during the day. At night he watches old black-and-white films that he downloads illegally from the Net. Are you coming in with me?"

"Wouldn't miss it for the world," Jacob said, climbing out of the car.

The held each other's hand as they walked up to the huge building.

The structure was an old-style farmhouse, with four chimneys, two floors, and a loft tall enough to stand up in. The red iron-oxide paint had peeled off decades ago and the wooden walls shone a grayish white in the early light.

Dessie opened the outside door without knocking and kicked off her shoes.

Apart from the sound from the television, the house was quiet. If anyone was here besides Granddad, they were sound asleep.

Her grandfather was sitting in his usual armchair, watching a film with Ingrid Bergman in it.

"Granddad?"

The old man turned around and took a quick look at her. Then he went right back to the television screen.

"Drag åta dörn för moija," he said.

Dessie shut the outside door.

"This is Jacob, Granddad," she said, walking toward him, still holding Jacob by the hand.

Her grandfather hadn't aged much, she thought. Maybe it was because his hair had been white for as long as she could remember, and his face had always had the same miserable scowl. He didn't seem the least bit surprised to see her in his living room for the first time since her mother's funeral. Instead, he just glowered suspiciously at Jacob.

"Vo jär häjna för ein?"

"Jacob mostly does rough work," Dessie said, taking the remote and turning off the television.

Then she sat down on the table directly in front of the old man.

"Granddad, I want to ask you something. If I'm on the run from the police and haven't got any money and want to hide out in Finland, what should I do?"

Chapter 129

THE OLD MAN'S EYES twinkled. He cast a quick, approving look at Jacob, straightened up in his armchair, and regarded Dessie with new interest.

"*Vo håva jä djårt?*"

"What language is that?" Jacob asked, bewildered. "It doesn't sound like any Swedish I've heard."

"*Pitemål,*" Dessie said. "It's an almost extinct dialect from where he grew up. It's further from Swedish than either Danish or Norwegian. This farm belonged to my maternal grandmother's family. No one around here really understands him."

She turned to her grandfather again.

"No," she said, "we haven't done anything bad. Not yet, anyway. I'm just wondering, purely hypothetically."

"*Sko jä håva nalta å ita?*"

"Yes, please," Dessie said. "Coffee would be good, and a sandwich, if you've got any cheese."

The old man stood up and staggered off toward the

kitchen. Dessie took the opportunity to go out into the gloom of the hall and crawl in under the stairs, where the only toilet in the house was situated.

When she got back, the old man had prepared some bread and cheese and had boiled water for instant coffee. He was sitting with his hands clasped on the wax tablecloth, his eyes squinting as he mulled over Dessie's question.

"Å djööm sä i Finland," he said. *"Hä gå et…"*

Dessie nodded and took a bite of the sweet bread and Port Salut.

Then she interpreted simultaneously for Jacob so he could follow.

Hiding in Finland wouldn't work. The Finnish police were far more effective, and brutal, than the Swedes. Any Finns on the run came over to Sweden as quickly as they could.

But if you absolutely had to get to Finland, that was no problem, as long as you had a freshly stolen car, of course.

Anyone could cross the Torne River wherever they liked. There were bridges in Haparanda, Övertorneå, Pello, Kolari, Muonio, and Karesuando. Each had its advantages and disadvantages. Haparanda was the biggest and slowest, but the guards there were the laziest, so you might not get questioned. Kolari was the least used and fastest, but you were more likely to be noticed there. You had to choose your route in Morjärv — north toward Överkalix or south to Haparanda. Then you just had to aim straight for Russia as quickly as you could.

"Russia?" Jacob said. "How far away is that?"

"Jä nögges tjöör över Kuusamo, hä jär som rättjest…"

"Three hundred kilometers," Dessie said.

"Christ," Jacob said. "That's nothing. Manhattan to the end of Long Island."

According to Dessie's grandfather, it was hard to get into Russia, and it always had been.

In his day, the no-man's-land along the border had been mined with explosives, but they were all gone now. Nowadays it was the most remote boundary of the European Union. It was tricky but not impossible.

The biggest problem wasn't getting out of the EU, but into Russia. You had to leave the car and then walk across, maybe just north of Tammela. There was a main road on the other side of the border that would take you to Petrozavodsk, and from there to St. Petersburg.

Dessie and Jacob sat in silence until the old man had finished.

Then he stood up, put the coffee cups on the draining board, and wandered off toward the television again.

"Stäng åta dörn för moija då jä gå," he said.

"We have to shut the door to stop the midges from getting in when we leave," Dessie said. "I think he likes you."

Chapter 130

THEY FILLED THE CAR with diesel from the farm's illegal agricultural tank.

Then Jacob took the wheel.

"Where am I going?"

"Straight on until you see 'Suomi Finland' on the signs," Dessie said, putting the seat back down and stretching out.

He aimed north and emerged onto the main road again.

If the Rudolphs managed to reach Russia, he'd never see them again, that much he was sure of. Anyone with a lot of money could buy protection there, and anyone without it could disappear among the country's homeless millions.

He stiffened his grip on the wheel and pressed the accelerator. His head still felt groggy from his long nap. The car was small and sluggish, with a weirdly noisy engine. He'd never driven a diesel before.

The landscape glided past and it really was astonishingly beautiful. Craggy cliffs falling to the sea. Blue peaks rising to the north. The road wound its way along the coast, getting ever narrower and more twisted and scenic.

He was on his way toward the end of the world. The Rudolphs were on their way there, too.

Dessie's cell phone started to ring on the dashboard.

He glanced at the woman beside him. She was fast asleep, mouth open in a narrow line.

Jacob grabbed the phone and said, "Yeah?"

"We've found the left-luggage locker," Gabriella said. "It was in the basement of the Central Station. You were right. Both of you were."

He clenched his fist in triumph.

"It contained everything you suspected: light shoes, brown wig, coat, trousers, sunglasses, Polaroid camera, a couple of packs of film, pens, stamps, postcards, eyedrops, and a really sharp stiletto knife, as well as some other stuff."

She fell silent.

"What?" Jacob said. "What else was there?"

His raised voice woke Dessie, and she sat herself up beside him.

"We found the passports and wallets of all the murder victims—apart from Copenhagen and Athens and Salzburg."

He braked and stopped the car by a twenty-four-hour café. He was searching for words but couldn't find any.

"Your daughter's were there," Gabriella said quietly. "I've got them on the desk in front of me. Her fiancé's as well. You'll get them when you're back."

"Okay," he muttered.

"You wanted to know if any cars had been stolen in northern Sweden late yesterday, didn't you? A farmer north of Gysinge has just reported the theft of a Volvo two forty-five. A nineteen eighty-seven model, red. License number CHC four-one-one.

"A two forty-five—that's a sedan?"

"A wagon. I'm sending a text message with all the details."

He put the car in gear and looked round. They were in a small village. A tractor trailer pulled out of the parking lot just ahead of him.

"How far have you gotten?" Gabriella asked.

Jacob pulled out onto the road behind a gigantic lumber truck billowing smoke.

"Halfway. Thanks for the call," he said.

"I wish there were more I could have done," Gabriella said quietly.

Dessie looked at him.

"Call your cousin," Jacob said. "We have the make of the potential getaway car."

She took the phone.

The sun was just rising to the north.

Chapter 131

THE FOREST GREW THICKER after Örnsköldsvik, and signs of habitation thinned out. Between the towns of Umeå and Skellefteå, a distance of almost 150 kilometers, Jacob hardly saw a single house. The end of the world was getting closer and closer, wasn't it?

In the town of Byske, the jet lag struck him like a sudden fog. The last traces of his ability to judge distances abandoned him and he woke Dessie to take over at the wheel.

Even with the sun in his eyes, he fell into a restless sleep.

Kimmy was there with him.

She looked like she had when she set off for Rome. She had on her new winter coat and her yellow woolly hat. So beautiful and talented.

Jacob could see she was upset, crying. She was standing in a glass box, banging her fists against the transparent walls and calling for him, calling for her dad. He tried to answer, but she couldn't hear him.

Kimmy! he shouted in the dream. *I'm here! I'm coming!*

"Jacob?"

He woke with a start.

"What?" he said.

"You were shouting. Having a bad dream."

He sat up and rubbed his eyes hard with his fists.

The car had stopped. They were on the outskirts of a town.

On the left was a large warehouse, and on the right, a long row of office buildings. It was full daylight, a dull sort of light, filtered through a thin cloud cover. The landscape was flat and bare, not like anything he'd ever seen before.

"Where are we?"

"The bridge over to the Finnish side is only a kilometer from here. Robert's a bit closer, on the other side of the rotary. Nothing came through during the night. No red Volvo. No young couple."

He blinked and looked around.

"This is Haparanda?"

"*Kyllä.*"

He looked at her, confused.

"Finnish for *yes,* babe. Let's go. Robert's waiting for us."

She started the car and drove toward a large rotary with what was practically a small forest at its center.

"He's got men watching all the bridges across the river, and a couple at the main harbors for small boats. No one's seen anything. Robert's men are vigilant."

"Thank god for organized crime," Jacob said.

"Robert's rough, but he's a good guy."

A huge building with an immense parking lot spread out to the left of the car.

"What the hell is that?" he asked.

"That's the most northerly IKEA in the world. And there's Robert!"

They stopped beside a customized Toyota Land Cruiser, the latest model. Leaning against the gleaming paintwork was a giant of a man with a blond ponytail and biceps like logs.

Dessie hurried out of the car and threw herself into his arms. The giant received her with a big grin on his face.

A pang of jealousy hit Jacob in the solar plexus. Slowly he got out of the car and approached the enormous man holding on to Dessie.

Robert's arms were covered in clumsy tattoos. He was missing two front teeth.

He would have been perfect, just as he was, as the leader of one of Los Angeles' infamous motorcycle gangs.

"So you're the American?" he said in a thick Swedish accent, holding out his paw.

Jacob's hand disappeared in the iron grip of the fist.

"Yep," he replied. "That's me."

Cousin Robert pulled him closer and lowered his voice.

"Don't think you can hide just because you're from the States. If you treat Dessie badly, I'll find you."

"That's good to know," Jacob said.

The giant let go of Jacob's hand.

"We've been keeping an eye on the junction in Morjärv all night," Robert said. "They passed it half an hour ago in a red Volvo with false plates. They took the E-ten down toward Haparanda."

Jacob felt adrenaline explode throughout his body. This was it. *The end of the tale, at the end of the world.*

The gangster looked at his watch, a diamond-encrusted Rolex.

"They could be here any minute."

Chapter 132

TIME NEARLY STOPPED FOR Jacob.

He checked his cheap plastic watch every minute.

8:14, then 8:15, then 8:16.

The early morning mist was lingering, making the land-scape seem eerie, scary-looking.

Robert's sidekick brought them coffee, juice, and ham sandwiches, which they ate in the car. They were both very hungry.

"How close are you two?" Jacob asked, nodding toward the enormous man leaning on his car a hundred yards away. The car sagged from his weight.

Dessie was doing her best to scrape the ham off the bread.

"Robert?" she said. "He's my favorite cousin. His mom was in and out of prison when he was young, so he spent a lot of time with us on the farm. He's two years younger than me, but he was always bigger and stronger than me."

Dessie put the sandwich down on her lap.

"I've always wondered if we're more than cousins," she said.

Jacob stopped chewing.

"What do you mean?"

She took a gulp of orange juice.

"I don't know who my dad is," she said quietly. "My mother always said he was an Italian prince who would come and fetch us both one fine day. I have *no idea* what she meant."

She gave him a quick embarrassed look.

"I know," she said. "All a bit like a fairy tale. One of my uncles is probably my father, or maybe even Granddad himself." She shivered and was silent.

Jacob turned to look through the windshield. What could you say to something like that?

Dessie stretched out as much as she could and looked in the rearview mirror.

"Red car," she said.

Jacob adjusted the mirror so he could see for himself. Sure enough, a red car was approaching from behind.

"It's a Ford," he said. "Four people. It's not them. It's probably not them."

Chapter 133

THEY SAT IN SILENCE, watching the passengers as the Ford went past on its way to the border crossing: two elderly couples, the men in the front, the women in the back.

Dessie turned to him, hesitated for a moment, then asked, "Who was Kimmy's mother?"

Now it was his turn to put his sandwich down.

"Her name's Lucy," he said. "We grew up together in Brooklyn. She was a singer, blues and jazz, really talented. We were both eighteen when she got pregnant. When Kimmy was three months old, she left us."

"Left you? To do what?"

Jacob shrugged.

"Live another life, I guess. Drugs, money, music... The first few years, she saw Kimmy a couple of times, but that died out. It must be fifteen years since I last saw her."

"Does Lucy know... about Kimmy...?"

Jacob shook his head.

"No. At least, I haven't told her. I don't know where she is. I don't even know if she's still alive."

"She sounds like an idiot to me."

"We were both young, both idiots."

Silence fell inside the car.

A green VW Passat drove past.

Jacob looked at his watch. 8:54.

A blue Saab sped past them. They could hear the sound of rock and roll coming from the open windows. Two young males. Punk-style haircuts.

Jacob looked at his watch. 8:55. He was conscious that he was doing it obsessively, but he couldn't help it.

Dessie's phone rang. She listened in silence, said not a word, then turned to Jacob.

"They've passed through Salmis and Vuono," she said. "Two villages just outside this town. Still in the red Volvo. They're almost here."

"Robert's men, are they reliable?"

Dessie nodded. "Very."

"I don't want them involved at the border. I'll take it from here."

She passed on the message and hung up.

Chapter 134

NINE O'CLOCK CAME AND WENT.

No red Volvo. No Rudolphs.

The road beyond the rotary was full of cars now, mostly trailers and trucks. Due to the hunt for the Postcard Killers, security at the border crossing had been stepped up and all vehicles were forced to go through the checkpoint, next to a small wooden building up on the left.

Jacob looked at his watch again.

Half past nine. Jesus. The time was crawling.

Big tourist buses had started to arrive in the lot outside IKEA. They seemed to come from the whole of the Arctic region. Jacob saw license plates from Norway, Finland, and Russia. It was like IKEA was a county fair.

Soon there was a line of cars waiting to get into the parking lot.

"This is the Thursday before Midsummer's Eve," Dessie said. "It's the high point of Sweden's busiest shopping week. It's even bigger than Christmas."

Jacob didn't say anything.

He realized he was grinding his teeth. He needed to stop that. Yes, as soon as they caught the Rudolphs.

A line of shoppers was starting to form outside the entrance to the superstore. These country folks were clearly nuts.

Jacob looked at the time.

Three minutes before ten.

He glanced up into the rearview mirror.

Just a line of cars: blue, red, white, black, all full of crazy-ass Arctic shoppers.

He pressed the palms of his hands to his forehead.

The doors to the store opened.

People flooded into the hangarlike building.

Jacob felt like he was going to burst out of his skin.

"What the hell is this?" he yelled suddenly. "Where have they gone?"

Dessie didn't answer.

"They must have taken another road," Jacob said. "They're not coming through Haparanda. That criminal hooligan you call your cousin was wrong. Maybe he's in league with them now. Maybe he's fooled us into sitting here so they can get away. They could have bribed him."

"Jacob, calm down! You don't know what you're saying. *Stop it.*"

Jacob turned the key, and the engine coughed into life.

"What are you doing?" Dessie asked.

"I can't wait here any longer," Jacob said. "I'm going completely fucking mad just sit—"

"Hang on," Dessie interrupted. "Just hang on. A red car—there's a red car. I think it's a Volvo."

Jacob looked in the rearview mirror again.

It was a Volvo wagon, an old model, definitely red.

There were two people inside.

A young blond man and a dark-haired woman.

The Rudolphs were here.

Chapter 135

THE VOLVO CREPT SLOWLY toward the big rotary with all the bushes and trees in the middle.

Jacob pulled out into the traffic right behind them. His heart was thumping so hard that he could hardly hear anything going on around him.

The pair in the Volvo stopped in the rotary. The line to the border crossing snaked forward ahead of them.

"They've realized they can't get through this way," Dessie said. "Not in that car. So what do they do about it?"

Jacob pulled handcuffs from the inside pocket of his jacket and stuffed them under his belt behind his back. Then he leaned forward and took the Glock out of its holster strapped to his ankle. Suddenly he was glad he hadn't turned it over to the authorities as requested but had checked it in an airport locker while he traveled to and from Los Angeles. It looked like he'd need it now.

He heard Dessie's breath catch.

"Jacob, what are you doing? You can't use that gun here. You'll go to jail."

Just then the red Volvo swerved out of the traffic line. The driver wrenched the car to the left and squeezed past a trailer and a small van with Cyrillic lettering scrawled along the side.

Jacob found first gear and pushed his foot all the way to the floor. A moment later he was forced to brake sharply to avoid a truck that was halfway into the rotary.

"Hell! We're losing them!"

"They're going straight on," Dessie cried, leaning her head out of the window. "Now they're turning right! *They're in the IKEA parking lot!*"

Jacob drove too fast past the truck. He scraped the side of a Peugeot and forced his way into the lot as the driver of the Peugeot sat angrily on his horn behind them.

The parking lot for IKEA was complete chaos. Cars and buses and trailers were all battling with huge shopping trolleys and children's strollers and hundreds of people.

Jacob stopped the car and looked around wildly.

"Where the hell have they gone? We've lost them! They got away!"

"I think they were heading for where the buses park," Dessie said, pointing. "There. *There!* That's Sylvia Rudolph, isn't it?"

The dark-haired woman opened the door and started to run. She was athletic, fast on her feet.

"No!" Jacob cried, trying to drive after her. An entire family—grandma, mother, four kids, and a dog—blocked his way. Then the driver of the Peugeot suddenly appeared, banging furiously on the windshield. Jacob showed him the pistol, and the man backed away, hands up.

"To hell with this!" Jacob said, throwing the door open and racing toward the buses.

Chapter 136

IT WAS THE RUDOLPHS, he was sure of that much. He recognized Malcolm's relaxed movements and the woman's thick head of dark hair.

The killers were moving quickly through the parking lot, getting away. People who saw him running with his pistol drawn screamed and threw themselves out of his way. Someone yelled, "Madman!" at him. That was correct.

Dessie was coming up behind him. She had her cell phone in one hand. She was keying in a number as she ran.

The Rudolphs disappeared between two big buildings.

Jacob raised the pistol as he approached the corner. He didn't know what weapons the Rudolphs might have.

No one was there.

He rushed through the passageway and emerged from the far end.

Four buses, with toilets and curtains, were parked there. Even if one of the vehicles was unlocked, they couldn't hide for long, not here.

With his Glock drawn he ran over to the first bus.

No one.

The second one.

No one.

The third . . .

"Drop the gun!"

The voice came from behind him, a woman's voice, struggling to stay calm and collected.

He spun around, aiming the Glock, ready to kill.

Chapter 137

SYLVIA RUDOLPH WAS HOLDING Dessie in front of her as a shield. She had a knife to her throat. It was a carving knife, maybe a butcher's knife.

Jacob's head was spinning. For a moment he imagined it was Kimmy standing there with the knife to her throat. He couldn't let her die.

"Drop the gun," Sylvia Rudolph said. "Put it on the ground—or she dies. I have no problem with that."

Dessie's face was deathly pale. Her cell phone was still in her hand.

Malcolm Rudolph was standing some ten feet away, looking bewildered and lost.

Jacob stood still, his weapon raised.

All at once the situation was clear to him. Another part of the mystery had just been solved.

It wasn't the brother who was the killer.

It was the sister, Sylvia. *La señorita.* The girl who found her parents dead in their beds, or who had killed them with her own hands. Why, though? For the sake of art?

"Do as I say," Sylvia said, "or I'll cut her throat! She'll die right here."

Her voice was becoming less controlled, but Jacob believed every word she said.

He tightened his hold on the grip of the pistol. Instinctively he adopted the posture he had practiced so many times back home in New York.

He closed an eye, focusing his aim, slowing his breathing as best he could.

He studied Sylvia's ice-cold expression next to Dessie's terrified face. There she was, the woman who had killed his Kimmy, holding a knife to Dessie's throat. Another knife but the same killer.

Suddenly he felt his pulse relax.

"Put the gun down!" Sylvia roared. *"I'll cut her throat! Put it down! You want her to die?"*

So much for all her talk of art and conceptual creation.

When it came down to it, she just wanted to save herself. And maybe her crazy brother, her lover.

He squeezed the trigger: a cautious click, then the explosion and recoil.

Dessie dropped her cell and screamed. She screamed and screamed. *Oh god, no, he'd missed!*

Dessie must have moved at the last second.

What had he done?

Chapter 138

DESSIE WAS COVERED IN blood, and she was still screaming. But then Jacob realized it wasn't her blood after all.

It was Sylvia's. It was pieces of Sylvia's brain that were splattered across Dessie's face and Windbreaker. It was Sylvia who sank to the ground, who dropped the knife, as Malcolm came running over to her.

Dessie staggered away and leaned against one of the buses. Jacob rushed at Malcolm with his pistol raised.

"Get on your knees, hands above your head!" he shouted at the top of his voice.

He was screaming to make himself heard above the ringing in his own ears, but Malcolm seemed not to hear him. The man sank down beside his sister's body and took her in his arms. With a wild howl, he rocked Sylvia back and forth, back and forth, completely deaf to the uproar around them.

Jacob went up to him, weapon aimed at his chest.

He fished out the handcuffs from under the belt of his

trousers with one hand as he tried to make contact with the dazed man.

"Malcolm Rudolph—the police are on their way. Put the body down. Get on your knees. Hands behind your head!"

The howling subsided. Malcolm's shoulders slumped. He laid his sister's body gently on the asphalt.

Jacob saw that he had hit her between the eyes, just above them in the forehead. The entry wound gaped red, and the woman's eyes stared blindly at the sky. The back of her head had been blown away.

"You killed her," Malcolm said. His arms hung by his sides. His back was bent like an old man's. "You killed my Sylvia."

"You and your sister killed my daughter," Jacob said.

He opened the handcuffs and leaned down to secure Malcolm Rudolph's arms behind his back.

From this angle, Sylvia's dead eyes seemed to be watching him.

He didn't see the knife coming.

In a fast move, the brother leapt up and stabbed the knife toward Jacob's chest. Instinctively, Jacob shifted a few inches to the right.

The blade cut through the outside and lining of his suede jacket, biting into skin and sinew and muscle. Then it tore veins and arteries and lung tissue.

Jacob heard someone scream, a woman screaming.

He felt warm blood pulsing out of his body and saw the world spin and turn sideways, as if he could fall right off it. A shot rang out, the echo ringing through his head.

The killer in front of him sank to the ground with his hands over his stomach.

Then someone was holding him, laying him on the ground, tearing his shirt away.

It was Dessie, his Dessie. No, it was Kimmy, *his Kimmy*. Of course it was!

"Kimmy," Jacob whispered. "I knew you'd come back."

Epilogue

Chapter 139

Bay Ridge, Brooklyn, USA

THE WIND CARRIED WITH it the smell of the sea and also exhaust fumes from Leif Ericson Drive. It made the leaves above his head rustle, the electrical wires sing.

Jacob was sitting on the porch outside his small house, watching the boys from the neighborhood play baseball on the patch of grass on the other side of the street.

The heat and extreme humidity had finally broken, leaving a hint of autumn behind it.

The sun was no longer high in the sky, and the leafy trees threw deep shadows along the street.

His lung had healed. The pain in his arm was almost gone. The wound had started to itch instead. Sometimes he thought that was worse.

He looked down toward Shore Road.

Still no taxi.

He pulled at the shoulder sling in irritation.

Next week he could take it off.

They said he must have had a guardian angel.

The little town on the Arctic Circle where his lung had been punctured and his arm almost sliced off had had no hospital, but there had been a local health center with an emergency room and a Hungarian doctor who specialized in microsurgery. The Hungarian had stitched his muscles and blood vessels together while they emptied the center's supply of blood plasma into his body, and somehow he had survived.

Malcolm Rudolph hadn't been so lucky.

Jacob's wild shot had hit his liver. The killer bled to death in the helicopter ambulance. Good riddance to him, and his sister, too. Horrifying bastards.

When Jacob woke up and remembered what had happened, he started to prepare himself to face the Swedish judicial system. He assumed that he would get away with the actual shots. After all, Gabriella had heard the whole sequence of events over Dessie's phone. It was obvious that he had fired only in self-defense.

On the other hand, he would have to explain his weapon, the one he'd purchased in Italy.

The Europeans were very serious about the illegal possession of firearms.

When Mats Duvall had visited him in the hospital, Jacob had been expecting to face charges.

But the police superintendent had merely informed him that a preliminary investigation could not be carried out. All suspicions had been dropped through lack of evidence. That was what happened in cases like this, he had explained curtly.

The Swedes weren't quite as rigid as he had thought.

But his gun was confiscated when he left the country.

Jacob watched as the neighbor's son got a clean hit on the other side of the street. The ball shot off like a missile toward Johnson's Garage (which, naturally, was no longer Johnson's, but belonged to a Polish family, whatever their name was). Jacob held his breath until the ball hit the brick wall, just inches from a window.

Once upon a time he had played baseball on that same patch of grass. He had broken the windows of Johnson's Garage on a couple of occasions. He still lived in the house where he'd grown up, where his father had grown up, where Kimmy had grown up.

Maybe he could take off the wretched rag around his neck. What was the worst that could happen? His arm was hardly going to fall off, was it?

A taxi came slowly along the street and stopped at the sidewalk below the porch.

Jacob raised his good arm and waved. He even managed to smile.

Chapter 140

JACOB DIDN'T GET UP as Lyndon Crebbs got out of the backseat with his scruffy navy bag in tow.

"So, here you sit, you one-armed bandit!" the FBI agent said.

Jacob shifted to make room on the step for his old mentor. "How did the operation go?" he asked.

Lyndon sighed as he sank beside him on the steps.

"Well, I'll never use my dick for anything but pissing from now on, but you have to be grateful. Small mercies."

They sat there next to each other. Good friends, the best kind. Through thin and thinner.

The ball-playing boys on the other side of the street started arguing about something, and a halfhearted fight broke out before they drifted off home, one by one.

"What happened up in Montecito?" Jacob asked.

"They found the remains of a woman behind the Mansion," Crebbs said. "She wasn't buried very deep. Hadn't been there long. Four or five years, according to the coroner."

"Any ID?"

"Not yet, but it's probably the missing girl, Sandra Schulman. Her throat was cut. More of Sylvia's artwork, I'm sure."

They sat in silence for a while.

"What about the murder of the guardian?" Jacob asked. "And the parents?"

Lyndon Crebbs shook his head.

"Still open cases. My guess is that they'll stay that way.... Do you want to know what I found out about Lucy?"

Jacob looked over toward Johnson's garage. It was Lucy Johnson's childhood home.

"Not right now."

Lyndon Crebbs glanced at Jacob.

"How did it go with the girl from Stockholm? The one named after the princess?"

"She's going to finish her doctorate," Jacob said. "As far as I can tell, it's going pretty well."

"Isn't that what I've always said? The smart ones are always best. Where did she end up, anyway?"

Jacob felt his face crack into a grin.

"There she is, down there," he said, pointing with his healthy arm toward Narrows Avenue.

The only thing Dessie had bought since she moved in was a seven-speed women's bicycle with a shopping basket on the front. And now she was pedaling along Seventy-seventh Street with the basket full of leeks and other rabbit food.

Leaving the bike and the groceries in the driveway, she came over to the steps.

"Mr. Crebbs? I've heard a lot about you."

Dessie and Jacob's friend shook hands.

"Nothing but crap, I hope."

Dessie smiled at Jacob.

"From a romantic guy like this? What'd you expect?"

Acknowledgments

Liza's thanks:

Tove Alsterdal, Thomas Bodström, Kent Widing, Eva Marklund, Peter Rönnerfalk, and Neil Smith for their professional advice and great patience. And the Museum of Modern Art in Stockholm, its staff and website, for information and theories about famous works of art.

Jim's thanks:

Liza, for jumping into this book with stunning enthusiasm, skill, and no ego. And Linda Michaels, for getting us together, and just for being *Linda*.

About the Authors

JAMES PATTERSON has had more *New York Times* bestsellers than any other writer, ever, according to *Guinness World Records*. Since his first novel won the Edgar Award in 1977, James Patterson's books have sold more than 180 million copies. He is the author of the Alex Cross novels, the most popular detective series of the past twenty-five years, including *Kiss the Girls* and *Along Came a Spider*. Mr. Patterson also writes the bestselling Women's Murder Club novels, set in San Francisco, and the top-selling New York detective series of all time, featuring Detective Michael Bennett.

James Patterson also writes books for young readers, including the award-winning Maximum Ride, Daniel X, and Witch & Wizard series. In total, these books have spent more than 200 weeks on national bestseller lists, and all three series are in Hollywood development.

His lifelong passion for books and reading led James Patterson to launch a new website, ReadKiddoRead.com, to give adults an easy way to locate the very best books for kids. He writes full-time and lives in Florida with his family.

LIZA MARKLUND is an international bestselling author and the creator of the Annika Bengtzon series, which has sold 9 million copies in 30 languages. She lives in Sweden and Spain.

Books by James Patterson

FEATURING ALEX CROSS

I, Alex Cross
Alex Cross's Trial (with Richard DiLallo)
Cross Country
Double Cross
Cross
Mary, Mary
London Bridges
The Big Bad Wolf
Four Blind Mice
Violets Are Blue
Roses Are Red
Pop Goes the Weasel
Cat & Mouse
Jack & Jill
Kiss the Girls
Along Came a Spider

THE WOMEN'S MURDER CLUB

The 9th Judgment (with Maxine Paetro)
The 8th Confession (with Maxine Paetro)
7th Heaven (with Maxine Paetro)
The 6th Target (with Maxine Paetro)
The 5th Horseman (with Maxine Paetro)
4th of July (with Maxine Paetro)
3rd Degree (with Andrew Gross)
2nd Chance (with Andrew Gross)
1st to Die

FEATURING MICHAEL BENNETT

Worst Case (with Michael Ledwidge)
Run for Your Life (with Michael Ledwidge)
Step on a Crack (with Michael Ledwidge)

FOR READERS OF ALL AGES

Daniel X: Demons and Druids (with Adam Sadler)
Maximum Ride: The Manga, Vol. 3 (with NaRae Lee)
FANG: A Maximum Ride Novel
Maximum Ride: The Manga, Vol. 2 (with NaRae Lee)
Witch & Wizard (with Gabrielle Charbonnet)

Daniel X: Watch the Skies (with Ned Rust)
MAX: A Maximum Ride Novel
Maximum Ride: The Manga, Vol. 1 (with NaRae Lee)
Daniel X: Alien Hunter (graphic novel; with Leopoldo Gout)
The Dangerous Days of Daniel X (with Michael Ledwidge)
The Final Warning: A Maximum Ride Novel
Maximum Ride: Saving the World and Other Extreme Sports
Maximum Ride: School's Out — Forever
Maximum Ride: The Angel Experiment

OTHER BOOKS

The Postcard Killers (with Liza Marklund)
Private (with Maxine Paetro)
The Murder of King Tut (with Martin Dugard)
Swimsuit (with Maxine Paetro)
Against Medical Advice (with Hal Friedman)
Sail (with Howard Roughan)
Sundays at Tiffany's (with Gabrielle Charbonnet)
You've Been Warned (with Howard Roughan)
The Quickie (with Michael Ledwidge)
Judge & Jury (with Andrew Gross)
Beach Road (with Peter de Jonge)
Lifeguard (with Andrew Gross)
Honeymoon (with Howard Roughan)
santaKid
Sam's Letters to Jennifer
The Lake House
The Jester (with Andrew Gross)
The Beach House (with Peter de Jonge)
Suzanne's Diary for Nicholas
Cradle and All
When the Wind Blows
Miracle on the 17th Green (with Peter de Jonge)
Hide & Seek
The Midnight Club
Black Friday (originally published as *Black Market*)
See How They Run (originally published as *The Jericho Commandment*)
Season of the Machete
The Thomas Berryman Number

For previews of upcoming books by James Patterson
and more information about the author,
visit www.JamesPatterson.com.